Fault Lines of the Heart

Donald J. Wright

About the author

My career, spanning over four decades, has been a testament to the power of strategic vision and leadership. From the vibrant sales floors of Bashinski's Gems and jewelry to the strategic boardrooms of Reeds Jewelers and Friedman's incorporated, I have navigated the intricate world of diamonds, gems, and the buying sector with a blend of scientific precision and creative flair as a geologist and chemist. My passion for storytelling is not just a personal interest but a reflection of my professional journey. It is beyond the sparkle of a well-cut diamond, weaving narratives that resonate with the heart and mind—my passion is clear in my published five nonfiction books and the twenty-plus novels. As an author, I understand the value of legacy, whether it the timeless beauty of a family heirloom or the enduring impact of a well-told tale. My books are more than just collections of words. They are vessels of 'knowledge, experience, and imagination' destined to inspire and enlighten. I hope you find these sources of information and entertainment too.

Contents

Chapter 1: Fault Lines of the Heart

The lecture hall smelled of chalk dust and nervous energy, two hundred undergraduate faces turned toward Professor Elias Quinn like sunflowers tracking light. He stood at the podium in his favorite worn corduroy jacket, the one with patches on the elbows that his colleagues teased him about and felt the familiar electricity that came with teaching—that moment when minds opened and possibilities expanded.

"Who can tell me," he began, his voice carrying easily to the back rows, "what happened in the Indian Ocean on December 26th, 2004?"

Hands shot up. A young woman in the third row called out, "The tsunami!"

"Exactly. A magnitude 9.1 earthquake triggered one of the deadliest tsunamis in recorded history." Elias clicked his remote, and images filled the projection screen—devastating waves, destroyed coastlines, rescue operations. "But here's what's fascinating. In many affected areas, something extraordinary happened in the hours before the waves hit."

He paused, letting the anticipation build. This was his favorite part—the moment before revelation.

"The animals knew."

Another click brought up video footage: elephants in Thailand trumpeting and heading for higher ground, dogs refusing to walk on beaches, birds abandoning their roosts en masse.

"Elephants broke their chains to flee inland. Dogs wouldn't go near the water. Horses refused to be led to the beach. Water buffalo gathered on hilltops. Even domestic cats were hiding in the highest places they could find." His voice gained momentum, passion bleeding through academic restraint. "The animals felt something we couldn't—or wouldn't—acknowledge."

A student in a West Virginia University sweatshirt raised her hand. "But Professor Quinn, isn't that just... instinct? Animals reacting to sound waves or vibrations?"

"Ah, Sarah, excellent question." Elias smiled, recognizing the young woman from his Introduction to Cultural Anthropology class. "And that's precisely the point. We dismiss it as 'just instinct' because we've forgotten how to listen to the same signals our ancestors once heeded."

Behind him, lying in his customary spot by the radiator, Koa lifted his head. The Australian Shepherd's ears twitched, and a low, almost inaudible growl rumbled from his throat.

Elias glanced back at his dog, frowning slightly. Koa had been coming to his lectures for three years, ever since... well, since Elias couldn't bear to leave him alone in the empty house. The dog was usually perfectly behaved, a beloved fixture that students often stayed after class to pet.

"Indigenous cultures worldwide have stories of animals warning of disasters," Elias continued. However, part of his attention remained on Koa, who had risen to his feet, hackles slightly raised. "Aboriginal Australians speak of kangaroos fleeing before earthquakes. Native Americans tell of horses refusing to cross certain paths before landslides. Ancient Greeks recorded dogs howling before volcanic eruptions."

Koa's growl grew louder, a sound that made several students turn around.

"The Romans," Elias pressed on, raising his voice slightly, "actually appointed official observers to watch animal behavior before making important decisions. They understood something we've forgotten in our rush to quantify and digitize everything—that intuition isn't the opposite of data. Sometimes, it *is* data."

Now Koa was on his feet, pacing restlessly, his claws clicking against the linoleum floor. The dog whined, a high, distressed sound that carried clearly through the suddenly quiet lecture hall.

"Professor?" Sarah called out, concern in her voice. "Is your dog okay?"

Elias felt his cheeks warm. This had never happened before. "I'm sorry, everyone. Koa's usually very well-behaved." He moved toward his dog, who was now staring intently at the windows, tail stiff, every muscle tense. "Maybe we should take a short break—"

"Actually," interrupted Dr. Harrison from the back of the room, where he'd been observing from the doorway, "this seems like perfect timing to discuss the difference between verifiable scientific data and, shall we say, wishful thinking."

Elias's jaw tightened. Dr. Harrison, the department's resident skeptic, had made no secret of his disapproval of what he called Elias's "soft science approach." The man's presence at his lecture was unexpected and unwelcome.

"Dr. Harrison," Elias replied carefully, "I'm simply presenting documented historical patterns—"

"Patterns that have never held up to rigorous statistical analysis," Harrison cut him off, stepping into the room with the confidence of a man who'd never doubted his own intelligence. "Correlation isn't causation, Professor Quinn. The fact that some animals happened to behave unusually before some disasters doesn't prove they can predict anything."

The students' heads swiveled between the two professors like spectators at a tennis match. Elias felt the energy in the room shift, his carefully constructed lesson slipping away.

Koa's whine became sharper, more urgent. The dog moved to the window, pressing his nose against the glass, fogging the glass with his breath.

"With respect, Dr. Harrison," Elias said, forcing his voice to remain steady, "dismissing centuries of recorded observations simply because we don't yet understand the mechanism—"

"Is exactly what science is supposed to do," Harrison finished. "We follow evidence, not folklore."

A distant rumble rolled across the campus, barely audible but felt in the chest—the kind of sound that might be thunder, or construction, or the ghost of some larger disturbance. Several students glanced toward the windows.

Koa barked once, sharp and insistent.

"Class dismissed," Elias said quietly, his face burning. "We'll pick this up next Thursday."

***

The campus quad was unusually quiet as Elias walked toward the old oak grove that bordered the western edge of the university grounds. Students hurried between buildings with their heads down, focused on phones or laden with backpacks, but something felt off. The usual chatter was muted, the energy subdued.

Koa trotted beside him, but his gait was wrong—tense, alert, with frequent stops to test the air. When they reached the edge of the grove, the dog planted his feet and refused to move forward.

"Come on, boy," Elias coaxed, tugging gently on the leash. "It's just trees."

But Koa whined and backed away, pulling toward the open quad. Above them, Elias noticed, the oak branches were unusually still. Not just still empty. Where normally dozens of squirrels would be chattering and racing along the branches, where birds would be calling from their perches, there was only silence.

A squirrel scurried past them, not in the typical zigzag pattern of campus foraging, but in a straight, purposeful line away from the trees. Then another. Then three more, all heading in the same direction, toward higher ground.

Elias pulled out his phone and opened the Prometheus app. The interface was crude—he'd coded it himself, more passion project than professional software—but the data streams were comprehensive. Real-time feeds from weather stations, seismic monitors, and most importantly, the behavioral tracking system he'd spent two years developing.

Animal behavioral anomalies in the past hour: forty-seven reports within a fifty-mile radius.

His breath caught. Forty-seven was more than he usually saw in a week.

A rumble rolled across the hills again, this time more distinct. Not thunder, the sky was clear. Not construction—it was Saturday afternoon. The sound seemed to come from below, a deep bass note that resonated in his bones.

Koa pressed against his legs, trembling.

"I know, boy," Elias murmured, scrolling through the Prometheus data. "I'm seeing it too."

Dogs refusing walks. Cats hiding. Farm animals clustering in far corners of fields. Birds abandoning roosts. All within the past six hours, all within an expanding circle centered roughly...

Elias calculated quickly, his anthropologist's training in pattern recognition kicking in. The center point was approximately twelve miles southeast of campus, in the hills where the old mining operations used to run.

Another rumble, longer this time. Koa whimpered and tugged insistently toward the main campus buildings.

"Okay," Elias said, pocketing his phone. "We're listening."

***

Elias's office occupied the fourth floor of Chitwood Hall, a cramped space he'd inherited when he took the position three years ago. Books lined every wall from floor to ceiling—not just anthropology texts, but geology, biology, psychology, computer science, even veterinary medicine. In one corner, a bank of computer monitors displayed the constant data streams that fed Prometheus.

The AI wasn't much to look at—a custom-built system housed in three humming towers that he'd assembled himself from salvaged university equipment and parts ordered online. The monitors showed scrolling feeds of numbers, graphs, and occasional alert notifications that most people would find incomprehensible.

To Elias, it was beautiful.

He'd named it Prometheus after the Titan who stole fire from the gods—a being who saw what others couldn't and paid a price for bringing that knowledge to humanity. The mythology felt appropriate.

Koa had claimed his usual spot on the threadbare rug beside the desk, but his eyes remained alert, tracking sounds and movements that Elias couldn't detect.

"Let's see what you're trying to tell me," Elias murmured, settling into his chair and pulling up the full Prometheus interface.

The system collected data from dozens of sources: weather stations, geological surveys, wildlife cameras, even social media posts tagged with animal behavior keywords. But its most valuable inputs came from the network of volunteers he'd cultivated over the past two years—farmers, park rangers, veterinarians, and pet owners who'd agreed to report unusual animal behavior to his database.

The reports from the past six hours painted a clear picture: something was wrong.

A farm thirty miles south reported cattle refusing to graze in their usual pasture, instead clustering near the barn. A veterinary clinic in Bridgeport noted an unusual number of pets brought in for "anxiety" symptoms. Wildlife cameras in the Monongahela National Forest showed deer moving away from their usual feeding grounds.

Elias pulled up the seismic data from the US Geological Survey. No earthquakes reported in the region. No tremors registered on any official monitors.

But the animals knew something.

He leaned back in his chair, thinking about the lecture that had gone so wrong, about Dr. Harrison's dismissive certainty, about the decades of human wisdom that modern academia had forgotten.

His wife would have understood.

The thought came unbidden, as it often did when he was wrestling with data that felt important but inexplicable. Elena had been the one with true scientific training—a behavioral biologist who'd spent her career studying migration patterns and environmental adaptation. But she'd also possessed something rare in academia: an absolute trust in phenomena that couldn't yet be explained.

"Just because we can't measure it doesn't mean it isn't real," she used to say, usually while analyzing some impossible pattern in her own research. "Science is about asking questions, not limiting them."

Elias saved the Prometheus data and locked his computer. The system would continue collecting information, building its models, learning from patterns that human consciousness was too limited to perceive.

As he stood to leave, his phone chimed with an email notification.

The sender address was a random string of characters he didn't recognize. The subject line read: "Regarding your early work on predictive behavioral modeling."

Elias frowned. His early papers—published during his graduate work almost fifteen years ago—were obscure theoretical pieces that had been largely ignored by the academic community. He rarely received correspondence about them, and never from anonymous accounts.

He opened the email.

Professor Quinn,

I've been following your research with great interest, particularly your recent applications of behavioral analysis to environmental prediction. Your work shows remarkable insight, though I suspect you don't yet realize its full implications.

I represent certain interests that would benefit from discussing your findings in more detail. The attached file contains preliminary data that might prove useful to your current research.

A word of caution: there are those who would prefer your work remain theoretical. I would suggest discretion in any future publications or presentations.

We should meet soon.

Regards, A concerned colleague

Elias stared at the screen, his pulse quickening. The email felt wrong in ways he couldn't articulate—too vague, too cryptic, carrying undertones of both opportunity and threat.

An attachment icon showed a compressed file labeled "Seismic_Behav ioral_Correlation_Data.zip."

His finger hovered over the attachment. Every instinct told him to delete the email, to forget about it, to stick to his small corner of academic research where the stakes were low and the dangers theoretical.

But the same instinct that drove him to trust animal behavior, to build Prometheus, to search for patterns others missed, whispered that this might be important.

He clicked download.

***

The memorial bench sat beneath a spreading maple tree on the eastern edge of campus, overlooking the hills that rolled away toward the distant mountains. A small brass plaque read: "In memory of Dr. Elena Vasquez Quinn—Scientist, Teacher, Beloved Wife. 'Listen to what the world is trying to tell you.'"

Elias sat on the bench as he did most Saturday evenings, a ritual that had become both comfort and self-imposed penance. Koa settled beside him, finally relaxed now that they were away from whatever had disturbed him earlier.

The sun was setting behind them, casting long shadows across the campus quad. Students moved between the dormitories in chattering groups, their laughter carrying on the evening air. Normal college sounds. Normal college rhythms.

Elena would have been forty-one next month.

"I got a strange email today," he said aloud, a habit he'd developed in the months after the accident. Talking to Elena, sharing his day, pretending for a few minutes that she might respond. "Someone who claims to know my work. Claims to have data that might help."

A breeze stirred the maple leaves above them, the sound like a whispered conversation.

"You'd tell me to be careful, wouldn't you? You'd say I'm too trusting, too eager to believe that everyone shares my passion for the truth."

The last light faded from the hills. Somewhere in the distance, a train whistle echoed—mournful, lonely, but familiar. Comforting in its predictability.

"The animals were agitated today. Really agitated. Koa wouldn't go near the oak grove, and the Prometheus data shows behavioral anomalies all across the region." He pulled out his phone and showed the screen to the empty space where Elena should have been sitting. "Forty-seven reports in six hours. That's unprecedented."

The phone screen illuminated the bench, casting blue light across the memorial plaque.

"I know what you'd say. You'd tell me to trust the data, follow the patterns, and not let people like Harrison make me doubt what I'm seeing." His voice grew softer. "You'd tell me that intuition isn't unscientific—it's just science our conscious minds haven't learned to process yet."

Elena had been driving home from a conference in Pittsburgh when the semi-truck ran the red light. Eighteen months ago. The driver had fallen asleep, investigators concluded. No animals had warned anyone about that collision.

"I miss having someone who understood," Elias whispered. "I miss having someone who believed."

Koa nuzzled his hand, a warm comfort in the cooling evening air.

The walk back to his small house on Faculty Row took fifteen minutes. Elias had chosen the rental specifically because it allowed dogs and because Elena had loved the view of the mountains from the kitchen window. Now the house felt too large for one person and one Australian Shepherd, but moving would mean admitting that his life in Morgantown was temporary.

He wasn't ready for that admission.

The kitchen still smelled faintly of the coffee he'd made that morning. Elias opened a can of dog food for Koa, then assembled a peanut butter sandwich for himself—the sort of meal Elena would have scolded him for.

"Proper nutrition supports proper thinking," she used to say, usually while preparing elaborate dinners that somehow never took more than thirty minutes to cook.

"I'm eating," he told the empty kitchen. "Peanuts are protein."

Koa finished his dinner and padded over to rest his head on Elias's knee, a gesture of solidarity that never failed to touch him. The dog seemed calmer now; whatever had disturbed him earlier apparently resolved.

"What do you think, boy? Should I open that attachment?"

Koa's tail thumped once against the floor.

Elias carried his laptop to the kitchen table and opened the email again. The attachment had finished downloading, the compressed file sitting in his downloads folder like a small, digital bomb.

There are those who would prefer your work remain theoretical.

What did that mean? Was it a warning or a threat? And who would care enough about his obscure research to send anonymous messages?

His finger moved to the trackpad, cursor hovering over the file.

I would suggest discretion in any future publications or presentations.

The lecture hall fiasco with Dr. Harrison flashed through his mind. Had word of his work somehow reached people outside the university? People with enough influence to make his professional life difficult?

He clicked on the file.

The compressed folder contained dozens of documents—seismic reports, behavioral studies, geological surveys, and what appeared to be correspondence between various government agencies. Most were dated within the past five years, but some went back decades.

One file caught his attention: "Appalachian_Seismic_Behavioral_Correlation_1987-1992.pdf"

Elias opened it and felt his breath catch. The document was a comprehensive study of animal behavioral patterns in the Appalachian region, correlated with seismic activity, conducted by the US Geological Survey in partnership with several universities. The methodology was sophisticated, the data extensive, the conclusions...

The conclusions matched everything his own research had suggested.

Animals in the Appalachian region showed measurable behavioral changes an average of 18-72 hours before seismic events. The larger the event, the more widespread the behavioral anomalies. The correlation was statistically significant across multiple species and geographic areas.

But according to the document's metadata, the study had never been published. Never released to the academic community. Never cited in any of the literature Elias had reviewed during his own research.

Why would a study this comprehensive, this conclusive, be suppressed?

His phone rang, the sudden sound making him jump. Koa lifted his head, ears pricked.

The caller ID showed only a number he didn't recognize.

"Hello?" Elias answered cautiously.

"Professor Quinn?" The voice was electronically distorted, processed through some kind of modulation software. "I trust you received my email."

Elias's heart rate spiked. "Who is this?"

"Someone who appreciates your work. Someone who understands that you're very close to something important."

"What do you want?"

"To warn you. The data I sent you represents twenty years of suppressed research. Studies that were conducted, conclusions that were reached, and findings that were buried by people who preferred the public remain unaware of certain... vulnerabilities."

Elias glanced at his laptop screen, at the USGS study that had somehow vanished from the historical record. "Why are you showing me this?"

"Because recent patterns suggest an event may be imminent. An event that will validate everything you've been working toward. But there are those who would prefer that validation never occur."

The line crackled with static. When the voice returned, it was urgent.

"They're watching your work, Professor Quinn. Be very careful who you trust."

The call ended.

Elias stared at his phone, pulse hammering. The kitchen suddenly felt too exposed, too vulnerable. He moved to the window and peered through the curtains, scanning the street for unfamiliar cars, strange figures, anything out of place.

Faculty Row was quiet. Porch lights glowed warmly from neighboring houses. A cat picked its way delicately across the wet street.

Normal. Everything looked completely normal.

But Koa was pacing again, restless energy returning. The dog moved from window to window, checking, alert.

Elias returned to his laptop and scrolled through more of the suppressed documents. Study after study, all reaching similar conclusions, all apparently classified or buried. Seismic prediction through animal behavior wasn't just possible—it had been proven possible decades ago.

So why wasn't it being used?

His email chimed with a new message. Same anonymous sender.

They're watching your work.

Nothing else. Just that single line, and an attachment.

This time, the attachment was a photograph.

Elias opened it and felt the world tilt.

The image showed him sitting at this very kitchen table, taken through his window, apparently from across the street. The timestamp indicated it had been captured less than an hour ago.

Someone was watching him. Right now.

Koa growled low in his throat, staring at the front door.

Elias closed the laptop and reached for his dog's leash.

It was time to go.

Chapter 2: The Skeptic Arrives

Dr. Mara Lang's office smelled of fresh paint and possibility. She stood in the doorway of Brooks Hall, Room 314, surveying the space that would be her academic home for the foreseeable future—assuming she could rebuild her career from the ashes of her previous position.

The room was smaller than she'd hoped but larger than she'd feared, with two tall windows facing the Appalachian foothills and enough wall space for the geological survey maps she'd spent the weekend unrolling and categorizing. Sunlight streamed across the empty desk, highlighting dust motes that danced in the still air.

"Fresh start," she murmured, setting down the first of several boxes marked "Dr. Lang - Office Materials" in her precise handwriting.

Mara had arrived in Morgantown three days earlier, driving her Honda Civic loaded with everything that remained of her professional life after the debacle at Virginia Tech. The forced resignation, the whispered conversations that stopped when she entered a room, the gradual isolation as colleagues distanced themselves from the controversy—all of it packed into boxes and transported to this small West Virginia university that had been willing to take a chance on damaged goods.

She opened the first box and began arranging her books on the metal shelving unit. Geological Survey manuals. Seismic analysis textbooks. Peer-reviewed journals dating back to her graduate school days. Each volume was placed with the same methodical precision she applied to everything in her life. This learned behavior had kept her sane through eighteen months of professional exile.

The second box contained her research materials: binders full of data, computer drives with backup files, and the rolled geological surveys that had become her obsession since the Cross incident. Mara spread the largest map across her desk—a comprehensive survey of the central Appalachian region dating back to the early 1980s.

The survey showed the familiar mountain ranges and valley systems she'd studied for her doctoral dissertation. Still, now she was looking for different patterns. Anomalies. Inconsistencies. The kind of subtle discrepancies that might indicate seismic instability.

Dr. Richard Cross had taught her to look for such patterns, back when she'd been naive enough to trust his guidance. Before she'd learned that his brilliance came with a price, that his mentorship was conditional on absolute loyalty, and that questioning his methods would result in systematic character assassination.

"Trust the data," she said aloud, running her finger along a fault line that didn't quite match the topographical features. "The data doesn't lie. People do."

The third box held her personal items—a small plant that had somehow survived the move, a photograph of her parents at her PhD graduation, and a coffee mug that read "World's Okayest Geologist." The mug had been a joke gift from her graduate school roommate. Still, Mara had kept it through every career move as a reminder not to take herself too seriously.

She was arranging the items on her desk when she noticed something odd about the geological survey. A series of small notations in the margins, barely visible unless you looked at just the right angle. Someone had marked specific locations with tiny symbols—not part of the original survey, but added later in different ink.

Mara pulled out her magnifying glass and studied the markings more closely. The symbols appeared to correlate with areas of known seismic activity, but the notation style wasn't familiar. Each mark was accompanied by a date and initials: "L.V."

She made a mental note to research the initials later. For now, she had more pressing concerns—like figuring out how to rebuild her reputation in a department where everyone would inevitably learn about her past.

A knock on her door interrupted her unpacking. "Dr. Lang?"

Mara looked up to see a woman in her fifties wearing a floral dress and a warm smile. "I'm Dr. Patricia Welsh, department chair. I wanted to welcome you to West Virginia University."

"Thank you," Mara replied, standing to shake hands. "I appreciate the opportunity."

"I know your transition here has been... complicated," Dr. Welsh said carefully. "I want you to know that we judge people by their work, not by academic politics from other institutions."

The kindness in her voice was unexpected, and Mara felt her carefully constructed professional facade waver slightly. "That means more than you know."

"There's a faculty mixer this evening in the student union. Nothing formal, just a chance for everyone to catch up before the semester begins. I hope you'll join us."

Mara's instinct was to decline—she'd learned to avoid social gatherings where whispered conversations might dissect her professional disgrace. But isolation hadn't helped her at Virginia Tech, and Dr. Welsh's invitation seemed genuine.

"I'll be there," she said.

After Dr. Welsh left, Mara returned to her maps, but her concentration was broken. The move to West Virginia represented more than a career change—it was a chance to remember who she'd been before Cross had twisted her research into something unrecognizable, before her name had become associated with fraudulent data and compromised ethics.

She traced the fault lines on the survey with her finger, following the geological story written in the landscape. The Appalachian region was old, stable, and predictable, not like the volatile tectonics of California or the volcanic systems of the Pacific Northwest. Here, the mountains had been wearing down for millions of years, their violent youth long past.

Safe. Boring. Perfect for rebuilding a damaged career.

Her phone buzzed with a text message from her sister: "How's the new job? Any cute professors?"

Mara smiled despite herself. Sarah always knew how to lighten her mood. She typed back: "Day one. Ask me again in a month."

The afternoon passed quickly as she organized files and prepared for her first classes. By evening, her office looked almost professional—books arranged, maps displayed, computer set up and running. The space felt like hers now, a small claim staked in the academic world that had nearly rejected her entirely.

***

The faculty mixer occupied the main ballroom of the student union, a space that managed to feel both too large and too crowded as professors clustered in comfortable groups, wine glasses in hand, conversations flowing with the easy familiarity of colleagues who'd worked together for years.

Mara stood near the entrance, nursing a glass of white wine and observing the social dynamics with the same analytical eye she applied to geological formations. Academic gatherings followed predictable patterns: senior faculty held court in central locations while junior professors orbited at respectful distances. Administrative staff moved efficiently between groups, facilitating introductions and managing logistics. Graduate students hovered at the periphery, eager to impress but uncertain of their place in the hierarchy.

"You must be the new geology professor," said a voice behind her.

Mara turned to see a man in his late thirties approaching with a friendly smile and an Australian Shepherd at his side. He was tall and lean, with dark hair that looked like he'd been running his hands through it, and the kind of easy confidence that suggested he was comfortable in his own skin.

"Dr. Mara Lang," she replied, extending her hand. "And you are?"

"Elias Quinn, anthropology. And this is Koa." He gestured to the dog, who sniffed politely in Mara's direction before settling at Elias's feet. "Fair warning—Koa's something of a celebrity around here. Students love him more than they love most of their professors."

"Including you?"

"Especially me." Elias's grin was self-deprecating and surprisingly charming. "What brings you to the wilds of West Virginia?"

It was a simple question, but Mara felt the familiar tightness in her chest that came with explaining her career transition. "Fresh start," she said, opting for the abbreviated version. "Sometimes a change of scenery helps with research focus."

"Ah, a woman of mystery." Elias's tone was light, but his eyes showed genuine interest. "What kind of research?"

"Seismic analysis. Earthquake prediction models, geological surveys, that sort of thing." She gestured vaguely toward the windows that overlooked the campus. "The Appalachian region is geologically fascinating—old mountain systems, complex fault structures, millions of years of tectonic history to unravel."

"Prediction models," Elias repeated thoughtfully. "That's interesting. I work with predictive systems myself, though from a very different angle."

"Oh?"

"Behavioral analysis. Animal behavior patterns that might correlate with environmental changes." His enthusiasm was immediate and infectious. "There's growing evidence that animals can sense environmental shifts before our instruments detect them. Seismic events, weather changes, even volcanic eruptions—nature has early warning systems that we're only beginning to understand."

Mara felt her academic hackles rise. "With respect, Dr. Quinn, animal behavior is notoriously unreliable as a predictive tool. Too many variables, too much subjective interpretation. Scientific prediction requires quantifiable data, not folklore."

"But what if folklore is just data we haven't learned to measure properly?" Elias leaned forward, his interest clearly piqued by her skepticism. "Indigenous cultures worldwide have animal-based prediction systems that have worked for centuries. The Romans appointed official observers to watch animal behavior before making military decisions. Even today, there are documented cases—"

"Correlation without causation," Mara interrupted, falling back on the fundamental principle that had guided her entire career. "Just because two events occur in sequence doesn't mean one causes the other. Animals might behave unusually before earthquakes, but they also behave unusually before thunderstorms, or when they're sick, or when humans change their feeding schedules. Without controlled conditions and rigorous statistical analysis—"

"Dr. Lang, Dr. Quinn," interrupted a new voice. "I hope I'm not interrupting anything important."

They turned to see an elderly woman approaching with the careful gait of someone whose bones had accumulated decades of wisdom along with wear. She was small and wiry, with silver hair pulled back in a neat bun and eyes that seemed to see more than they revealed.

"Dr. Voss," Elias said warmly. "Mara, I'd like you to meet Dr. Lenora Voss, retired volcanology professor and local legend. Lenora, this is Dr. Mara Lang, our new geology professor."

"Volcanology," Mara said, shaking the older woman's hand. "That must have been fascinating work."

"It had its moments," Dr. Voss replied, though something in her tone suggested not all of those moments had been pleasant. "I understand you're interested in seismic prediction."

"That's right. Though Dr. Quinn and I were just debating the reliability of unconventional prediction methods."

Dr. Voss's eyes crinkled with what might have been amusement. "Ah yes, the eternal debate between quantifiable data and indigenous wisdom. I've had that argument with myself for forty years."

"You must come down on the side of data," Mara said. "Volcanology is a hard science."

"Indeed, it is. But I've learned that dismissing traditional knowledge is often a mistake." Dr. Voss paused, studying Mara with an intensity that was slightly unsettling. "The land has ways of speaking to those who know how to listen. Animals, plants, even the rocks themselves—they respond to changes we can't yet measure with our instruments."

"With respect, Dr. Voss, that sounds dangerously close to mysticism."

"Does it?" The older woman's smile was enigmatic. "Tell me, Dr. Lang, have you had a chance to review the historical geological surveys for this region?"

The question seemed to come from nowhere, but Mara nodded. "I've been studying the 1980s surveys, actually. Looking for baseline data to inform my research."

"Interesting period," Dr. Voss said quietly. "A lot of... unusual readings during those years. Most of them were dismissed as equipment malfunctions or human error."

"Were they?"

Dr. Voss didn't answer directly. Instead, she turned to Elias. "How is your animal behavioral research progressing, Dr. Quinn? Still finding correlations where others see coincidence?"

"Always," Elias replied. "Though I get the impression Dr. Lang thinks I'm wasting my time chasing shadows."

"Not shadows," Mara corrected, surprised by her own diplomatic tone. "I just think there are more reliable methods for environmental prediction. Methods that don't require subjective interpretation of animal moods."

"Moods," Elias repeated, and she could hear the edge in his voice. "Is that what you think this is about?"

"I think," Mara said carefully, aware that their conversation was drawing attention from nearby faculty members, "that science works best when it follows established protocols. Peer review, controlled conditions, statistical significance. The scientific method exists for a reason."

"And what about when the scientific method fails?" Dr. Voss interjected softly. "When our instruments miss what indigenous peoples have known for generations? When our models fail to predict events that traditional knowledge systems see coming?"

The question hung in the air, charged with implications that Mara wasn't sure she wanted to explore. Around them, the mixer continued—wine glasses clinked, conversations flowed, professors debated the minutiae of academic life. But she felt as though she'd stumbled into a different kind of discussion, one that challenged assumptions she'd never thought to question.

"Traditional knowledge systems fail too," she said finally. "And when they do, people die."

Dr. Voss nodded slowly. "Yes, they do. But so do people when we ignore warnings because they don't fit our paradigms."

***

The conversation with Dr. Voss left Mara unsettled in ways she couldn't quite articulate. She found herself gravitating back toward Dr. Quinn—Elias—despite their philosophical differences, drawn by his obvious passion for his work and his willingness to engage with ideas that challenged conventional thinking.

"I'm sorry if I came across as dismissive," she said when they found themselves alone near the refreshment table. "It's not that I don't appreciate unconventional approaches. It's just that I've learned to be... cautious about research that can't be easily verified."

"Cautious," Elias repeated, and she heard understanding in his voice. "Someone burned you."

It wasn't a question, and Mara felt her defenses rise automatically. "What makes you say that?"

"Academic caution usually comes from academic trauma. Someone twisted your work, or took credit for it, or used it in ways you never intended." His expression was gentle, nonjudgmental. "I'm right, aren't I?"

Mara stared at him, surprised by his perceptiveness. Most people who learned about her situation at Virginia Tech focused on the professional implications—the damaged reputation, the forced resignation, the difficulty finding new positions. Few understood the deeper wound: the betrayal of trust that made her question not just her colleagues but her own judgment.

"Something like that," she admitted.

"For what it's worth, I think your skepticism is healthy. Science needs people who ask hard questions, who demand evidence, who won't accept conclusions just because they sound compelling." Elias paused, studying her face. "But it also needs people who are willing to consider possibilities that don't fit existing models."

"Like animal behavior predicting earthquakes?"

"Like animal behavior predicting earthquakes," he agreed. "Would you be interested in seeing some of my data? Not to convince you of anything, just to show you what I'm working with?"

The offer surprised her. Most researchers guarded their preliminary data jealously, especially from skeptical colleagues who might find flaws in their methodology. Either Elias was supremely confident in his work, or he was naive about academic politics.

"I'd like that," she heard herself saying.

"Fair warning—my research setup is pretty informal compared to what you're probably used to. I work mostly alone, with equipment I've assembled myself." He smiled self-consciously. "Not exactly cutting-edge scientific infrastructure."

"Some of the best research happens in informal settings," Mara replied, thinking of her own graduate school days when breakthrough insights had come from late-night conversations in cluttered laboratories rather than formal presentations in sterile conference rooms.

"Coffee tomorrow morning? I can show you the behavioral tracking system I've been developing."

"I'd like that," she said again, and realized she meant it.

As the mixer wound down and faculty members began making their excuses, Mara found herself walking toward the parking garage with a sense of anticipation she hadn't felt in months. The conversation with Elias had been intellectually stimulating in a way that reminded her why she'd fallen in love with research in the first place—the excitement of exploring unknown territories, the thrill of discovering patterns hidden in seemingly random data.

Maybe West Virginia would be more interesting than she'd anticipated.

***

Mara's flat was a small, furnished unit near campus that came with the basic necessities and none of the personal touches that might make it feel like home. She'd deliberately chosen temporary housing, unwilling to commit to permanence until she was certain the position would work out.

The geological surveys were spread across her dining room table, weighted down with coffee mugs and textbooks to keep them from rolling closed. She'd been studying them for hours, following the fault lines and geological formations, trying to understand the region's seismic history.

The anomalous markings she'd noticed earlier were more extensive than she'd initially realized. The mysterious "L.V." had made dozens of notations across multiple surveys, each one carefully dated and positioned. The marks seemed to cluster around areas of known seismic activity, but the dating didn't match any earthquakes in the official records.

Mara pulled out her laptop and cross-referenced the marked locations with historical seismic data from the US Geological Survey. Most of the dates corresponded to minor seismic events—tremors too small to cause damage, barely registering on seismographs, the kind of micro-earthquakes that happened constantly throughout geologically active regions.

But the markings predated the seismic events. By weeks, sometimes months.

She stared at the screen, double-checking her calculations. The pattern was clear: someone had identified areas of seismic instability before the earthquakes actually occurred. Either the mysterious "L.V." had been extraordinarily lucky in their guesses, or they'd had access to predictive methods that weren't reflected in the official geological literature.

Her phone rang, interrupting her analysis. The caller ID showed a number she recognized with a mixture of dread and resigned acceptance.

"Hello, Richard."

"Mara." Dr. Cross's voice carried the same smooth charm that had once made her feel like the most promising student in his program. Now it made her skin crawl. "I heard you'd settled in at West Virginia University. How are you adjusting?"

"Fine," she replied curtly. "What do you want?"

"Just checking in on a former colleague. Academic transitions can be challenging, especially when one's reputation has been... complicated by unfortunate circumstances."

The veiled reference to her forced resignation made her jaw clench. Cross had orchestrated those "unfortunate circumstances" through a careful campaign of professional sabotage, but he'd been too clever to leave fingerprints on his betrayal.

"I'm managing," she said.

"I'm glad to hear it. West Virginia is a lovely state, though somewhat isolated from the major research centers. I imagine it must feel quite different from the collaborative environment you were used to at Virginia Tech."

Everything about his tone suggested sympathy, but Mara had learned to read the subtext in Cross's communications. He was reminding her that her career had been effectively exiled to an academic backwater, that her opportunities for high-profile research were now severely limited.

"The work environment here is very collegial," she said, refusing to take the bait.

"Excellent. And your new colleagues—are they supportive of your research interests? I know you were working on some quite innovative seismic prediction models before... well, before you decided to make a change."

Before you destroyed my credibility and forced me to resign, she thought but didn't say.

"I'm still exploring research opportunities," she replied carefully.

"Wise to take your time. It's important to be selective about collaboration, especially given your recent experiences. Some colleagues can be..."

He paused, as if searching for the right word. "Unreliable. I'd hate to see you get involved with researchers whose methods might not meet the rigorous standards you're accustomed to."

The warning was subtle but clear: Be careful who you trust, because your reputation can't survive another scandal.

"I appreciate your concern," Mara said, though appreciation was the last thing she felt.

"Of course. We may have had our differences, but I still consider myself something of a mentor to you. If you ever need advice about navigating... challenging colleagues... please don't hesitate to call."

The line went dead, leaving Mara staring at her phone with a familiar mixture of anger and anxiety. Cross had a talent for making her feel simultaneously threatened and protected, as if he were the source of both her problems and their solutions.

She set the phone aside and returned to the geological surveys, but her concentration was shattered. Cross's call hadn't been coincidental—he'd learned about her position at WVU somehow, which meant he was keeping tabs on her career. The reference to "unreliable colleagues" suggested he might even know about her conversation with Elias.

The thought sent a chill through her. Cross's influence extended far beyond his own university, and his ability to manipulate professional networks had been instrumental in her downfall at Virginia Tech. If he decided that her new position represented a threat to his interests...

A low rumble interrupted her spiraling anxiety, a sound so faint she almost missed it beneath the ambient noise of her apartment's heating system. The windows rattled slightly, just enough to make the geological surveys shift on the table.

Mara froze, listening intently. The sound faded after a few seconds, leaving only the ordinary nighttime sounds of a university town—distant traffic, muffled music from neighboring apartments, the hum of electrical appliances.

Construction, she told herself. Or a heavy truck on the nearby highway. The kind of minor vibration that could easily be mistaken for seismic activity by someone whose professional paranoia had been activated by mysterious phone calls and cryptic survey markings.

But as she rolled up the geological surveys and prepared for bed, Mara couldn't shake the feeling that the rumble had come from below rather than above, from the earth itself rather than human activity on its surface.

She made a mental note to check the regional seismic monitoring data in the morning. Just to be sure.

After all, the data didn't lie.

People did.

Chapter 3: Academic Collision

The morning air carried an unusual stillness as Elias walked across campus toward the Earth Sciences building, Koa trotting beside him with less than his usual enthusiasm. The dog kept pausing to sniff the air, ears swiveling toward sounds only he could detect, and twice he'd tried to steer them away from their normal route through the quad.

"What's gotten into you lately, boy?" Elias murmured, though he suspected he already knew the answer. The Prometheus data from the past forty-eight hours showed no signs of improvement—if anything, the behavioral anomalies were spreading and intensifying.

He pulled out his phone and checked the overnight reports. Sixty-three new incidents within a hundred-mile radius. Horses refusing to cross bridges. Farm dogs digging frantically as if trying to escape something underground. A veterinary clinic in Fairmont reporting a forty percent increase in anxiety-related visits.

And now he was about to spend two hours in a classroom with Dr. Mara Lang, trying to present a unified front while teaching radically different approaches to environmental prediction.

This should be interesting.

The co-taught seminar had been Dr. Welsh's idea—a way to give students exposure to interdisciplinary thinking while showcasing the department's collaborative spirit. "Environmental Prediction: Science, Culture, and Human Response" was listed as a 400-level course, which meant the twenty students enrolled were serious about their academic work and unafraid of complex concepts.

Elias had spent the previous evening preparing his portion of the lesson plan, focusing on historical examples of successful prediction through observing animal behavior. He'd selected case studies from around the world: the dogs of Helice who fled before the earthquake that destroyed the ancient Greek city, the snakes that emerged from hibernation before the devastating Haicheng earthquake in China, the horses that refused to enter the Yellowstone backcountry in the days before the 1988 fires.

Each example demonstrated the same principle: animals possessed sensory capabilities and environmental awareness that humans had either lost or learned to ignore. The challenge was translating that awareness into actionable intelligence.

Mara, he suspected, had prepared something entirely different.

***

Room 237 in the Earth Sciences building was a modern classroom equipped with dual projection systems, whiteboards on three walls, and flexible seating that could be arranged for traditional lectures or small group discussions. Elias arrived fifteen minutes early to find Mara already there, connecting her laptop to the presentation system.

She wore a charcoal blazer over dark jeans and boots that looked both practical and elegant—the kind of outfit that suggested someone who was equally comfortable in the field or the boardroom. Her dark hair was pulled back in a neat ponytail, and she moved with the efficient precision he was beginning to recognize as characteristic.

"Good morning," he said, setting his own materials on the desk. "Ready for our academic cage match?"

Mara glanced up, and for a moment, he caught something unguarded in her expression—amusement, maybe, or anticipation. But it was quickly replaced by professional courtesy.

"I prefer to think of it as intellectual discourse," she replied. "Though I suppose the students might enjoy the spectacle of two professors disagreeing in real time."

"Disagree? We're not going to disagree." Elias grinned. "We're going to have a spirited exchange of ideas that will demonstrate the importance of considering multiple perspectives when approaching complex problems."

"Is that what we're calling it?"

There was something in her tone—dry humor, maybe, or the beginning of a smile—that made him want to keep the conversation going. But students were beginning to file into the classroom, backpacks slung over their shoulders, coffee cups in hand, the slightly dazed look of people adjusting to morning schedules.

"Dr. Quinn! Dr. Lang!" A young woman with long black hair and an eager expression approached the front of the room. "I'm so excited about this class. I've been reading about both of your research areas, and the potential for integration is fascinating."

"Sierra Patel," Mara said, consulting her class roster. "Graduate student in geological engineering, undergraduate degree from Carnegie Mellon. Impressive academic record."

Sierra beamed at the recognition. "Thank you, Dr. Lang. I'm particularly interested in how traditional knowledge systems might complement modern predictive technologies. There's so much we might be missing by focusing exclusively on instrumental data."

Elias felt a surge of satisfaction. At least one student was approaching the topic with an open mind.

"That's exactly what we hope to explore," he said. "The intersection between scientific methodology and indigenous wisdom, between quantifiable data and observational knowledge."

"Though we should be careful not to romanticize traditional systems," Mara added, her tone diplomatic but firm. "Historical accuracy requires acknowledging both successes and failures."

The comment was clearly directed at him, though her expression remained professionally neutral. Elias felt his competitive instincts engage—not hostile, exactly, but the kind of intellectual challenge that made teaching exciting.

"Absolutely," he agreed. "Which is why we'll be examining case studies from multiple perspectives, looking at both the documented successes and the instances where traditional methods fell short."

More students had arrived, claiming seats and pulling out notebooks. Elias recognized several faces from his other classes, including a few who'd been present during his disastrous lecture with Dr. Harrison. He hoped today would go more smoothly.

"Shall we begin?" Mara asked, and Elias noticed the way she unconsciously smoothed her blazer. This small gesture suggested nerves beneath her composed exterior.

"After you," he said, gesturing toward the podium.

***

"Environmental prediction," Mara began, her voice carrying easily through the classroom, "is fundamentally about risk assessment. We study patterns in the physical world—geological, meteorological, biological—to anticipate events that might threaten human safety and economic stability."

She clicked her remote, and the projection screen filled with a map showing earthquake probability zones across the United States. Bright red areas marked regions of high seismic risk, while blue and green zones indicated relative stability.

"This map represents decades of data collection and analysis. Seismic monitoring networks, geological surveys, and historical records of past events. We can predict with reasonable confidence where earthquakes are most likely to occur, and roughly how severe they might be."

Sierra raised her hand. "But not when they'll occur?"

"Correct. Timing remains our greatest challenge. We can identify fault systems under stress, we can model the physics of rock failure, but we cannot predict the precise moment when that failure will occur."

Mara's presentation was polished, professional, and backed by solid data and clear visual aids. She spoke about magnitude calculations, probability distributions, and the mathematical models used to assess seismic hazards. Everything she said was accurate, well-researched, and utterly conventional.

Elias found himself watching her more than listening to her words. There was something compelling about her certainty, the way she moved through complex concepts with apparent ease. But he also noticed the subtle tension in her shoulders, the way her eyes occasionally flicked toward him as if gauging his reaction.

"Dr. Quinn," she said, turning toward him with what might have been a challenge in her voice, "would you like to present an alternative perspective?"

"I'd be happy to," he replied, standing and moving to the other side of the room. "Dr. Lang has given you an excellent overview of how modern science approaches environmental prediction. Now let me ask you a different question: what if we're only seeing part of the picture?"

He clicked his own remote, and the screen filled with a photograph of elephants moving in single file across the African savanna.

"December 26th, 2004. Two hours before the Indian Ocean tsunami struck the coasts of Thailand, elephants at the Khao Lak beach resort began acting strangely. They trumpeted in distress, broke their chains, and moved inland—carrying tourists on their backs to higher ground."

Several students leaned forward, intrigued. Sierra was taking notes rapidly.

"The elephants had no access to seismic data, no knowledge of plate tectonics, no understanding of wave propagation physics. But they knew something was wrong, and they acted on that knowledge in ways that saved human lives."

"Anecdotal evidence," Mara interjected, though her tone was more curious than dismissive. "Compelling, but not scientifically rigorous."

"You're right," Elias agreed. "A single incident proves nothing. But what about patterns? What about consistent, documented cases of animal behavior changes preceding seismic events?"

He advanced to the next slide, showing a data table with dates, locations, and behavioral observations.

"Friuli, Italy, 1976. Cats and dogs fled their homes in the hours before a magnitude 6.5 earthquake. Haicheng, China, 1975. Snakes emerged from hibernation in the dead of winter, livestock refused to enter barns, and dogs howled continuously for days before a magnitude 7.3 quake. L'Aquila, Italy, 2009. Residents reported unusual animal behavior for weeks before the earthquake that killed 308 people."

The classroom was quiet, students dividing their attention between Elias and Mara, clearly sensing the intellectual tension building between their professors.

"The question," Elias continued, "isn't whether these correlations exist—they're well documented. The question is whether we're arrogant enough to dismiss information sources we don't fully understand."

"It's not arrogance," Mara replied, rising from her chair with fluid grace. "It's methodology. Scientific prediction requires reproducible results, controlled conditions, and statistical significance. Animal behavior is influenced by dozens of variables—weather, human activity, disease, seasonal changes. How do you separate genuine precognitive abilities from random behavioral variations?"

"The same way we separate genuine seismic patterns from random geological noise," Elias shot back. "Through careful observation, data collection, and pattern analysis. The only difference is that we've chosen to trust our instruments more than our environmental partners."

"Our environmental partners?"

"Every animal that shares this ecosystem with us. Every creature whose survival depends on reading environmental cues we've forgotten how to perceive."

Mara stepped closer to the center of the room, and Elias found himself acutely aware of her proximity, the way the morning light from the windows caught the subtle highlights in her dark hair.

"That's a beautiful philosophy," she said, and he couldn't tell if she was being sarcastic or sincere. "But philosophy doesn't save lives when the earth starts shaking."

"Neither do prediction models that consistently fail to predict anything," he replied, then immediately regretted the harsh tone. This was supposed to be an academic discussion, not a personal attack.

But Mara didn't seem offended. If anything, she looked energized by the confrontation.

"Touché," she said. "Though I'd argue that imperfect science is still more reliable than perfect folklore."

Sierra raised her hand again, and both professors turned toward her.

"Actually," the graduate student said, "I have some personal experience that might be relevant to this discussion."

"Please," Mara said, gesturing for her to continue.

Sierra took a breath, as if steeling herself for something difficult. "My family is from West Virginia—coal mining country, about sixty miles southeast of here. My grandfather worked the mines for thirty-seven years, and my father followed him underground until the industry collapsed."

She paused, looking around the classroom at her fellow students.

"There's a story my family tells about something that happened in 1987, when I was just a baby. My grandfather was working the late shift at the Beckley mine when he noticed something strange—the pit ponies were acting up. They'd kept ponies underground in those days to help with the carts, and these animals had been working the same tunnels for years without any problems."

The classroom was completely quiet now, every student focused on Sierra's words.

"But that night, the ponies were refusing to go into the deep sections. They'd get to a certain point in the main tunnel and just stop, no matter how much the miners coaxed or pushed. My grandfather said he'd never seen anything like it—animals that had been perfectly obedient suddenly becoming stubborn and scared."

Elias felt his pulse quicken. He glanced at Mara and saw that she was listening intently, her scientific skepticism temporarily suspended.

"Most of the miners thought it was just animal foolishness," Sierra continued. "But my grandfather had been underground long enough to respect what the ponies knew about the mountain. He convinced his crew to end their shift early and come back to the surface."

She looked directly at Mara, then at Elias.

"Three hours later, there was a methane explosion in the deep tunnels. The same tunnels the ponies had refused to enter. Seven men were killed in the blast—men who were supposed to be working alongside my grandfather's crew."

The silence that followed was profound. Even the usual background sounds of the building seemed muted.

"The official investigation blamed faulty ventilation equipment," Sierra said quietly. "But my family has always believed that the ponies saved our lives. Animals know things we don't, feel things we can't. Sometimes listening to them is the difference between going home at the end of the day and never going home at all."

Elias saw Mara swallow hard, her composed expression wavering slightly. When she spoke, her voice was softer than before.

"That's a powerful story, Sierra. And I don't want to diminish its emotional impact. But one incident, even a compelling one, doesn't establish a predictive principle we can rely on."

"But it does suggest," Elias said gently, "that dismissing animal behavior entirely might be premature. Maybe the question isn't whether we should trust animals instead of instruments, but whether we can find ways to integrate both sources of information."

Mara met his eyes, and for a moment, the professional distance between them seemed to evaporate. He saw something vulnerable in her expression, as if Sierra's story had touched on experiences she wasn't ready to share.

"Integration," she repeated thoughtfully. "That's... not impossible. If we could develop rigorous protocols for behavioral observation, control for environmental variables, establish statistical baselines..."

"Exactly," Elias said, feeling a surge of excitement. "Combine traditional knowledge with modern methodology. Use technology to amplify indigenous wisdom rather than replace it."

The remainder of the class passed in animated discussion, with students asking questions and proposing their own examples of environmental prediction. Elias found himself stealing glances at Mara throughout the session, noticing the way she tilted her head when considering a complex question, the small smile that appeared when a student made a particularly insightful comment.

By the time the session ended, he was convinced that teaching with her again would be not just intellectually stimulating, but genuinely enjoyable.

***

The hallway outside Room 237 was filled with the usual post-class chatter as students gathered their belongings and discussed the morning's topics. Elias lingered near the doorway, ostensibly organizing his materials but actually waiting for Mara to finish her conversation with Sierra.

"Dr. Lang," Sierra was saying, "I'd love to discuss some research opportunities with you. I'm particularly interested in how geological monitoring systems might be enhanced by incorporating behavioral data."

"That's an intriguing idea," Mara replied. "Why don't you stop by my office hours this week? We can explore some possibilities."

After Sierra left, Mara turned to find Elias still standing near the door, his laptop bag slung over one shoulder, Koa sitting patiently at his feet.

"Good class," she said, and he thought he detected genuine warmth in her voice.

"It was," he agreed. "Your students seem exceptionally engaged. Sierra especially—she's going to make a significant contribution to whatever field she chooses."

"She reminds me of myself at that age," Mara said. "Passionate, idealistic, convinced that the right combination of intelligence and determination can solve any problem."

"And now?"

Mara's expression grew more guarded, but not unfriendly. "Now I know that intelligence and determination aren't always enough. Sometimes the problems are bigger than our ability to solve them."

There was something in her tone that suggested personal experience with unsolvable problems, and Elias found himself wanting to know more about what had brought her to West Virginia, what had put that note of caution in her voice.

"Coffee?" he asked impulsively. "I know a place off campus that makes excellent espresso and doesn't water down their coffee with academic politics."

For a moment, he thought she might accept. Something flickered in her expression—interest, maybe, or the beginning of a smile. But then the professional mask returned.

"I appreciate the offer, but I have office hours starting in twenty minutes. Maybe some other time."

"Of course," Elias said, trying not to let disappointment show in his voice. "Another time."

But as Mara gathered her materials and headed toward the elevator, she paused and looked back.

"For what it's worth," she said, "your approach to environmental prediction isn't as unscientific as I initially thought. Integrating traditional knowledge with modern methodology... there might be something there."

"High praise from a geologist," Elias replied, grinning.

"Don't let it go to your head, anthropologist."

The exchange was light, teasing, but Elias detected something underneath—a recognition of intellectual respect, maybe even the beginning of personal interest. As the elevator doors closed behind her, he found himself looking forward to their next collaboration with an anticipation that had nothing to do with academic research.

***

The campus coffee shop occupied a corner of the student union, its wide windows overlooking the central quad and the distant Appalachian foothills. Elias claimed a small table near the back, ordered a double shot of espresso, and tried to analyze his reaction to Mara's polite rejection.

It wasn't as if he'd been asking her on a date. Coffee with colleagues was routine academic behavior, the kind of informal interaction that facilitated collaboration and built professional relationships. Her decision to prioritize office hours over casual conversation was entirely reasonable.

So why did he feel like he'd been turned down for something more significant than a professional coffee meeting?

Koa settled under the table with a contented sigh, apparently relieved to be away from whatever environmental disturbances had been affecting him lately. The dog's behavior was one of many data points that had been troubling Elias over the past few days—subtle signs of distress that didn't seem to have obvious explanations.

He pulled out his phone and checked the latest Prometheus reports. The behavioral anomalies were continuing to spread, now encompassing a roughly circular area with a hundred-mile radius centered on the southern Appalachian region. Livestock are refusing to graze in certain fields. Domestic animals showing signs of anxiety. Wild creatures are avoiding their usual habitats.

If he were to present these patterns to a scientific panel—to colleagues like Mara who demanded rigorous methodology and statistical significance—they would rightfully point out the lack of controlled conditions, the subjective nature of behavioral assessment, the absence of clear causal mechanisms.

But the patterns were undeniable, and they were intensifying.

His phone buzzed with an incoming call from a number he didn't recognize.

"Professor Quinn? This is Sheriff Tom Granger from Pendleton County."

"Sheriff," Elias replied, immediately alert. Calls from law enforcement rarely brought good news. "What can I do for you?"

"I understand you're some kind of expert on animal behavior," Granger said, his voice carrying the measured cadence of someone accustomed to dealing with both routine complaints and genuine emergencies. "I've been getting some unusual reports from farmers in my jurisdiction, and I was hoping you might have some insight."

Elias felt his pulse quicken. "What kind of reports?"

"Livestock acting strange. Horses refusing to cross bridges they've crossed for years. Cattle clustering in the corners of fields won't spread out to graze. Dogs digging holes like they're trying to escape something underground. Started about a week ago, but it's gotten worse the past couple of days."

"How many reports?"

"Dozen or so, scattered across maybe thirty square miles. Might not sound like much, but these are people who've been working with animals their whole lives. They know when something's not right."

Elias pulled out a pen and started taking notes. "Any common factors? Geographic clustering, weather patterns, changes in local industry?"

"Nothing obvious. Mix of elevation levels, different types of farming operations, no recent construction or industrial activity. But there's something else that's got me concerned."

Granger paused, and Elias heard papers rustling in the background.

"There's a fellow who has been making the rounds, talking to the farmers, asking questions about their animals and their land. Claims to be some kind of researcher, but he's got them all worked up, talking about government cover-ups and hidden dangers. Started showing up right around the time the animal problems began."

A chill ran down Elias's spine. "What kind of questions?"

"Property boundaries, mineral rights, whether they've noticed any unusual geological features. And he's been telling them that people like you—university researchers studying animal behavior—are part of some conspiracy to hide information from the public."

"Did you get a name?"

"Goes by Dr. Richard Cross. Drives a black SUV with Virginia plates. Professional-looking fellow, very persuasive. But he's got people scared, talking about evacuating their farms, selling their land below market value."

Elias felt the coffee turn bitter in his mouth. Cross—the same name Mara had mentioned in connection with her previous position, the colleague who had somehow betrayed her trust and forced her resignation.

"Sheriff, I'd like to come down and talk to some of these farmers myself, if they're willing. The animal behavior patterns you're describing... they might be significant."

"Significant how?"

Elias hesitated, aware that his next words might sound either prophetic or delusional.

"They might indicate some kind of environmental change that humans haven't detected yet. Something the animals are sensing before our instruments pick it up."

"Environmental change, like what?"

"I'm not sure yet. But I'd like to find out before Dr. Cross convinces everyone that the problem is government conspiracy rather than geological reality."

Granger was quiet for a moment. When he spoke again, his voice carried a note of concern that hadn't been there before.

"Professor Quinn, I've been a sheriff for eighteen years. I've seen people panic over rumors, seen communities torn apart by fear and misinformation. If there's something real happening here, something that might affect public safety, I need to know about it."

"I understand. And I promise you, if my research indicates any genuine threat to public safety, you'll be the first person I call."

"Fair enough. But Professor? If this Cross fellow is trying to create panic for his own purposes, that's a problem I can solve. Interfering with agricultural operations, spreading false information that affects property values—there are laws against that kind of behavior."

After ending the call, Elias sat staring out the coffee shop windows at the peaceful campus scene. Students walked between buildings, backpacks slung over their shoulders, absorbed in conversations or cell phone screens. Faculty members moved with the unhurried pace of people whose greatest concern was making it to their next class on time.

None of them seemed aware that something fundamental might be shifting beneath their feet.

Cross's presence in the region couldn't be coincidental. The man was somehow connected to Mara's professional troubles, and now he was actively working to discredit the very research that might provide early warning of environmental dangers.

The question was whether Cross was simply an opportunistic troublemaker exploiting local fears, or whether he knew something about the animal behavior patterns that made him want to suppress scientific investigation.

Either way, Elias was certain of one thing: the mysterious email sender's warning about being watched was proving disturbingly accurate.

Someone was definitely watching his work.

And they were taking active steps to interfere with it.

Chapter 4: The First Tremor

The morning air felt electric with the tension that preceded thunderstorms, though the sky remained cloudless. Elias walked across campus with Koa pressed unusually close to his legs, the dog's behavior growing more agitated with each step toward the academic buildings.

It wasn't just Koa. As they passed the landscaped areas around the library, Elias noticed that the usual chorus of campus wildlife had fallen silent. No squirrels chattered in the oak trees. No birds called from their perches. Even the ornamental koi pond near the student center sat motionless, its surface undisturbed by the fish that normally created ripples as they fed.

The absence of sound was more unsettling than any noise could have been.

His phone buzzed with notifications from the Prometheus system—a steady stream of behavioral reports that had accelerated dramatically overnight. A veterinary clinic in Bridgeport reported that three separate pet owners had brought in cats that were hiding and refusing to eat. The agricultural extension office had logged calls from five different farms about livestock clustering in unusual patterns. A park ranger in the Monongahela

National Forest noted that deer were moving away from their normal feeding areas, heading consistently toward higher elevations.

There have been seventy-eight anomalous reports in the past twelve hours. The pattern was unmistakable now, centered in a roughly circular area that encompassed the university and extended into the surrounding hills.

"Easy, boy," Elias murmured as Koa whined and tugged toward a different path. "I know something's wrong. I'm watching it too."

But watching and understanding weren't the same thing. The data painted a clear picture of widespread animal distress, but the cause remained elusive. No seismic activity registered on official monitors. No unusual weather patterns. No industrial accidents or environmental contamination that might explain such a broad behavioral response.

Unless...

Elias pulled up the GPS coordinates for the center of the anomaly zone and cross-referenced them with geological survey maps. The epicenter of the disturbance fell squarely over a region that geological surveys had identified as seismically stable—old mountain formations that hadn't experienced significant tectonic activity in recorded history.

But indigenous legends spoke of different truths. Stories passed down through generations of Cherokee and other Native American tribes described the southern Appalachians as a place where the earth occasionally "awakened," where ancient spirits stirred beneath the mountains and caused the ground to shake.

Folklore. The kind of traditional knowledge that Mara would dismiss as unscientific.

The kind of traditional knowledge might be the only early warning system they had.

***

Room 237 buzzed with nervous energy as students filed in for their second co-taught environmental prediction seminar. Elias arrived to find Mara already setting up her presentation materials, but her usual composed efficiency seemed strained. She moved with quick, jerky motions that suggested underlying anxiety.

"Everything all right?" he asked, settling his laptop bag on the desk.

"Just tired," she replied without looking up. "I was up late reviewing some geological surveys, and I didn't sleep well."

Koa padded to his usual spot near the radiator but remained standing, ears alert, occasionally whining softly. Several students noticed the dog's distress and exchanged concerned glances.

"Is your dog okay, Professor Quinn?" asked a young man in the front row. "He seems really upset about something."

"Animals are sensitive to environmental changes we can't always detect," Elias replied, which was true enough without being alarmist. "He's probably picking up on atmospheric pressure changes or something similar."

But even as he spoke, Elias noticed other signs of distress throughout the classroom. A student's service dog was refusing to settle, pacing restlessly despite its training. Through the windows, he could see maintenance staff dealing with what looked like a flock of birds that had apparently flown into the building's glass facade—unusual behavior for creatures that had navigated the same architectural features for years.

Mara began her portion of the lesson with a discussion of seismic hazard assessment, her voice steady despite the tension he could see in her shoulders. She clicked through slides showing probability maps and risk calculations, explaining how geologists identified areas of potential earthquake activity.

"The key principle," she said, gesturing toward a cross-section diagram of tectonic plates, "is that geological processes follow predictable patterns. Stress accumulates along fault lines over time, and we can measure that accumulation using sensitive instruments."

Sierra raised her hand. "But what about areas that don't show obvious fault activity? Places where the geological surveys suggest stability, but there might still be underlying risk?"

It was a perceptive question, and Elias saw Mara hesitate before answering.

"Those areas..." she began, then paused, glancing toward the windows as if distracted by something outside. "Those areas are generally considered low-risk, but you're right to ask about it. Sometimes our understanding of regional geology is incomplete."

The admission surprised Elias. It was the first time he'd heard Mara acknowledge limitations in scientific methodology without being pressed to do so.

"Which brings us to the value of multiple information sources," he interjected, taking his cue to present the alternative perspective. "When instrumental data is incomplete, traditional knowledge systems might provide additional insights."

He clicked to his first slide, showing a map of earthquake prediction successes from around the world.

"1975, Haicheng, China. Official seismic monitoring indicated elevated risk, but the decision to evacuate the city was triggered by reports of unusual animal behavior. Snakes emerging from hibernation, livestock refusing to enter barns, domestic animals showing signs of extreme agitation."

"The evacuation saved an estimated 150,000 lives," Sierra added, clearly having done additional research since their last class.

"Exactly. But here's what's interesting about the Haicheng case—the animal behavior changes began weeks before the earthquake, but they intensified dramatically in the final 24 hours before the event."

Elias advanced to the next slide, showing a timeline of behavioral observations.

"Small changes first. Subtle alterations in feeding patterns, minor variations in sleep cycles. Then escalating distress signals. Animals refusing to enter certain areas, persistent vocalizations, attempts to flee or hide."

Koa whined loudly, as if responding to the description, and several students turned to look at the dog with new concern.

"The pattern suggests," Elias continued, trying to keep his voice steady despite his growing unease, "that animals can detect precursor phenomena that our instruments miss. Possibly low-frequency vibrations, electromagnetic changes, or chemical emissions that precede major seismic events."

Mara stepped forward, and he noticed that her professional composure had returned, though her eyes remained watchful.

"The challenge with animal behavior data," she said, "is distinguishing genuine precognitive responses from random behavioral variations. Animals react to dozens of environmental factors—weather changes, human activity, seasonal cycles, illness, social dynamics within their communities."

"True," Elias agreed. "Which is why the key is looking for patterns rather than isolated incidents. Widespread behavioral changes across multiple species, consistent directional responses, and behaviors that persist despite normal environmental fluctuations."

As if summoned by their discussion, a campus maintenance worker appeared outside the classroom windows, using a leaf blower to clear what looked like dozens of dead birds from the walkway below. The sight sent a chill through the room, and Elias saw several students exchange worried glances.

"That's... unusual," Mara said quietly, staring out at the scene.

Sierra's hand shot up. "Professor Lang, could we actually be observing a real-time example of the kind of pattern Dr. Quinn is describing?"

Before Mara could answer, the building began to shake.

It started as a low rumble, barely perceptible at first—the kind of vibration that might be attributed to heavy construction equipment or a passing truck. But the sound deepened and strengthened, rising from below rather than arriving from outside.

The floor beneath their feet began to undulate with a gentle, rolling motion that made several students grab their desks for stability. Coffee cups rattled against tabletops. The projection screen swayed on its mounting brackets.

Koa barked once, sharp and urgent, then pressed himself against Elias's legs.

"Everyone, stay calm," Elias called out, his voice cutting through the rising murmur of student voices. "Get under your desks and cover your heads."

The earthquake intensified, the rolling motion becoming more pronounced. Books tumbled from shelves. The lights flickered. Through the windows, Elias could see trees swaying beyond their normal range of motion, their branches moving in patterns that had nothing to do with wind.

Mara moved with swift efficiency, helping students who seemed frozen by fear or confusion. "Away from the windows," she called out. "Find cover and hold on."

The shaking continued for what felt like an eternity, but probably lasted less than thirty seconds. As it gradually subsided, leaving behind an eerie stillness, Elias realized that one student—a young woman near the back of the room—was still standing, apparently too shocked to move.

The aftershock hit just as she took a step toward her desk.

The secondary tremor was briefer but more violent than the initial quake, a sharp jolt that sent the student stumbling toward the tall windows. Elias moved without thinking, crossing the room in three quick strides and catching her just as she lost her balance.

His momentum carried them both away from the glass, which cracked with a sound like gunshots as the building frame twisted. They ended up against the far wall, the student—he thought her name was Jessica—breathing heavily in his arms.

"You're okay," he said, steadying her until she could stand on her own. "Just breathe. It's over."

But even as he spoke the reassuring words, Elias's mind was racing. The earthquake had followed almost exactly the pattern he'd described in his lecture—weeks of subtle animal behavior changes, escalating to obvious distress signals, culminating in seismic activity.

Prometheus had been right. The animals had been right.

The question was what came next.

***

The aftermath of the earthquake transformed the campus into a scene of controlled chaos. Emergency vehicles arrived within minutes, their sirens adding to the cacophony of car alarms, building alarms, and the general commotion of people trying to assess damage and ensure everyone's safety.

Elias stood outside the Earth Sciences building with his students, conducting informal headcounts and checking for injuries while waiting for official word on building safety. The structure appeared intact from the outside, but several windows had cracked, and maintenance crews were already beginning their inspections.

"Professor Quinn," Sierra approached with her notebook in hand, "I was monitoring the university's seismic sensors during the earthquake. The preliminary data shows magnitude of 3.2, duration approximately 28 seconds, with an epicenter about twelve miles southeast of campus."

"Quick thinking," Elias said, impressed by her initiative. "Did you get readings on the aftershock?"

"Magnitude 2.1, much shorter duration. But here's what's interesting—the wave propagation patterns don't match what I'd expect for typical regional geology."

Elias felt his pulse quicken. "What do you mean?"

Sierra flipped through her notes. "The seismic waves traveled faster through the bedrock than the geological models predict. It's subtle—maybe not significant—but the timing suggests the subsurface structure might be different from what the surveys indicate."

Before Elias could respond, Mara appeared at his elbow, her professional composure intact despite the circumstances.

"How are your students?" she asked.

"Shaken but unharmed. Jessica nearly fell into the windows, but she's fine now. How about yours?"

"Everyone's accounted for, no injuries. Though several are pretty rattled." Mara glanced around at the emergency response activity. "I need to inspect the building damage before we resume classes. Want to help?"

The offer surprised him—Mara had been maintaining careful professional distance since their coffee shop encounter. But crisis situations had a way of breaking down social barriers.

"Of course," he said.

They spent the next two hours conducting a methodical survey of the Earth Sciences building, checking each floor for structural damage, documenting cracks in walls and ceilings, and noting areas where windows had been compromised. Mara moved with the practiced efficiency of someone accustomed to post-disaster assessments, photographing damage patterns and making detailed notes about their locations and severity.

"Look at this," she said, crouching beside a crack that ran along the base of the wall in the building's main corridor. "This isn't typical seismic damage."

Elias knelt beside her, acutely aware of her proximity, the way her dark hair fell across her face as she examined the crack with her magnifying glass.

"What makes it unusual?"

"The orientation," Mara replied, tracing the crack's path with her finger. "Most earthquake damage creates cracks that follow predictable stress patterns—usually radiating outward from points of structural weakness.

But this crack runs in a straight line, almost perpendicular to the building's foundation."

She stood and moved to another damaged area, her movements graceful despite the debris scattered across the floor.

"And here—same pattern. Linear cracks that don't correspond to the building's stress points." She looked up at him, and he saw genuine puzzlement in her expression. "It's almost as if the shaking came from directly below, pushing straight up instead of radiating outward from a distant epicenter."

"What would cause that kind of pattern?"

Mara was quiet for a moment, clearly wrestling with something. When she spoke, her voice carried a note of reluctance.

"Localized uplift. Geological processes happening directly beneath the building rather than at a distant fault line." She paused. "Or potentially... volcanic activity."

The word hung between them like a challenge to everything they thought they knew about regional geology.

"Volcanic activity?" Elias repeated. "In West Virginia?"

"It's not impossible," Mara said, though her tone suggested she wasn't entirely convinced by her own words. "Ancient volcanic systems can become active again under the right conditions. But the geological surveys for this region show no evidence of volcanic features."

"What if the surveys missed something?"

Mara's professional training warred visibly with the evidence in front of her. "Surveys can be incomplete," she admitted finally. "Especially older ones. But to miss an entire volcanic system..."

"Would require either incompetence or deliberate suppression," Elias finished.

They stared at each other, both understanding the implications of what they were discussing. If there was volcanic potential in the region, if previous geological assessments had somehow failed to identify it, then the earthquake they'd just experienced might be the beginning of something much more serious.

"I need to review the historical surveys more carefully," Mara said. "Cross-reference them with current data, look for inconsistencies or gaps in the geological record."

"And I need to check the Prometheus data," Elias replied. "See how the animal behavior patterns correlate with the seismic activity."

It was the first time they'd spoken about combining their research approaches without debate or skepticism. Crisis, Elias reflected, had a way of cutting through academic posturing to focus on practical necessities.

"Coffee tomorrow morning?" Mara asked. "To compare notes?"

This time, her invitation carried no undertones of professional obligation. This time, it sounded like something she genuinely wanted.

"I'd like that," Elias said.

***

That evening, Elias sat in his home office surrounded by printouts of Prometheus data, laptop screens displaying behavioral tracking information, and maps showing the geographic distribution of animal anomalies over the past week. Koa lay nearby, finally calm for the first time in days, as if the earthquake had somehow released the tension that had been building in his nervous system.

The correlation between animal behavior and seismic activity was undeniable. Beginning five days ago, reports of unusual animal behavior had begun clustering in a circular pattern centered approximately twelve miles southeast of the university campus. The same location where seismic analysis had placed the earthquake's epicenter.

Over the following days, the reports had spread outward in concentric rings, like ripples in a pond. Domestic animals are showing anxiety, livestock are avoiding certain areas, and wild creatures are moving away from their normal territories. All followed a predictable pattern that culminated in today's seismic event.

Prometheus had detected the pattern three days ago and flagged it as a significant anomaly requiring investigation. Suppose Elias had trusted the system's analysis and been willing to make public predictions based on animal behavior data. In that case, he might have provided advance warning of the earthquake.

Instead, he'd hesitated, constrained by the same scientific conservatism that Mara represented, unwilling to risk his professional reputation on what colleagues would dismiss as speculation.

His phone chimed with an email notification. The sender was Sierra Patel, and the subject line read: "Urgent—Seismic Data Anomalies."

Professor Quinn,

I've been analyzing the earthquake data more carefully, and I found something that concerns me. The seismic signatures suggest this wasn't an isolated event—the geological processes that caused today's earthquake are still active.

I've attached detailed analysis, but the summary is that we're likely to see additional seismic activity in the coming days or weeks. Possibly stronger than what we experienced today.

Also, I received a strange email from someone claiming to know about historical geological surveys that were suppressed by government agencies. The sender mentioned Dr. Voss by name and suggested she might have information about previous seismic events in the region that weren't included in official records.

I know this sounds conspiracy theory crazy, but given everything that's happened today, I thought you should know.

—Sierra

Elias opened the attachments Sierra had sent and felt his blood pressure spike. Her analysis was thorough and professionally executed, showing wave propagation models, stress distribution calculations, and statistical projections for future seismic activity.

The conclusions were sobering: today's earthquake had released only a fraction of the tectonic stress that appeared to be building in the region. If her calculations were correct, they could expect additional seismic events within the next two weeks, potentially reaching magnitudes of 4.5 or higher.

Magnitudes that could cause serious structural damage and threaten public safety.

His phone rang, interrupting his analysis of Sierra's data.

"Professor Quinn? This is Dr. Voss."

The elderly volcanologist's voice sounded strained, as if she'd been struggling with a difficult decision.

"Dr. Voss," Elias replied. "Are you all right? I know today's earthquake must have been unsettling."

"I'm fine, physically. But I'm calling because today's event has forced me to confront some difficult memories. Things I probably should have spoken about years ago."

Elias felt his pulse quicken. "What kind of things?"

"I need to show you some documents, Professor Quinn. Research conducted in this region during the 1980s found that certain findings were discouraged from publication. If you're serious about your animal behavior research, if you truly believe that traditional knowledge systems can provide early warning of geological events, then you need to see what was discovered here thirty years ago."

"Can you tell me over the phone?"

"Not safely. But I can meet you tomorrow evening, if you're willing. Bring Dr. Lang if you trust her—this concerns her field of expertise as much as yours."

After ending the call, Elias returned to his analysis of the Prometheus data, but his concentration was broken by movement outside his window.

A figure stood at the edge of the woods behind his house, partially obscured by shadows but clearly watching the building.

Elias moved to the window and peered through the curtains, trying to make out details. The figure was tall, wearing dark clothing, and positioned at an angle that provided a clear view of Elias's office windows.

As if sensing his observation, the figure stepped deeper into the shadows and disappeared among the trees.

But not before Elias caught a glimpse of the man's profile.

Dr. Richard Cross was no longer content to watch from a distance.

He was getting closer.

Chapter 5: Prometheus Rising

The basement of Chitwood Hall felt like descending into the digital heart of some mad scientist's laboratory. Fluorescent lights hummed overhead, casting harsh shadows between towers of computer equipment that Elias had assembled over the past three years. Cables snaked across the floor in organized chaos, connecting servers, monitors, and data collection devices that blinked and whirred with constant activity.

"Welcome to Prometheus," Elias said, gesturing toward the array of machinery that occupied most of the cramped space. "It's not much to look at, but it's mine."

Mara stood in the doorway, taking in the scene with the careful attention she applied to geological formations. The basement lab was clearly a labor of love—every piece of equipment positioned with purpose, every cable routed with consideration for both function and maintenance access. But it was also obviously the work of someone operating on a limited budget and unlimited determination.

"You built all of this yourself?" she asked, stepping carefully around a particularly dense cluster of ethernet cables.

"Mostly salvaged university equipment and parts I ordered online," Elias replied, moving to a central workstation dominated by three large monitors. "The university's IT department wasn't exactly enthusiastic about supporting behavioral prediction research, so I had to get creative."

Koa followed them down the stairs but immediately began pacing restlessly, his claws clicking against the concrete floor. The dog's ears swiveled constantly, tracking sounds that were inaudible to human perception, and twice he approached the main server tower only to back away with a low whine.

"He's been like this for days," Elias explained, watching his dog with concern. "Something's got him spooked, but I can't figure out what."

Mara knelt beside Koa, letting him sniff her hand before gently scratching behind his ears. The dog leaned into her touch but remained visibly tense, his body coiled with nervous energy.

"Animals process environmental information differently than we do," she said thoughtfully. "Higher frequency ranges, electromagnetic sensitivity, vibrations we can't detect. If something in the environment is changing—"

"He might be the first to know," Elias finished. "That's exactly the principle behind Prometheus."

He turned to the central workstation and began bringing systems online. The monitors filled with scrolling data streams, real-time feeds from dozens of sources, and visualizations that transformed raw numbers into comprehensible patterns.

"The core concept is integration," Elias explained, settling into a worn office chair that had seen better decades. "Traditional environmental monitoring focuses on specific variables—seismic activity, weather patterns, atmospheric conditions. But what if we're missing crucial information by treating these systems as separate phenomena?"

Mara pulled up a second chair, close enough to see the monitors clearly but not so close that their proximity felt inappropriate. Still, Elias found himself acutely aware of her presence—the subtle scent of her perfume, the way she leaned forward when something caught her attention, the small furrow that appeared between her eyebrows when she was processing complex information.

"Show me how it works," she said, and there was genuine curiosity in her voice that made his pulse quicken.

Elias clicked through several screens, explaining the data collection networks he'd established over the past two years. Weather stations throughout the Appalachian region fed atmospheric data into the system. Seismic monitors provided real-time earthquake information. Wildlife cameras captured animal movement patterns. Social media feeds were scraped for keywords related to unusual animal behavior.

"But the most valuable input comes from human observers," he continued, pulling up a map dotted with colored pins. "Farmers, park rangers, veterinarians, pet owners—people who interact with animals daily and can report behavioral changes that might not show up in automated systems."

"How do you control for subjective interpretation?" Mara asked the scientist in her, who immediately identified potential flaws. "Human observers are notoriously unreliable, especially when they're looking for patterns that might not exist."

"That's where the algorithms come in," Elias replied, clicking to a new screen filled with complex mathematical formulas. "Prometheus doesn't just collect reports—it weighs them based on the observer's credibility, cross-references them with environmental data, and looks for statistical correlations that exceed random chance."

He pulled up a specific example: the behavioral reports that had preceded a minor earthquake in eastern Kentucky six months earlier.

"Forty-eight hours before the quake, we started getting reports of unusual animal behavior within a fifty-mile radius of what turned out to be the epicenter. Dogs are refusing walks, cats are hiding, and livestock is clustering away from normal grazing areas. Individually, any of these reports could be explained by other factors. But when you see coordinated behavioral changes across multiple species and geographic areas..."

"The pattern becomes statistically significant," Mara said, leaning closer to study the data visualization. Her shoulder brushed against his as she pointed to specific data points, and Elias felt an unexpected jolt of awareness that had nothing to do with scientific collaboration.

"Exactly. And that's just a magnitude 4.2 event—barely strong enough to rattle windows. The behavioral precursors for larger events are even more pronounced."

Mara was quiet for several minutes, scrolling through historical data and asking technical questions about the system's architecture. Elias found himself watching her face as she worked, noting the way her expression shifted from skepticism to interest to what might have been grudging admiration.

"This is actually quite sophisticated," she said finally. "The data integration, the statistical analysis, the real-time processing capabilities—you've essentially built a prototype early warning system."

"Prototype being the keyword," Elias replied. "The interface is crude, the processing power is limited, and I'm still working out bugs in the correlation algorithms. But the core concept seems sound."

"Have you published any of this work?"

The question hit a nerve that Elias wasn't entirely prepared for. "I've submitted papers to several journals. So far, the response has been... lukewarm. Most peer reviewers have concerns about the methodology, the reliability of behavioral data, the lack of controlled experimental conditions."

"Standard scientific skepticism," Mara said, but her tone was sympathetic rather than dismissive. "Revolutionary ideas rarely receive immediate acceptance, especially when they challenge established paradigms."

"Revolutionary might be overstating it," Elias said with a self-deprecating smile. "I'm not trying to overturn the laws of physics. I'm just suggesting that we might be overlooking valuable information sources."

"Which is exactly what makes it revolutionary."

Their eyes met for a moment, and Elias felt something pass between them—recognition, maybe, or the beginning of an intellectual partnership. Mara looked away first, returning her attention to the monitors, but not before he caught a faint flush coloring her cheeks.

"Dr. Quinn? Dr. Lang?" Sierra's voice echoed down the stairwell, followed by the sound of careful footsteps navigating the cable-strewn floor.

"Down here, Sierra," Elias called, grateful for the interruption but also slightly disappointed that their private moment had been broken.

Sierra appeared at the bottom of the stairs, laptop bag slung over her shoulder and eyes bright with curiosity. "I hope I'm not interrupting anything important."

"Not at all," Mara said, though Elias thought he detected a note of regret in her voice. "Dr. Quinn was just showing me his behavioral prediction system."

"Prometheus!" Sierra's enthusiasm was immediate and infectious. "I've been reading about your work, Dr. Quinn. The integration of traditional knowledge with modern data analysis—it's exactly the kind of interdisciplinary approach that could revolutionize environmental monitoring."

"You're welcome to take a look," Elias said, gesturing toward the workstation. "Though I should warn you, the user interface isn't exactly intuitive."

Sierra settled into a third chair they'd dragged over from a storage area, and for the next hour the three of them worked through the system's capabilities. Sierra's technical background in geological engineering proved invaluable—she immediately grasped the mathematical concepts underlying the correlation algorithms and began suggesting improvements to the data visualization modules.

"The problem isn't the analysis," she said, pulling up a particularly dense screen of statistical output. "It's presenting the results in a way that non-specialists can understand and act upon. You need interface design that translates complex correlations into clear, actionable warnings."

"Exactly," Elias agreed. "Right now, only someone with an extensive background in both behavioral analysis and statistical modeling can interpret the output effectively. That severely limits the system's practical applications."

"I could help with that," Sierra offered. "User interface design was part of my undergraduate coursework, and I've been looking for a research project that combines engineering principles with environmental applications."

Mara looked up from the technical documentation she'd been studying. "That's a generous offer, Sierra. But research partnerships involve long-term commitments, and Dr. Quinn's work is still in the experimental stages."

"Which is exactly what makes it exciting," Sierra replied. "Established research is safe, but experimental work is where real breakthroughs happen."

Elias felt a surge of gratitude toward the graduate student, both for her technical expertise and for her willingness to take risks on unconventional ideas. But he also noticed the way Mara had phrased her concern—not discouraging Sierra's involvement, exactly, but highlighting the uncertainties that came with cutting-edge research.

"What do you think, Mara?" he asked, deliberately using her first name for the first time. "Would Sierra's interface improvements make Prometheus more credible to the broader scientific community?"

Mara considered the question carefully, her gaze moving between the monitors and the two researchers watching her with expectant expressions.

"User interface improvements would certainly help," she said finally. "But credibility ultimately comes from results. The system needs to demonstrate clear predictive success under rigorous testing conditions."

"Which brings us back to the fundamental challenge," Elias said. "How do you rigorously test a system designed to predict rare, unpredictable events?"

"You wait," Sierra said pragmatically. "You monitor, you collect data, and when the next major environmental event occurs, you analyze how well your system performed."

"That could take years," Mara pointed out. "And if the system fails to predict a significant event, the credibility damage could be irreversible."

The conversation continued as evening settled over the campus. Sierra worked on interface mockups while Elias and Mara discussed the theoretical foundations of behavioral prediction. The basement lab, initially cramped and intimidating, began to feel comfortable—a space where ideas could be explored without the formal constraints of academic propriety.

***

By nine o'clock, Sierra had produced preliminary designs for a much more intuitive user interface, complete with color-coded alert levels and geographic visualization tools that would make Prometheus accessible to emergency management professionals and even educated members of the general public.

"This is remarkable work," Elias said, studying the mockups on Sierra's laptop screen. "You've managed to preserve the analytical sophistication while making the output genuinely user-friendly."

"The key is progressive disclosure," Sierra explained. "Basic users see simple alerts and recommendations, but technical users can drill down through multiple layers to access the underlying data and analysis."

Mara leaned over to examine the designs, her proximity to Elias once again sending an unexpected jolt of awareness through his nervous system. He could feel the warmth radiating from her body, catch the subtle movement of her breathing, detect the faint vanilla scent of whatever shampoo she used.

"These interface improvements would address most of my concerns about practical implementation," she said, seemingly unaware of the effect her closeness was having on him. "If the system could present clear, actionable information to non-specialists..."

"It becomes a tool rather than an academic curiosity," Elias finished, though his concentration was divided between the technical discussion and his growing awareness of Mara as something more than a professional colleague.

"Exactly." She looked up, and their faces were suddenly only inches apart, close enough that he could see the flecks of gold in her dark eyes, the way her lips parted slightly when she was thinking.

For a moment, the lab fell silent except for the humming of computer equipment and Koa's restless pacing. Elias felt the air between them charge with possibility, the kind of electric tension that preceded either breakthrough discoveries or serious mistakes.

Then Sierra's laptop chimed with an incoming message, breaking the spell.

"Sorry," Sierra said, glancing at her screen. "Just an email from my advisor about next week's seminar."

Mara stepped back, creating professional distance that felt both appropriate and disappointing. "I should probably head home," she said, glancing at her watch. "It's getting late, and I have an early class tomorrow."

"Of course," Elias replied, though he found himself reluctant to end the evening. The collaboration had felt natural, productive, and energizing in ways that his solitary research never achieved. "Thank you for taking the time to understand what Prometheus is trying to accomplish."

"Thank you for showing me," Mara said, gathering her jacket and purse. "Your work is more rigorous than I initially assumed. There might be real potential here."

Sierra began packing up her laptop, but she moved slowly, as if sensing that the adults in the room needed a moment to navigate whatever was developing between them.

"Mara," Elias said, then paused, uncertain how to voice what he was thinking. "Would you be interested in collaborating more formally? Your geological expertise could help refine the environmental correlation algorithms, and Sierra's interface work could make the system genuinely practical."

Mara paused at the bottom of the stairwell, considering his proposal. "What kind of collaboration did you have in mind?"

"Regular data review sessions, joint analysis of significant behavioral patterns, maybe co-authoring papers if we develop findings worth publishing." He kept his tone professional, but he couldn't entirely suppress the hope that collaboration might lead to something beyond academic partnership.

"I'll think about it," she said, which felt like progress rather than rejection. "This work deserves serious consideration, regardless of my initial skepticism."

After Mara and Sierra left, Elias remained in the lab, ostensibly running system diagnostics but actually replaying the evening's conversations and trying to analyze his growing attraction to his geological colleague. The intellectual connection was undeniable—Mara's sharp questions had forced him to articulate concepts more clearly than he'd managed in months of solitary work. But there was something deeper developing, a personal interest that went beyond professional respect.

He was checking the overnight data collection protocols when Prometheus issued an alert—not the major emergency signal he'd programmed for catastrophic events, but a moderate-level warning indicating unusual patterns in the behavioral data streams.

Elias pulled up the relevant displays and felt his breath catch. Reports were flooding in from across the Appalachian region: animals showing distress behaviors, livestock refusing to graze in specific areas, domestic pets displaying anxiety symptoms. The geographic distribution formed a rough circle centered approximately forty miles southeast of Morgantown, and the intensity was unlike anything he'd recorded since beginning the project.

He was reaching for his phone to call Sheriff Granger when the system suddenly froze. All the monitors went blank for several seconds, then displayed a simple error message: "Data corruption detected. Recent files may be incomplete."

When the system came back online, Elias discovered that several hours of behavioral reports had been deleted—not the most recent data, but a specific time range from earlier in the week. The deletion appeared to be selective, targeting only certain geographic regions and behavioral categories.

Random system failures didn't delete data selectively. Someone with detailed knowledge of Prometheus's architecture had accessed the system remotely and removed specific information.

But why target behavioral data from several days ago rather than current alerts? And how had they gained access to a system that wasn't connected to the university's main network?

Elias spent the next hour running diagnostic protocols and checking security logs, but found no evidence of unauthorized access. Whatever had happened, it had been accomplished by someone with sophisticated technical skills and detailed knowledge of the system's vulnerabilities.

As he locked up the lab and headed home, Koa trotting nervously beside him, Elias couldn't shake the feeling that the evening's collaboration with Mara had been observed by unfriendly eyes. The data deletion felt like a warning—or perhaps a test to see how quickly he would notice and respond to sabotage.

Either way, it was clear that his research was attracting attention from people who preferred that certain patterns remain undetected.

The question was whether Mara's involvement would make her a target as well, or whether her geological expertise might provide the key to understanding why someone was so determined to suppress evidence of environmental instability in the Appalachian region.

As they walked across the darkened campus, Koa suddenly stopped and growled low in his throat, staring into the shadows between the academic buildings. Elias followed his gaze but saw nothing unusual—just the normal campus landscape, poorly lit and largely deserted at this hour.

But Koa's hackles remained raised, and his focus never wavered from whatever had captured his attention in the darkness.

Somewhere in those shadows, Elias was certain, unfriendly eyes were watching.

And planning their next move.

Chapter 6: Data and Desire

Three days later

The basement lab had transformed into something resembling a war room. Additional monitors lined the walls, displaying real-time feeds from across the Appalachian region. Whiteboards covered in equations and behavioral correlation charts created a maze of intellectual intensity. Coffee cups in various stages of emptiness marked the territory of two researchers who had fallen into a routine of late-night collaboration that felt both professionally productive and personally dangerous.

Elias glanced at the clock: 11:47 PM. Mara sat cross-legged on the floor beside Koa, who had finally relaxed enough to serve as an impromptu backrest while she reviewed printouts of the latest behavioral data. Her dark hair had escaped its professional ponytail hours ago, framing her face in a way that made concentration on statistical analysis considerably more difficult.

"The pattern is definitely expanding," she said, highlighting sections of a regional map with a yellow marker. "Behavioral anomalies are now reported within a hundred-and-twenty-mile radius, but the intensity decreases with distance from the central focal point."

"Like ripples in a pond," Elias agreed, though he was watching the way her fingers moved across the data rather than focusing on the geographical implications. "Something is definitely disturbing the environmental equilibrium, and it's radiating outward from a specific source."

Over the past three nights, they had fallen into an easy rhythm. Mara would arrive around seven, claiming she was just stopping by to check on their progress, but inevitably staying until midnight or later. They would order Chinese takeout or pizza, spread their work across every available surface, and lose themselves in the kind of intense intellectual collaboration that made time seem irrelevant.

Sierra joined them most evenings, contributing interface improvements and offering fresh perspectives on their data interpretation. But tonight she had begged off, citing an early morning presentation for her advisor, leaving Elias and Mara alone with their research and the growing awareness that their partnership was evolving beyond academic boundaries.

"Your correlation algorithms are remarkable," Mara said, setting aside the printouts and reaching for her laptop. "I've been running some geological analyses based on your behavioral focal points, and some interesting patterns are emerging."

She pulled up a topographical map overlaid with seismic monitoring data, the screen's blue glow highlighting the elegant line of her profile. Elias found himself studying the curve of her neck, the way she absently tucked a strand of hair behind her ear when she was concentrating.

"See these micro-tremor patterns?" she continued, pointing to clusters of barely visible dots on the display. "They're too small to register on standard earthquake monitoring systems, but when you aggregate them over the past six months, they form a clear geological structure."

Elias moved closer to see the screen better, their shoulders touching as he leaned in. The contact sent an unexpected jolt of awareness through him—the warmth of her body, the subtle scent of her perfume mixed with the coffee they'd been consuming all evening.

"A fault system," he said, though his voice came out rougher than intended.

"Not just any fault system," Mara replied, seemingly unaware of the effect her proximity was having on him. "This matches geological surveys from the 1980s that were never fully published. The same surveys that had those mysterious 'L.V.' markings I found in my office."

She clicked through several more displays, showing underground structure models and historical seismic data. The evidence was compelling, but Elias found his attention divided between the scientific implications and his growing awareness of Mara as a woman rather than just a colleague.

Koa lifted his head from where he'd been dozing, ears pricked toward some sound only he could detect. But instead of the nervous pacing that had characterized his behavior for weeks, the dog simply repositioned himself closer to Mara, as if her presence provided some kind of calming influence.

"Even Koa likes you," Elias observed, grateful for a topic that didn't require him to analyze his own emotional state.

Mara smiled, scratching behind the dog's ears with gentle familiarity. "He's a good judge of character. Dogs usually are."

"Elena used to say the same thing."

The name slipped out before Elias could stop it, carrying with it all the emotional weight he'd been carefully avoiding in their professional interactions. Mara looked up, her expression shifting from casual affection for his dog to something more serious and attentive.

"Elena was your wife," she said quietly. It wasn't a question.

Elias nodded, suddenly feeling exposed in a way that had nothing to do with academic vulnerability. "She died eighteen months ago. Car accident."

"I'm sorry." Mara's voice carried genuine sympathy, not the perfunctory condolences he'd grown accustomed to receiving. "That must have been devastating."

"It was." He found himself talking about Elena in ways he hadn't with anyone since the funeral. "She was a behavioral biologist, actually. Much more scientifically rigorous than I am. She would have loved what we're doing here—the integration of traditional knowledge with modern methodology."

Mara set aside her laptop, giving him her full attention. "Is that where the inspiration for Prometheus came from?"

"Partly. Elena always believed that animals possessed sensory capabilities we'd evolved away from. She used to say that civilization had made us deaf to conversations that were happening all around us—chemical communications, electromagnetic signals, vibrations that travel through ground and water. Her death made me realize how much knowledge dies with each person, how much wisdom we lose when we dismiss sources of information that don't fit our technological paradigms."

The lab fell quiet except for the humming of computer equipment and Koa's contented breathing. Mara studied Elias's face with the same careful attention she applied to geological formations, as if looking for patterns that might reveal hidden structures.

"Building Prometheus was a way of continuing her work," she said, understanding evident in her voice.

"Or trying to prove that her theories weren't just romantic idealism," Elias admitted. "Sometimes I think I'm more interested in honoring her memory than advancing scientific knowledge."

"Those aren't mutually exclusive goals."

The simple statement carried surprising emotional weight. Most people offered platitudes about moving on or finding closure, but Mara seemed to understand that love and loss could coexist with intellectual passion.

"What about you?" he asked, recognizing that personal revelations should be reciprocal. "What brought you to West Virginia? And don't say 'fresh start'—I can tell there's more to the story."

Mara was quiet for a long moment, her fingers absently stroking Koa's fur. When she finally spoke, her voice carried the careful tone of someone sharing painful experiences.

"Richard Cross was my graduate advisor at Virginia Tech. Brilliant researcher, charismatic teacher, the kind of mentor every student hopes to find. He took me under his wing, guided my dissertation work, made me feel like I was part of something important."

She paused, and Elias could see the tension building in her shoulders.

"It took me three years to realize that he was systematically appropriating my research, publishing papers based on my work without giving me credit. When I confronted him about it, he claimed that graduate student research belonged to the supervising professor. When I threatened to report him to the university ethics committee..."

"He destroyed your career," Elias finished, feeling anger on her behalf.

"He was more subtle than that. Suddenly, my methodology was questionable, my data analysis was flawed, and my conclusions were unsupported by evidence. He convinced other faculty members that I was an unreliable researcher who couldn't handle the pressures of academic life. By the time I realized what was happening, my reputation was too damaged to recover."

"So you resigned."

"I was given the choice between resignation and formal dismissal. Resignation looked better on my record, gave me a chance to find another position somewhere else." Her voice turned bitter. "Somewhere far enough from Virginia Tech that the rumors might not follow."

Elias felt a surge of protective anger that surprised him with its intensity. "He's the reason you're so skeptical of unconventional research."

"Cross taught me that brilliance and integrity don't always go together, that charismatic people can manipulate data to support whatever conclusions serve their purposes." Mara looked directly at him, her expression vulnerable but determined. "When I first heard about your behavioral prediction work, I assumed you were another brilliant narcissist using questionable methodology to gain attention."

"And now?"

"Now I think you're genuinely trying to understand something important, even if your methods don't fit conventional scientific paradigms." She smiled, and he felt something shift between them—a deepening of trust that went beyond professional collaboration. "Though I reserve the right to change my mind if you start claiming credit for my geological analysis."

"I would never—"

"I know," she said softly. "That's what makes this collaboration possible."

The moment stretched between them, charged with implications neither seemed ready to fully acknowledge. Elias became acutely aware of their proximity, of the way the basement's harsh fluorescent lights had been dimmed to reduce eye strain, creating an unexpectedly intimate atmosphere. Mara was sitting close enough that he could see the flecks of gold in her dark eyes, close enough that he could lean forward and...

A Prometheus alert chimed, breaking the spell with electronic insistence.

"Major behavioral anomaly detected," the system announced in the synthesized voice Elias had programmed for emergency notifications. "Multiple species, expanding geographic distribution, statistical significance exceeds baseline parameters by four hundred percent."

They both turned toward the monitors, the moment of personal connection reluctantly set aside for professional crisis. But as Elias pulled up the alert data, Mara moved to stand behind his chair, her hand briefly touching his shoulder in a gesture that felt both supportive and intimate.

"This is unprecedented," she said, studying the cascading data displays. "The behavioral reports are coming from every monitoring station in the network."

"And they're all showing the same pattern," Elias added, his fingers flying across the keyboard as he pulled up geographic visualizations. "Coordinated distress behaviors across multiple species, radiating outward from the same focal point we identified earlier."

The main display showed a real-time map of the Appalachian region, with colored dots representing behavioral anomaly reports. The pattern was unmistakable: a roughly circular area of intense animal distress, centered approximately sixty miles southeast of their location, with ripple effects extending outward like shock waves from some underground disturbance.

"If this were seismic activity," Mara said, her scientific training taking over, "I'd say we were looking at precursor signals for a major geological event."

"But it's not seismic activity," Elias replied, pulling up earthquake monitoring data that showed normal background levels throughout the region. "At least, nothing our instruments can detect."

They worked for another hour, analyzing the data from multiple angles, cross-referencing with historical patterns, and trying to develop meaningful predictions based on the unprecedented behavioral reports. The collaboration felt natural, energizing, as if their different expertise areas were combining to create insights neither could achieve alone.

It was nearly 2 AM when Mara finally stretched and announced that she needed to head home before she fell asleep at her desk. "My first class is at eight," she said, gathering her materials with obvious reluctance. "Though I hate to leave when we're making this kind of progress."

"Take a key," Elias said impulsively, pulling out his key ring and removing the spare he'd had made for Sierra. "To the lab, I mean. In case you want to check the data when I'm not here, or if you think of something that needs immediate attention."

Mara stared at the key as if it represented something more significant than simple access to a basement laboratory. "Are you sure? This is your research, your space..."

"It's our research now," he said, meaning it more completely than he'd expected. "And I trust you."

She closed her fingers around the key, the simple gesture feeling like a formalization of their partnership. "Thank you. For the access, and for trusting me with work that's obviously important to you."

They stood in the doorway of the lab, reluctant to end the evening despite the late hour and their mutual exhaustion. The basement hallway was dimly lit and completely deserted, creating an atmosphere of intimacy that made ordinary conversations feel charged with possibility.

"Mara," Elias began, then stopped, uncertain how to voice what he was thinking.

"Yes?"

"I'm glad you decided to collaborate with me. Not just because of your expertise, but because... working with you makes the research feel more meaningful."

She looked up at him, her expression shifting from professional courtesy to something warmer and more personal. "I feel the same way. This work, what we're discovering together—it's the most excited I've been about research in years."

They were standing close enough that Elias could see the way her lips parted slightly when she was thinking, close enough that leaning forward would close the distance between them entirely. The hallway seemed to hold its breath, waiting for one of them to acknowledge what was developing beyond academic collaboration.

Mara's phone rang, shrill and intrusive in the quiet hallway.

She glanced at the screen, frowned, and answered with obvious reluctance. "Dr. Lang."

Even from several feet away, Elias could hear the agitated voice on the other end of the line. Mara's expression shifted from mild annoyance to serious concern as she listened.

"Yes, Dr. Welsh, I understand your concerns," she said carefully. "No, I haven't discussed our research with anyone outside the university... Yes, I realize that collaboration requires departmental approval for anything involving potential publication..."

Cross, Elias realized with a sinking feeling. Somehow, Cross had learned about their collaboration and was applying pressure through official channels.

Mara ended the call and stood staring at her phone with an expression of frustrated anger.

"Problem?" Elias asked, though he suspected he already knew the answer.

"Dr. Welsh received a call from someone questioning my 'professional judgment' and 'choice of research collaborators,'" Mara said, her voice tight with controlled emotion. "Apparently, there are concerns about my involvement with work that might not meet appropriate academic standards."

"Cross."

"Has to be. The phrasing was too specific, too targeted to be coincidental." She looked up at him with an expression that mixed anger, fear, and determination. "He's trying to isolate me professionally, make it impossible for me to collaborate with anyone he considers a threat."

"We won't let him," Elias said firmly. "Our research is solid, our methodology is sound, and our findings speak for themselves."

"I hope you're right," Mara replied, but her voice carried doubt that hadn't been there before Cross's interference. "I can't afford another professional scandal, Elias. My career barely survived the first one."

As she walked toward the stairwell, Elias felt a surge of protective anger mixed with something deeper—a recognition that his feelings for Mara went beyond professional collaboration or intellectual attraction. Cross's attempts to sabotage her career felt like personal attacks, and he found himself willing to do whatever was necessary to protect both her research and her reputation.

He was locking up the lab when he noticed something that made his blood run cold.

A folded piece of paper had been slipped under the door—not there when they'd arrived that evening, positioned where it couldn't be missed when leaving.

Elias unfolded the paper with trembling fingers and read the message printed in block letters:

STOP DIGGING.

No signature, no identifying marks, just those two words that felt like a direct threat. Someone had been in the building, had known exactly where to find them, had waited until they were alone and vulnerable to deliver their warning.

Koa suddenly appeared at his side, growling low in his throat and staring at the stairwell as if sensing the presence of whoever had left the note. The dog's hackles were raised, his body tense with protective instincts.

"Mara!" Elias called, taking the stairs two at a time.

He found her in the main hallway, frozen beside the exit door, staring at something in her hands. Her face was pale, her breathing shallow with what looked like fear or shock.

"What is it?" he asked, though part of him already knew.

Without a word, she held up an identical piece of paper.

STOP DIGGING.

"Someone was watching us," she whispered, her voice barely audible. "They knew exactly when we'd be leaving, exactly how to deliver maximum intimidation."

Elias felt cold rage building in his chest. Bad enough that Cross was using official channels to undermine their research—but direct threats crossed a line that made personal safety a genuine concern.

"We should call campus security," he said, pulling out his phone.

"And tell them what? That someone left us anonymous notes that could be interpreted as anything from academic rivalry to student pranks?" Mara shook her head, though he could see the fear beneath her practical response. "Cross is too smart to leave evidence that could be traced back to him."

As they walked across the deserted campus toward the faculty parking area, Koa maintained his protective position between them and the shadows, alert to threats that human senses couldn't detect. The dog's behavior made it clear that danger was real and immediate, not just psychological intimidation.

"This changes things," Mara said when they reached her car. "If Cross is willing to resort to direct threats..."

"It means we're onto something important enough to scare him," Elias finished. "Important enough that he's willing to take risks to stop our research."

"Or it means he's escalating toward something more dangerous than professional sabotage."

The implication hung between them as Mara unlocked her car and tossed her laptop bag onto the passenger seat. The evening that had begun with scientific collaboration and personal revelation was ending with very real concerns about their safety.

"Be careful driving home," Elias said, hating how inadequate the words sounded. "And call me when you get there, just so I know you're okay."

"I will." She paused, key in hand, and looked back at him with an expression that mixed vulnerability with determination. "Elias? Whatever Cross is trying to hide, whatever he's so afraid we'll discover—I'm not backing down. Not this time."

"Neither am I," he replied, meaning it completely.

As Mara drove away, her taillights disappearing into the darkness beyond campus, Elias stood in the empty parking lot with Koa pressed against his legs, both of them alert to sounds and movements that might indicate continued surveillance.

The threatening notes had been intended to isolate them, to make them doubt their research and abandon their collaboration. But the effect had been exactly the opposite—they were more committed to their work than ever, and more invested in each other's safety and success.

Cross had made a tactical error. Instead of dividing them, he had forced them into a partnership that was becoming something deeper than academic collaboration.

The question was whether the partnership would be strong enough to survive whatever Cross was planning next.

Chapter 7: The Prediction

The basement lab hummed with an intensity that seemed to match the urgency building in the data streams. Elias stared at the central monitor, his coffee growing cold in his hands as Prometheus processed the overnight behavioral reports and cross-referenced them with geological data Mara had integrated into the system. Numbers cascaded across multiple screens, but it was the synthesis display that held his attention. This visualization transformed raw data into something that looked disturbingly like a countdown timer.

"This can't be right," he murmured, running the analysis for the third time in ten minutes.

The results were identical. Prometheus was generating its first major prediction: a significant seismic event, magnitude 6.5 or higher, with an epicenter approximately fifty-seven miles southeast of Morgantown. Timeline: seventy-two to ninety-six hours.

Koa lay at his feet, but the dog's restless energy had been replaced by something more ominous—a hypervigilant stillness, as if he were listening to sounds that existed just beyond human perception. Every few minutes, his ears would swivel toward the ceiling, tracking something moving through the building's structure or perhaps through the earth itself.

Elias reached for his phone to call Mara, then stopped. The prediction was revolutionary if accurate, career-ending if wrong. Before involving her in what might be professional suicide, he needed to verify every calculation, check every assumption, and confirm that Prometheus wasn't generating false positives from corrupted data.

He spent the next hour running diagnostic protocols and manually checking the correlation algorithms Sierra had helped refine. The mathematics were sound, the data integration was functioning properly, and the statistical confidence levels exceeded anything the system had previously generated.

Prometheus was telling him that the earth was about to move in ways that would affect tens of thousands of people, and it was doing so with the kind of certainty that demanded immediate action.

His phone buzzed with an incoming text from Mara: "In my office reviewing overnight seismic data. Something strange is happening. Can you meet me in an hour?"

The synchronicity sent a chill through him. Suppose Mara was seeing anomalies in the geological data that matched Prometheus's behavioral analysis. In that case, the prediction might have independent verification from entirely different sources.

He saved the analysis results to an encrypted drive, locked down the lab systems, and headed for the Earth Sciences building with Koa trotting nervously beside him.

***

Mara's office had been transformed into something resembling a geological war room. Maps covered every available surface, weighted down with coffee mugs and textbooks to prevent them from rolling closed. Her computer displayed multiple windows showing seismic monitoring data, underground structure models, and what appeared to be historical earthquake records dating back to the 1800s.

She looked up when Elias knocked on her open door, and he immediately noticed the tension in her expression—the kind of controlled concern that suggested she'd discovered something that challenged her fundamental understanding of regional geology.

"Thank god you're here," she said, gesturing for him to enter. "I've been staring at this data for three hours, and I keep reaching the same impossible conclusion."

"Which is?"

"That the Appalachian region is showing precursor signals for a major seismic event. Not microearthquakes or minor fault adjustments—something significant enough to cause structural damage across a wide area."

Elias felt his pulse quicken. "How significant?"

Mara pulled up a computer model showing underground stress patterns; the display filled with red and orange zones indicating areas of geological instability. "Based on the micro-tremor patterns and fault stress analysis, I'd estimate magnitude 6.0 to 7.0, centered somewhere in the southern Appalachian region."

"Prometheus is predicting 6.5 or higher, epicenter about sixty miles southeast of here, timeline seventy-two to ninety-six hours."

The words hung in the air between them, carrying implications that neither seemed fully prepared to acknowledge. Mara stared at him with an expression that mixed shock, disbelief, and something that might have been fear.

"Your system is predicting a specific timeline?" she asked quietly.

"Based on the behavioral escalation patterns and correlation with your geological data. The animal distress reports have reached critical thresholds across multiple species and geographic areas. According to the algorithms, that level of coordinated response typically precedes major seismic events by three to four days."

Mara turned back to her computer, pulling up additional displays with fingers that trembled slightly. "The historical records support that timeline. Every major earthquake in the Appalachian region over the past two centuries has been preceded by three to five days of what the reports called 'animal unrest' and 'atmospheric disturbances.'"

"You believe it," Elias said, recognizing the shift in her tone from skepticism to acceptance.

"I believe the data. And the data is telling us that something unprecedented is about to happen in a region that's supposed to be geologically stable." She looked at him with an expression that mixed professional excitement with personal fear. "If we're right, Elias, this could revolutionize earthquake prediction. But if we're wrong..."

"Our careers are over."

"Worse than that. Suppose we issue public warnings that cause panic and evacuations, and nothing happens. In that case, we'll have destroyed public trust in scientific prediction for decades. No one will listen to legitimate warnings ever again."

They stood in silence for several minutes, the weight of their potential discovery pressing down on them like a physical force. Outside Mara's window, the campus looked peaceful and normal—students walking between classes, faculty members heading to afternoon meetings, maintenance crews tending to landscaping. None of them was aware that two researchers in a cluttered office were grappling with information that might affect thousands of lives.

"Show me the complete analysis," Mara said finally. "Every data point, every calculation, every assumption. If we're going to stake our careers on this prediction, I want to understand exactly how Prometheus reached its conclusions."

They spent the next two hours dissecting the behavioral data, cross-referencing it with geological surveys, and running independent statistical analyses that confirmed the system's mathematical accuracy. Mara's scientific skepticism proved invaluable—she identified potential sources of error, suggested alternative interpretations, and forced Elias to defend every aspect of his methodology.

But with each challenge answered, each alternative explanation eliminated, the prediction looked more credible and more terrifying.

"The behavioral patterns are unprecedented," Elias said, pulling up geographic visualizations that showed the spread of animal distress reports. "I've never seen coordinated responses across this many species and such a wide area. It's as if every creature in the ecosystem is receiving the same warning signal."

"And the geological data supports it," Mara added, her voice carrying a note of wonder that mixed with apprehension. "The micro-tremor patterns, the underground stress analysis, even the subtle changes in groundwater levels—everything points to a major fault adjustment in the next few days."

They were leaning over her desk, studying a particularly complex correlation display, when their hands accidentally touched while reaching for the same printout. The contact sent an unexpected jolt of awareness through both of them—not just the familiar spark of attraction, but something deeper that had been building through weeks of collaboration and shared discovery.

Mara looked up, her face only inches from his, and for a moment the data analysis was forgotten in favor of more immediate concerns. Elias could see the flecks of gold in her dark eyes, could feel the warmth radiating from her body, could sense the way her breathing had changed when their skin made contact.

"Elias," she began, her voice softer than usual.

"I know," he replied, understanding without needing explanation. The professional boundary they'd been carefully maintaining was becoming impossible to sustain, especially when they were facing a crisis that demanded complete trust and cooperation.

"Dr. Quinn? Dr. Lang?" Sierra's voice echoed from the hallway, followed by the sound of footsteps approaching the office.

They stepped apart quickly, creating appropriate professional distance, but Elias caught the smile that flickered across Sierra's face when she appeared in the doorway. The graduate student was too perceptive to miss the charged atmosphere, though she was tactful enough not to comment directly.

"I finished the interface updates," Sierra announced, holding up her laptop bag. "The new visualization modules should make the prediction data much easier to interpret and present. Are you ready to test them?"

"Actually," Mara said, glancing at Elias with an expression that suggested significant decisions were being made, "I think we need to discuss the implications of what we've discovered before we worry about presentation formats."

Sierra's expression shifted from technical enthusiasm to serious concern as she absorbed the tension in the room. "You've found something major."

"Prometheus has generated its first significant prediction," Elias explained. "A major earthquake, magnitude 6.5 or higher, within the next four days. Mara's geological analysis supports the timeline and magnitude estimate."

Sierra stared at them, her engineering background immediately grasping the practical implications. "That's... that's incredible. And terrifying. What are you going to do?"

"That's what we need to figure out," Mara replied. "Do we report this to emergency management authorities based on untested predictive technology? Do we publish preliminary findings that might be completely wrong?

Do we wait and see if the prediction proves accurate before making any public statements?"

"People could die if you're right and you don't warn them," Sierra pointed out with characteristic directness. "But people could also die if you're wrong and cause panic evacuations."

The conversation was interrupted by a knock on the door frame. Dr. Lenora Voss stood in the hallway, her expression grave and her usual cheerful demeanor replaced by something more serious.

"Dr. Voss," Mara said, surprised. "What brings you to campus today?"

"You do, I'm afraid," the older woman replied, entering the office and glancing around at the maps and data displays. "I've been hearing rumors about earthquake predictions and behavioral analysis research. Given my own history with such matters, I thought it might be appropriate to offer some perspective."

She moved to the window, gazing out at the campus with eyes that seemed to see beyond the immediate landscape.

"This isn't the first time researchers have identified seismic threats in this region," she continued. "And it's not the first time those warnings have been ignored or suppressed."

"Suppressed?" Elias asked, feeling a familiar chill of recognition.

"In 1987, I was part of a USGS research team that identified what we believed to be precursor signals for a major earthquake in the southern Appalachian region. Our data showed fault stress patterns, behavioral anomalies, and atmospheric disturbances that suggested an imminent seismic event."

Dr. Voss turned back to face them, her expression carrying the weight of old disappointments and hard-learned wisdom.

"We prepared detailed reports, contacted emergency management agencies, and requested funding for additional monitoring equipment. Instead of support, we received visits from federal officials who questioned our methodology, our conclusions, and our professional competence. Our funding was cut, our research was classified, and our findings were buried in bureaucratic files that never saw public distribution."

"What happened to the earthquake?" Sierra asked.

"It occurred exactly as predicted, two weeks later. Magnitude 6.2, centered near the Virginia-West Virginia border. Forty-three people died, hundreds were injured, and millions of dollars in damage could have been prevented if authorities had heeded our warnings."

The office fell silent except for the humming of Mara's computer and the distant sounds of campus activity. Dr. Voss's revelation cast their current dilemma in a new and disturbing light—they weren't just dealing with scientific uncertainty, but with institutional forces that had a history of suppressing inconvenient predictions.

"The officials who silenced your research," Mara said carefully, "do you remember their names?"

"The lead investigator was a Dr. Richard Cross from the National Science Foundation. He is very charismatic and persuasive in his arguments about scientific credibility and public safety. He convinced my colleagues that issuing earthquake warnings based on incomplete data would cause more harm than good."

Elias felt the pieces of a larger conspiracy clicking into place. Cross hadn't just betrayed Mara's trust at Virginia Tech—he'd been suppressing earthquake prediction research for decades, using his institutional authority to silence scientists who threatened whatever agenda he was serving.

"Dr. Voss," he said urgently, "we need to know everything you remember about Cross's involvement in suppressing your research. Names, agencies, specific methods he used to discredit your findings."

"Why?" the older woman asked, though her expression suggested she already suspected the answer.

"Because he's doing it again," Mara replied grimly. "Cross has been interfering with our research, pressuring university administrators, and making direct threats against our continued collaboration."

Dr. Voss nodded slowly, as if this confirmation matched her own fears about why she'd felt compelled to visit them today.

"Then you need to understand something crucial," she said, moving closer to the desk where their data displays showed the unfolding crisis. "Cross didn't just suppress our 1987 research to protect his bureaucratic reputation. He actively prevented emergency preparations that could have saved lives, and he did so knowing that people would die as a result of his interference."

"You think he knew the earthquake was coming?" Sierra asked.

"I think he had access to information sources that confirmed our predictions, and he chose institutional control over public safety. The question you need to ask yourselves is whether he's making the same choice now."

As if summoned by their discussion, a sound echoed across the campus—distant, mournful, and unmistakably organic. Through the office window, they could see flocks of birds rising from the trees in coordinated waves, their cries creating a chorus of distress that seemed to speak of dangers the human world was only beginning to recognize.

Koa, who had been lying quietly in the corner, suddenly stood and began pacing, his movements agitated and purposeful. Other dogs could be heard barking from various locations around campus, their voices joining the avian warnings in a symphony of environmental alarm.

"The land's warnings were ignored before," Dr. Voss said quietly, watching the birds disappear over the distant hills. "Forty-three people paid the price for bureaucratic arrogance and institutional cover-ups. How many will pay this time if the same warnings are suppressed again?"

The question hung in the air like a challenge, demanding an answer that none of them felt prepared to give. But as the animal voices grew louder and more urgent, Elias realized that their choice was becoming increasingly clear.

They could protect their careers by staying silent, or they could risk everything to protect the people who might die if their prediction proved accurate.

Looking at Mara's determined expression, at Sierra's technical confidence, and at Dr. Voss's hard-earned wisdom, he knew which choice they were going to make.

The only question was whether they could act quickly enough to overcome Cross's interference and reach the people who needed to hear their warning.

Outside, the animal voices continued their urgent chorus, as if time were running out faster than any of them realized.

Chapter 8: The Skeptic's Wall

The Mountainlair conference room smelled of stale coffee and skepticism. Mara adjusted the laptop one final time, her fingers trembling slightly as she checked the HDMI connection. Through the floor-to-ceiling windows, the Appalachian hills rolled beneath a gray morning sky that threatened rain—or perhaps something worse, given what Prometheus had been showing them.

"You've got this," Sierra whispered, making a last adjustment to the visualization software she'd spent the night perfecting. The graduate student's eyes were rimmed with exhaustion, but her smile was encouraging. "The data speaks for itself."

Mara wished she shared Sierra's confidence. The university board members filed in like judges to an execution: Dr. Harrison Chen, the pragmatic Dean of Sciences; Margaret Whitfield from Budget and Finance, whose expression suggested she'd already made up her mind; and three other administrators whose names Mara knew but whose support she couldn't count on.

"Dr. Lang," Chen nodded, settling into his chair with the careful precision of someone who'd sat through too many presentations that promised the world and delivered disappointment. "We're eager to hear about this... collaborative project with Professor Quinn."

The way he said "collaborative" made it sound like a disease.

Mara clicked to her first slide—a clean, professional display of seismic data overlaid with Prometheus's behavioral correlations. "Thank you for your time. What we're presenting today isn't just academic theory. It's a potential early warning system that could save lives."

She moved through the technical data with practiced efficiency, watching their faces for any sign of engagement. Whitfield took notes—probably calculating how much funding to cut. Chen's expression remained neutral, though his fingers drummed against the table when she showed the prediction timeline.

"The correlation between animal behavioral anomalies and seismic events shows a statistical significance of—"

The door opened.

Dr. Marcus Cross entered like a stage actor arriving for his big scene. His Italian suit was immaculate, his smile warm and apologetic. "I'm so sorry to interrupt. I was in town for a conference and heard my former colleague was presenting. I hope you don't mind if I observe?"

Mara's stomach clenched. Chen brightened immediately. "Marcus! Of course, please join us. Your expertise would be invaluable."

Cross took a seat directly in Mara's line of sight, his presence radiating the easy confidence of someone who'd never had a paper rejected or a grant denied. He gave her a slight nod, almost sympathetic, like a chess master acknowledging a novice's opening move.

"Please, continue," Cross said smoothly. "This sounds fascinating."

Mara forced herself to return to the presentation, but her rhythm was broken. Every slide felt like a target Cross was preparing to destroy. When she reached the Prometheus predictions, she saw him typing rapidly on his phone, not even pretending to pay attention.

"These behavioral patterns," she continued, her voice steadier than she felt, "particularly in domestic animals, show a consistent—"

"May I ask a question?" Cross interjected, his tone respectful but with an undertone that made Mara's skin crawl. "This AI system—Prometheus, you call it—how many successful predictions has it made?"

"We've accurately identified patterns in three minor tremor events—"

"Three." Cross let the number hang in the air like an indictment. "And the prediction window?"

"Between 48 and 72 hours, with increasing precision as—"

"So we're talking about a system that might give us three days' warning, based on three minor events, using data that's largely... intuitive?" His smile was patient, almost pitying. "Mara, I admire your ambition, but surely you can see the liability issues here. What happens when Prometheus cries wolf?"

Sierra started to speak, but Cross raised a hand. "I'm sure Ms. Patel's visualizations are impressive, but pretty graphics don't change the fundamental problem. You're asking the university to stake its reputation on what amounts to digital tea-leaf reading."

Whitfield looked up from her notes. "Dr. Cross raises valid concerns about liability."

"The system is still being refined—" Mara began.

"Which is why we need continued funding," Sierra interjected, pulling up a new visualization. "Look at the pattern recognition improvements over just the last week—"

Cross's phone buzzed. He glanced at it, and something flickered across his face—satisfaction? "I'm sorry, but I think the board should see this." He turned his phone toward them. "The Herald just posted an article about your press conference announcement. The headline is... unfortunate."

Chen pulled up the article on his tablet, his frown deepening. "'University Researchers Claim to Predict Disasters Using Dog Behavior.' The comments section is... not favorable."

Mara's phone vibrated with incoming messages. She glimpsed the screen—Twitter notifications, emails, all with variations of mockery and disbelief. Someone had leaked a deliberately misleading version of their data, complete with out-of-context quotes that made them sound like conspiracy theorists.

"This is taken completely out of context," Mara protested, but she could see she'd already lost them. The board members were scrolling through their devices, watching their university become a viral punchline in real-time.

"I think we've heard enough," Whitfield said, closing her notebook with finality. "Dr. Lang, while we appreciate your... innovative approach, the university cannot afford—financially or reputationally—to support research that generates this kind of public response."

"You're making a decision based on a misleading article?" Sierra's voice cracked with frustration.

"We're making a decision based on risk assessment," Chen replied, though he looked uncomfortable. "Dr. Lang, Professor Quinn, you're free to continue your research, of course. But without university backing or funding."

Cross stood, straightening his jacket. "For what it's worth, Mara, I think your passion is admirable. Sometimes our reach exceeds our grasp. No shame in that." He paused at the door. "Though you might want to be more careful about who you trust with preliminary data. Academic competition can be... cutthroat."

The threat was subtle enough that the board members missed it, but Mara heard it clearly. Cross had orchestrated this—the leak, the timing, everything.

After the board filed out, Sierra slammed her laptop shut. "This is bullshit. He played them like a violin."

"He's had years of practice," Mara said quietly, staring at the empty room. The walls felt like they were closing in, the fluorescent lights suddenly too bright. "I need some air."

Sierra gathered their equipment. "Want me to find Elias?"

"No." The word came out sharper than intended. "I just... I need to think."

Mara escaped through a side door, avoiding the main corridors where she might encounter colleagues who'd undoubtedly seen the article. The woods behind the Mountainlair building offered sanctuary, though even the trees seemed to whisper accusations.

Her phone buzzed incessantly. Texts from concerned friends, emails from reporters wanting comments, and three missed calls from Elias. She turned it off and kept walking, following a deer trail deeper into the forest.

The first drops of rain began to fall, matching her mood perfectly. She'd been so careful, so methodical in preparing the presentation. But Cross had destroyed it all with a few well-placed words and a leaked article. Just like before. Just like with her dissertation research when he'd—

"Your methodology is flawed," she said aloud, mimicking his patronizing tone. "But don't worry, I'll help you fix it." And then he'd published her corrected work under his name, with her relegated to a footnote.

A branch cracked behind her.

"Thought I might find you here," Elias said softly. Koa bounded past him, tail wagging despite the rain, and pressed against Mara's leg.

"Sierra told you?"

"She's worried. So am I." He kept his distance, giving her space. "I saw the article. Cross's fingerprints are all over it."

"It doesn't matter whose fingerprints are on it. The damage is done." Mara's voice broke slightly. "They think we're crackpots, Elias. My career is over."

"Your career is not over."

"Easy for you to say. You have tenure. You can afford to be the eccentric professor with his unconventional theories. I'm just the geologist who got seduced by pseudoscience."

"Is that what you think happened? I seduced you into this?"

She turned to face him, rain streaming down her face. "No. I seduced myself. I wanted to believe that maybe, just maybe, there was something more than just data points and measurements. That intuition could matter. Your wife was right about that, and I was starting to see it too. But Cross just proved that the real world doesn't care about intuition or doing the right thing. It cares about reputation and funding and not rocking the boat."

Elias stepped closer, rain darkening his hair. "My wife also believed that the truth has a way of surfacing, even when people try to bury it. Cross is scared, Mara. That's why he's attacking so hard."

"Scared of what?"

"Of being wrong. Of us proving that his entire worldview—that only his kind of data matters—is limited." Elias pulled out his phone, showing her Prometheus's latest readings despite the rain. "Look at this. The patterns are intensifying. The animals know something's coming, and the rocks are starting to agree with them."

"It doesn't matter if we can't warn people."

"Then we find another way." His intensity made her look up. "University funding isn't the only source of support. Sierra's already got a crowdfunding page started. Three thousand dollars in the last hour from people who believe in what we're doing."

"Three thousand dollars won't run Prometheus for a month."

"It's a start. And there are grants, private foundations, people who understand that innovation doesn't always follow conventional paths." He reached out, hesitating before touching her shoulder. "But none of that matters if you give up. Cross wins if you give up."

Mara wanted to believe him, wanted to feel his optimism. But all she could see was her professional reputation crumbling, her colleagues' respect evaporating, her future narrowing to nothing.

"The board's not just cutting funding," she said quietly. "Chen pulled me aside after. They're reviewing my appointment. Questioning whether I'm 'aligned with the university's academic standards.' That's administrative speak for 'start looking for another job.'"

Elias's jaw tightened. "They can't do that. You have a contract—"

"Which includes clauses about maintaining professional standards and not bringing the university into disrepute." She laughed bitterly. "Cross probably helped write those clauses. He thinks of everything."

They stood in the rain, the forest around them dripping and silent except for Koa's occasional whine. The dog kept looking east, toward the mountains, his ears perked at something only he could hear.

"What if we're wrong?" Mara asked suddenly. "What if Cross is right and we're just seeing patterns that aren't there?"

Elias was quiet for a moment, rain running down his face. "Then we're wrong with good intentions, trying to protect people. But what if we're right and we let Cross silence us? How many lives is your reputation worth?"

The question hung between them like a challenge.

"That's not fair."

"Neither is what Cross is doing to you. To us." He paused. "To the people who might die because someone decided their career mattered more than the truth."

Before Mara could respond, both their phones buzzed simultaneously—an emergency alert. She turned hers back on to see a notification from the USGS: a 4.1 magnitude earthquake had just struck 30 miles east, exactly where Prometheus had indicated increasing instability.

They looked at each other, rain forgotten.

"That's not a coincidence," Elias said.

"No," Mara agreed, her scientific mind already racing through the implications. "It's not."

Her phone rang—Sierra. "Did you see? Prometheus called it within a six-hour window! And there's more—the local news wants a statement. They're asking if we knew it was coming."

Mara looked at Elias, seeing her own mixture of vindication and dread reflected in his eyes. They were right. The system worked. But Cross had already poisoned the well of public opinion.

"Tell them no comment for now," Mara said. "We need to check the data first."

She ended the call and found Elias watching her with something that might have been pride.

"That sounded like someone who hasn't given up," he said softly.

"Cross doesn't get to win," she replied, surprising herself with the steel in her voice. "Not this time."

They started back toward campus, Koa leading the way with urgent purpose. The rain was lessening, but the real storm was just beginning. As they emerged from the woods, Mara's phone buzzed with an email from an unknown sender. The subject line made her blood run cold:

"You have 24 hours to retract your predictions or lose everything. -A concerned friend"

Attached was a photo—her dissertation data, the original version, before Cross had "corrected" it. Data she thought had been destroyed. Data that, taken out of context, could end her career permanently.

She showed it to Elias, whose face darkened. "He's escalating."

"Which means we're getting close to something he doesn't want found," Mara said, her mind shifting from despair to determination. "The question is: what is Marcus Cross so afraid of?"

In the distance, thunder rolled across the mountains. Or perhaps it wasn't thunder at all. Koa whined, pressing closer to their legs, his ancient instincts sensing what their instruments were only beginning to detect.

The earth was waking up, and someone was desperate to keep them from sounding the alarm.

Chapter 9: Cabin in the Hills

The headlights carved through mountain darkness as Elias's truck wound higher into the Appalachian hills. Mara gripped the door handle, not from fear of his driving but from the weight of the email still glowing on her phone. Twenty-four hours. Cross had given them twenty-four hours before he destroyed what was left of her career.

"You're going to burn a hole through that screen," Elias said gently, reaching over to lower her phone. "We need a few hours to think clearly. To breathe."

"We don't have time to breathe. Prometheus is showing—"

"Prometheus will keep monitoring. Sierra's watching the feeds. Right now, we need perspective." He glanced at her, his face illuminated by the dashboard's green glow. "Trust me?"

She wanted to say no, that trust was a luxury she couldn't afford. But something in his voice, a quiet certainty mixed with vulnerability, made her nod.

"The Seneca called these hills the 'Endless Mountains,'" Elias said, his voice taking on the storytelling cadence she recognized from his lectures.

"They believed the ridges were sleeping giants, guardians who would wake when the land was threatened."

"Comforting," Mara said dryly, though she found herself listening despite her anxiety.

"My wife loved those stories. Said indigenous peoples had thousands of years of observational data we dismissed as mythology." He navigated a sharp curve, the trees pressing close on both sides. "She spent months with the Eastern Band of Cherokee, recording their earthquake stories. Found patterns that matched geological records going back centuries."

The truck's headlights flickered.

"Electrical storm coming in," Elias muttered, though the sky had been clear when they left campus.

The lights died completely.

For a heart-stopping moment, they coasted in absolute darkness. Then the headlights sputtered back to life, weaker than before. In the restored light, Mara saw a deer standing in the road, its eyes reflecting green. But it wasn't running. It stood perfectly still, head cocked as if listening to something beneath the asphalt.

Elias stopped the truck, waiting. The deer remained frozen for another beat, then bounded into the forest with urgent grace.

"That's the third one doing that today," he said quietly. "Standing still, listening."

The power outage had killed the radio, leaving only static. Mara's phone showed no signal. They were completely cut off, driving deeper into isolation with only failing headlights to guide them.

"How much farther?" she asked, hating how small her voice sounded.

"Just around this bend."

The cabin materialized from the darkness like something from a fairy tale—or a ghost story. Built from local timber, it nestled against the hillside as if it had grown there. Solar panels on the roof provided independent power, their backup batteries glowing faintly through a window. But what struck Mara most was how alive it felt, despite being a shrine to someone dead.

Koa jumped from the truck bed and immediately began patrolling the perimeter, his nose to the ground, occasionally stopping to stare into the dark forest with an intensity that raised the hair on Mara's neck.

"He's been doing that more lately," Elias said, unlocking the heavy wooden door. "Like he's standing guard."

The interior was exactly what Mara had expected and nothing like it at all. Yes, there were photos of Elias's wife—a vibrant woman with wild curly hair and eyes that sparkled with intelligence. Yes, there were her field journals stacked on shelves, her rain jacket still hanging by the door. But it wasn't a mausoleum. It was a working space, a continuation of research rather than a memorial to it.

"Sarah," Elias said, noticing Mara's gaze on a photo of his wife releasing a tagged hawk. "Dr. Sarah Chen-Quinn, officially. She kept her name, said Quinn was too boring for a behavioral ecologist."

"She was beautiful," Mara said, meaning more than just physically. The woman in the photos radiated purpose.

"Brilliant, stubborn, absolutely impossible to argue with." His smile was soft, pained. "You would have liked each other. Or hated each other. Probably both."

He moved through the cabin with practiced ease, lighting a fire in the stone fireplace, checking the battery backup system. Mara found herself drawn to Sarah's journals, their covers worn from field use.

"May I?" she asked.

"She would have wanted them read. Especially by someone who might understand."

While Elias cooked—the domestic simplicity of it somehow intensifying the intimacy—Mara opened a journal at random. Sarah's handwriting was precise but urgent:

May 15th - The crows know. Thirty-seven birds abandoned their roost this morning, three days before the landslide Johnson's team predicted would happen "sometime this month." The birds were specific. Why can't we be?

Another entry:

August 3rd - E thinks I'm becoming too mystical, but there's something about being in the field that pure data can't capture. The forest feels different before a disturbance, like holding your breath. Indigenous knowledge isn't primitive—it's sophisticated pattern recognition developed over millennia. We've just forgotten how to listen.

"She was trying to bridge the gap," Mara said, looking up to find Elias watching her from the kitchen. "Between intuition and empirical data."

"She called it 'embodied knowledge.' The idea that we perceive more than we consciously process." He brought over two glasses of wine, sitting beside her on the couch—close enough that she could feel his warmth but not touching. "She was working on a paper about it when—"

He stopped, taking a sip of wine.

"When she died?" Mara prompted gently.

"When she didn't come back from a field study. Flash flood in a canyon she knew like the back of her hand. Every sign said it was safe. All the data, the weather reports, the hydrological models." His voice was steady, but his knuckles were white around the glass. "But the ravens had left that morning. She mentioned it in her last voice message, almost as a joke. 'The birds disagree with NOAA today.'"

Mara set down Sarah's journal and placed her hand over his. "It wasn't your fault."

"I know. Intellectually, I know. But I keep thinking if I'd paid more attention to her theories, if I'd helped her develop better predictive mo dels..."

"You're doing that now. Prometheus is her work continued."

"Our work," he corrected, turning his hand to interlock their fingers. "She would have been amazed by what you've brought to it. The geological data, the mathematical rigor. You're making it real in a way I never could alone."

The firelight cast dancing shadows on the walls, making Sarah's photos seem to move. Outside, wind rattled the windows—or perhaps it wasn't wind. The house creaked in a way that suggested the earth itself was shifting, settling, preparing.

"I should check Prometheus," Mara said, but didn't move.

"In a minute," Elias agreed, also not moving.

They sat in the flickering light, hands linked, surrounded by the ghost of his past and the uncertainty of their future. The wine was warm in Mara's stomach, or maybe that was something else—a feeling she'd thought Cross had killed along with her ability to trust.

"Tell me about him," Elias said suddenly. "Cross. What did he do to make you so afraid?"

Mara stiffened, but his thumb traced gentle circles on her palm, grounding her.

"He was my advisor. Brilliant, charismatic, everything a young graduate student could want in a mentor." She stared into the fire. "He took an interest in my work on micro-fractures in Appalachian bedrock. Said I had a 'unique perspective' that could revolutionize our understanding of regional seismology."

"Let me guess—your unique perspective became his groundbreaking paper?"

"Three papers, actually. With my data 'corrected' and my name buried in acknowledgments." The bitterness in her voice surprised her. "But that wasn't the worst part. The worst part was how he made me doubt my own observations. Every time I questioned his changes, he had an explanation that made me feel stupid for not seeing it myself. Gaslighting dressed up as mentorship."

"And now he's trying to do it again."

"No." Mara turned to face him fully. "Now he's scared. You were right about that. The question is why? What does he know that we don't?"

Before Elias could answer, Koa burst through the dog door, barking urgently. The Prometheus tablet on the coffee table lit up with alerts. The coffee table lit up with alerts—not from the tablet, but from the laptop Elias had synced to the cabin's system.

They leaned over the screen together, their earlier intimacy replaced by professional focus. The data was staggering. Micro-tremors had increased by 300% in the last two hours. Temperature readings from mountain springs showed a three-degree spike. And the animal behavior data...

"Jesus," Elias breathed. "Look at the migration patterns."

Every tracked species was moving. Birds, mammals, even insects—all flowing away from a specific point in the mountains, roughly thirty miles from their current location.

"That's not possible," Mara said, her scientific mind reeling. "This kind of coordinated movement... it would take a massive trigger."

"Or advanced warning of one." Elias pulled up the geological surveys. "This area has no history of volcanic activity. The last major seismic event was—"

"1897," Mara finished, remembering suddenly. "There was a mine collapse. Officially blamed on poor engineering, but..." She grabbed Sarah's journal, flipping through the pages urgently. "Your wife mentioned it. Here—'October 1897 mine disaster preceded by three weeks of animal evacuations. Local newspapers called it superstition, but indigenous oral histories describe the earth 'breathing fire' before the collapse.'"

They looked at each other, the implications crystallizing.

"Cross's company has mining interests in these mountains," Mara said slowly. "Old copper mines they've been trying to reopen for years. If there's volcanic activity..."

"It would destroy billions in potential profits. And if he knew, if he's been suppressing data—"

The lights flickered again. This time, they didn't come back on immediately. In the darkness, they heard it—a sound like distant thunder, but too rhythmic, too deep. The windows vibrated slightly.

Emergency power kicked in, bathing them in red light. Koa pressed against their legs, whining. On the Prometheus screen, a new alert appeared: CRITICAL THRESHOLD APPROACHING.

"We have to warn people," Mara said.

"With what authority? Cross has destroyed our credibility."

"Then we rebuild it. Fast." She was already pulling up contacts on her phone, which had found a weak signal. "I know journalists who still trust me. Scientists who remember my work before Cross. We can—"

Elias caught her hand. "Mara. If we do this, if we go public against Cross directly, there's no going back. He'll destroy us both."

She looked at him in the red emergency lighting, seeing Sarah's photos watching from the walls, feeling the mountain trembling beneath them like a sleeping giant beginning to stir.

"Some things are worth being destroyed for," she said.

He pulled her closer, his forehead touching hers. For a moment, the world narrowed to just them—two people standing on the edge of disaster, choosing to face it together.

The laptop beeped. A new message had arrived, sender unknown:

Check the 1897 survey reports. Cross's grandfather was the mining engineer. History repeats when we let it. - A friend

Attached was a scanned document, yellow with age. Mara opened it, her blood running cold as she read.

"Elias," she whispered. "This isn't the first time. The Cross family has been suppressing volcanic activity data in these mountains for over a century."

Outside, Koa began howling—a sound Mara had never heard him make before. Other dogs answered from distant farms, their voices carrying on the wind like a warning.

The power died completely. In the darkness, lit only by the dying fire, they heard it clearly now—the mountain breathing, just as the indigenous stories had described. Breathing fire.

Chapter 10: Fire Beneath the Hills

The Morgantown Historical Society occupied a Victorian house that had seen better centuries. Paint peeled from its wraparound porch like old skin, and the floorboards groaned a symphony of protest as Elias and Mara climbed the front steps. Koa hung back, hackles raised, until Elias coaxed him forward with a gentle tug on his leash.

"Charming," Mara muttered, eyeing a broken shutter that hung at a drunken angle.

"Don't let appearances fool you," Elias replied, pushing open the heavy oak door. "Margaret Henley keeps the most comprehensive collection of local history in three states."

The interior was a dragon's hoard of documents. Papers towered in precarious stacks, maps papered every wall, and the air tasted of old leather and older secrets. Margaret herself emerged from behind a fortress of filing cabinets—a bird-like woman with silver hair pinned in a bun that defied several laws of physics.

"Dr. Quinn," she said, her voice surprisingly strong. "I wondered when you'd come asking about the old stories."

"You know why we're here?"

Her eyes, sharp as flint, flicked to Mara. "The whole town knows about your earthquake prediction. Some folks think you're fear-mongering. Others..." She gestured to a corner table where yellowed maps lay waiting. "Others remember what their grandparents whispered about the mountains' anger."

They spent the next hour poring over documents that predated West Virginia's statehood. Indigenous accounts spoke of "the burning breath beneath stone" and "the time when mountains wept fire." One map, drawn in 1847, showed cave systems that didn't appear on any modern survey.

"Here," Margaret said, producing a leather journal with reverent care. "Jeremiah Voss's personal account. Lenora's great-grandfather."

Mara's head snapped up. "Voss mentioned family stories, but..."

"Read," Margaret commanded.

The journal's cramped handwriting told of the 1920s mining disaster everyone had forgotten. Not a collapse, as official records claimed, but something stranger. Animals fleeing the mountains for days before. Wells are running hot. The ground itself groaning like a living thing.

"'The earth gave warning,'" Elias read aloud. "'But the company men wouldn't listen. Said the mountain was solid, had always been solid. Then came the night of fire.'"

"Fire?" Mara leaned closer, her shoulder pressing against his.

"'Flames from below,'" he continued. "'Not coal fire—something deeper. Twenty-three souls lost before they sealed the shaft. The company paid for silence, but the mountain remembers.'"

Koa whined, low and urgent. The sound raised goosebumps along Elias's arms.

"There's more," Margaret said, producing a manila folder marked with government stamps. "Lenora gave me this before they forced her into retirement. Said someone should know the truth."

Inside was Voss's suppressed 1983 report. Whole sections had been redacted with thick black marks, but what remained painted a chilling picture. Thermal anomalies. Mineral deposits consistent with ancient pyroclastic flows. A recommendation for detailed volcanic assessment—denied and buried.

"Jesus," Mara breathed. "She had proof. Thirty years ago, she had proof."

"And they destroyed her career for it," Margaret said quietly. "Called her an alarmist. Said she was seeing volcanos where none could exist."

Elias photographed every page, his hands steady despite the adrenaline coursing through him. The pieces were falling into place—not just the geological evidence, but a pattern of suppression, of willful blindness.

"The cave," he said suddenly. "The 1847 map showed a cave system near Backbone Mountain. If there's physical evidence—"

"—we need to see it," Mara finished. Their eyes met, and he saw his own mixture of excitement and dread reflected there.

Margaret walked them to the door, pressing a hand-drawn map into Elias's palm. "My grandfather explored those caves as a boy. Said they sang sometimes—a deep humming that made your bones ache. Be careful. The mountain doesn't like visitors."

Outside, Morgantown carried on its normal afternoon routines, oblivious to the history of warnings buried in one old house. As they loaded Koa into Elias's Jeep, Mara spotted something that made her freeze.

"That car," she said, nodding toward a black sedan parked across the street. "It was outside the university this morning."

Elias studied it, memorizing the license plate. The windows were tinted too dark to see inside. As they pulled away, the sedan's engine started.

"Coincidence?" Mara asked, though her tone suggested she didn't believe it.

"In my experience, coincidences are just patterns we haven't recognized yet."

They lost the sedan in Morgantown's winding streets, but the feeling of being watched lingered like smoke.

****

The cave entrance was exactly where Margaret's map indicated, hidden behind a curtain of kudzu and time. The afternoon sun barely penetrated the forest canopy, leaving them in a green twilight that felt older than memory.

Koa flat-out refused to approach. He planted all four paws and pulled against his leash, a keening whine escaping his throat.

"I've never seen him like this," Elias said, kneeling beside the trembling dog. "Even during thunderstorms, he's braver than this."

Mara checked her equipment—headlamp, sample bags, and geological hammer. "We could leave him in the Jeep?"

But Elias shook his head. Something told him they'd need Koa's instincts. He secured the dog's leash to his belt, speaking in soothing tones that didn't quite mask his own apprehension.

The cave mouth exhaled cold air that smelled wrong—not the usual mustiness of underground spaces, but something sharper. Sulfurous.

"You smell that?" Mara asked, her scientific excitement overriding caution.

"Hydrogen sulfide. Shouldn't be present in these rock formations unless..."

"Unless there's volcanic activity." She was already moving forward, headlamp cutting through the darkness.

The passage descended at a steep angle, narrow enough that they had to proceed single file. Koa pressed against Elias's legs, nearly tripping him twice. The walls were smooth—too smooth for natural erosion.

"Look at these marks," Mara said, running her hand along the stone. "This was carved. Widened deliberately."

"The miners," Elias realized. "They must have found this natural cave and expanded it."

Deeper they went, the stronger the sulfur smell growing stronger. The cave began to sing—a low vibration that seemed to come from the stone itself. Koa's whining became constant, punctuated by warning growls aimed at nothing they could see.

"Elias." Mara's voice was tight. "The temperature's rising. According to this, it's fifteen degrees warmer than it should be at this depth."

He checked his own instruments, confirming her reading. The vibration grew stronger, and with it came sounds that shouldn't exist—whispers that might have been wind, or water, or something else entirely.

Betrayed.

The word echoed off the walls, so clear that both of them stopped.

"Did you—"

"I heard it," Mara confirmed, her rationalism warring with evidence. "Acoustic phenomenon. Has to be."

But her hand found his in the darkness, fingers interlacing with desperate strength.

They reached a chamber where the passage widened dramatically. Their lights revealed a ceiling lost in shadow and walls that gleamed with moisture. In the center, a pile of rocks that looked deliberately placed.

"This must be where they sealed the lower passages," Elias said, approaching carefully.

That's when Koa went berserk. The dog lunged backward, nearly pulling Elias off his feet. His barking echoed off the walls, multiplying into a chorus of alarm.

"Koa, what—"

The rocks shifted.

Not all of them—just one, near the top of the pile. It teetered, then fell, starting a cascade. Elias realized with crystal clarity that the pile had been rigged, balanced to collapse at the slightest disturbance.

"Move!" He grabbed Mara, pulling her backward as tons of stone crashed down where they'd been standing. Dust filled the air, choking and blinding. Koa's leash tangled around Elias's legs, sending him sprawling.

A massive boulder, dislodged from above, plummeted toward Mara. Time slowed. Elias saw her eyes widen, saw her try to dodge, knew she wouldn't make it—

He lunged, tackling her sideways. The boulder crashed past, missing them by inches, the wind of its passage ruffling their hair. They hit the ground hard, Elias taking the brunt of the impact with Mara cushioned against his chest.

For a moment, they lay frozen, breathing hard, acutely aware of every point of contact between their bodies.

"You saved my life," Mara whispered.

"You would have done the same," he managed, though speaking required remembering how to breathe.

She lifted her head, looking down at him in the wild play of their scattered headlamps. Something shifted in her expression—walls crumbling like the rocks around them. She leaned down, and for a heart-stopping moment, he thought she might kiss him.

Instead, she pulled back, professional mask sliding into place. "We sho uld... we should collect samples. Before anything else happens."

They worked in tense silence, gathering rock samples from the revealed lower passage. The stones were wrong—volcanic basalt where there should be sedimentary limestone. Proof of ancient fire, exactly as Voss had predicted.

"This is impossible," Mara muttered, turning a sample over in her hands. "The geological surveys—"

"Were either wrong or deliberately falsified." Elias packed the evidence carefully. "Someone didn't want this found."

A scratching sound made them both freeze. It came from above, like claws on stone. Or feet trying to find purchase.

"We need to go," Elias said. "Now."

They retreated quickly but carefully, Koa leading the way with new-found urgency. Behind them, the scratching sounds multiplied, echoing strangely in the cave's acoustics.

They burst into fading daylight like swimmers breaking the surface. Koa immediately ran to the Jeep, pawing at the door. They followed, not speaking until they were inside with the doors locked.

"That was deliberate," Mara said finally. "That rock fall. Someone set that trap."

"The question is whether it was meant for us specifically, or any curious explorers."

"Given that we were followed..." She trailed off, checking the mirrors. No sign of the black sedan, but that meant nothing.

Elias started the engine, eager to distance themselves from the cave. As they pulled onto the access road, his phone buzzed. No signal out here—the message must have been waiting.

Margaret Henley's number. Her text was brief: "Someone came asking about you after you left. City type. Expensive suit. Watch yourselves."

"Cross," Mara said flatly. "Has to be."

"How would he know we're here?"

"Same way he always knows. He has eyes everywhere." Her voice carried years of bitter experience.

They drove in silence, processing what they'd found. The evidence was undeniable now—ancient volcanic activity, suppressed reports, and someone willing to kill to keep it hidden.

"We should make camp soon," Elias said as dusk painted the mountains purple. "I know a spot, isolated. We can plan our next move."

Mara nodded. "And figure out who's trying to stop us."

***

The campsite was a small clearing blessed with a freshwater spring and shielded by old-growth pines. They worked together with practiced efficiency—Elias setting up the tent while Mara built a fire. Koa finally relaxed, though he kept positioning himself between them and the forest.

"One tent?" Mara asked, eyebrow raised.

"I... there's a tarp in the Jeep. I can—"

"It's fine," she said quickly. "We're adults. And after today, I'd rather not be alone out here."

They shared a simple meal, the fire casting dancing shadows that made the forest seem alive. Conversation came easier in the darkness, as if the night granted permission for vulnerability.

"Tell me about her," Mara said suddenly. "Your wife."

Elias poked at the fire, sending sparks spiraling upward. "Sarah was... incandescent. She saw the world differently than everyone else. Where I saw data points, she saw stories. Where I needed proof, she had faith."

"You miss her."

"Every day. But lately..." He paused, choosing words carefully. "Lately, the grief feels different. Less like drowning, more like... like carrying a stone in my pocket. Present, but not overwhelming."

"That's good," Mara said softly. "That's healing."

"Tell me about Cross. The real story."

She was quiet so long he thought she wouldn't answer. Then: "We were partners. Research partners," she clarified quickly. "I thought we were building something important. Turns out he was building his career on my work. He didn't just steal my data—he poisoned it. Made sure everyone would question anything I produced afterward."

"Why?"

"Because I was better than him. And he couldn't stand it." She threw a pine cone into the fire, watching it flare and crumble. "The worst part was how he did it. So subtle, so careful. Compliments that were actually undermining. Concern that was really controlled. By the time I realized what was happening, my reputation was in ruins."

Elias shifted closer, drawn by the pain in her voice. "You rebuilt. You're here."

"Here. Chasing what might be a ghost story through caves that try to kill us." She laughed, but it was brittle. "Maybe he was right about me being too trusting."

"No." The word came out fiercer than intended. "Trust isn't weakness, Mara. What he did—using your trust against you—that's the weakness. His weakness."

She looked at him across the fire, eyes reflecting the flames. "You really believe that?"

"I believe in you," he said simply. "I've watched you work. Seen your integrity, your brilliance. Cross tried to dim your light because he couldn't stand being in your shadow."

Something broke in her expression—a wall finally crumbling. "I haven't let anyone close since him. Haven't trusted my own judgment about people."

"And now?"

"Now..." She stood abruptly. "Now I'm going to check the equipment. Make sure everything's secure for tomorrow."

Elias watched her go, recognizing the retreat for what it was. He banked the fire and made his own patrol of the campsite, Koa shadowing his steps.

That's when he found it.

The device was small, no bigger than a quarter, attached to the inside of his equipment bag with magnetic backing. A tiny LED blinked red in steady intervals. GPS tracker.

His blood turned to ice. They'd been marked, followed, monitored. Every move reported to someone—Cross, most likely, but possibly others.

He almost called out to Mara, then stopped. She was already on edge, already fighting her own demons. This confirmation of her fears might push her to run. And they needed to stay together, needed to see this through.

He pocketed the device, mind racing. He could disable it, but that would alert whoever was monitoring them. Better to know you're being watched than give away that knowledge.

A sound made him turn—the distinct whir of drone rotors, faint but growing closer. He grabbed Koa, pulling the dog into the shadow of the trees. The drone passed overhead, infrared camera sweeping the campsite. Looking for them. Recording them.

The implications were staggering. This wasn't just academic rivalry or corporate espionage. Someone with resources—serious resources—wanted to track their every move.

The drone disappeared into the night, but Elias knew it would be back. They were being hunted, and the cave trap hadn't been meant to kill. It had been meant to scare them off.

Which meant someone believed they were close to something important.

He returned to find Mara already in the tent, arranging sleeping bags with meticulous care to maintain a professional distance. The space felt impossibly small with both of them inside.

"Everything secure?" she asked.

"For now." He wanted to tell her about the tracker, about the drone, but the words stuck in his throat. Tomorrow. When they were safely away from here.

They lay in darkness, hyperaware of each other's breathing. Outside, the forest carried on its nocturnal symphony, but underneath it, Elias imagined he could hear something else. A rumbling, almost below perception. The mountain's restless sleep is disturbing.

"Elias?" Mara's voice was barely a whisper.

"Yeah?"

"I'm glad you're here. I couldn't do this alone."

He reached across the space between them, finding her hand in the darkness. She squeezed back, holding on like an anchor.

"We're going to figure this out," he promised. "Whatever Cross is planning, whatever's happening with the mountain—we'll stop it."

"Together?"

"Together."

They fell asleep like that, hands clasped across the divide, while above them the drone circled back for another pass.

In the distance, so faint it might have been imagination, the ground trembled. The mountain was waking, and someone desperately wanted to keep that secret buried.

But Elias had learned something important tonight. Secrets, like volcanos, never stayed buried forever. They always found a way to erupt.

The tracker in his pocket blinked its steady rhythm, marking time until morning would force him to reveal one more betrayal in a story already full of them. He only hoped Mara's newfound trust could survive it.

Koa, curled between them, growled softly in his sleep. Even in dreams, the dog sensed what was coming.

The mountain remembered, and soon, everyone would know its secret.

Chapter 11: Prometheus Speaks

The basement lab hummed with an electric anticipation that made the hair on Elias's arms stand on end. Three computer monitors cast an ethereal blue glow across his face as he leaned forward, fingers dancing across the keyboard. Behind him, Mara paced like a caged animal, her footsteps sharp against the concrete floor. Sierra sat cross-legged on a cleared patch of workbench, her laptop balanced precariously on her knees as she refined the visualization protocols.

"There," Elias breathed, pointing at the central monitor. "Prometheus just completed its analysis."

The screen erupted in a cascade of data points, algorithms churning through millions of calculations per second. Animal migration patterns overlapped with seismic readings, creating a three-dimensional web of interconnected warnings. At the center, pulsing like a malevolent heart, was a heat signature deep beneath the Appalachian bedrock.

"Sierra, can you—"

"Already on it." Her fingers flew across her keyboard, translating the raw data into something visual, something visceral. The monitors flickered, then displayed a cross-section of the earth beneath West Virginia. Rivers of orange and red flowed through digital rock, converging on a chamber that shouldn't exist according to any geological survey.

Mara stopped pacing. "That's... that's not possible."

"The data doesn't lie," Elias said softly. He pulled up a secondary window showing animal behavior patterns from the past six months. "Look at this. Every species within a hundred-mile radius has shown signs of distress. Migration patterns are shifting, breeding cycles are disrupted, and territorial behaviors are abandoned. The correlation coefficient is 0.94."

Sierra's visualization zoomed in, revealing the magma chamber in horrifying detail. Heat readings suggested temperatures exceeding 1,200 degrees Celsius, with pressure building at an exponential rate. Animated flow patterns showed magma forcing its way through ancient fissures, following paths that hadn't been active for millennia.

"The indigenous legends Voss mentioned," Elias continued, his voice gaining strength. "They speak of the earth's warning voices—not metaphorically, but literally. Animals fleeing before 'the mountain's angry breath.' Prometheus found seventeen separate accounts that match our current data patterns."

Koa, who had been sleeping in the corner, suddenly lifted his head and whined. The sound sent a chill through the room.

"How long?" Mara asked, her scientific skepticism warring with the evidence before her eyes.

Elias clicked through to the temporal analysis. The graph that appeared made Sierra gasp.

"Six weeks," he said. "Maybe eight if we're lucky."

"Six weeks?" Mara spun to face him, her dark eyes flashing. "You're telling me there's a volcanic eruption brewing beneath West Virginia—a region with no history of volcanism for 250 million years—and we have six weeks?"

"The Appalachians were formed by massive tectonic activity," Elias countered. "Just because the volcanism has been dormant doesn't mean it's extinct. Prometheus identified a deep mantle plume, probably triggered by the New Madrid fault system's recent activity."

"That's hundreds of miles away!"

"Connected by the same tectonic structures." He pulled up another visualization, this one showing fault lines spreading like spider webs beneath the continent. "The earth doesn't recognize our arbitrary boundaries, Mara."

She shook her head, moving closer to examine the data. Her shoulder brushed his, and for a moment, the contact distracted them both. "Even if I accept your mantle plume theory—which is a massive leap—volcanic eruptions don't just happen. There are precursors, centuries of buildup, clear geological evidence."

"Which is exactly what Voss's suppressed data showed," Sierra interjected, pulling up the digitized files they'd recovered. "Look at the thermal anomalies from the 1980s. The mineral deposits indicate past eruptions. Someone knew this was possible and buried it."

"Because it was inconclusive!" Mara's voice rose, frustration bleeding through. "You're asking me to stake my reputation—our reputations—on a computer model that contradicts everything we know about this region's geology."

Elias stood, facing her fully. The lab's fluorescent lights caught the gold flecks in her brown eyes, and he had to force himself to focus. "I'm asking you to trust the data. To trust what we've built together."

"Trust?" She laughed, but there was no humor in it. "You sound like Cross did, right before he—" She cut herself off, jaw clenching.

The mention of Cross hung between them like a blade. Elias saw the old wound in her eyes, the betrayal that had shaped her into someone who needed proof for everything, who couldn't afford to believe in intuition.

"I'm not Cross," he said quietly. "And this isn't about ego or career advancement. This is about lives."

"Don't you think I know that?" Her voice cracked slightly. "If we're wrong—if your wishful thinking leads us to cause a mass panic—"

"Wishful thinking?" Now it was Elias's turn to feel the sting. "Is that what you think this is? That I want there to be a disaster?"

"I think you want to be right about intuition mattering as much as hard data. I think you've built your entire worldview around the idea that feelings and hunches can predict what science can't, and now—"

"Stop." Sierra's voice cut through their argument like a scalpel. Both turned to look at her, having almost forgotten she was there. "While you two are having your philosophical divorce, maybe look at what Prometheus just flagged."

She gestured to her screen, where a new alert pulsed urgent red. Elias moved first, Mara close behind, their argument momentarily forgotten.

"Micro-tremors," Sierra explained. "Too small for humans to feel, but Prometheus detected them through the university's research seismographs. They started..." She checked the timestamp. "Forty-seven minutes ago. Increasing in frequency."

Mara's face paled. She knew, as they all did, that micro-tremor swarms often preceded larger seismic events. Her fingers flew across the keyboard, pulling up real-time data from the USGS.

"They haven't registered anything," she muttered.

"Because they're not looking for it," Elias said. "Their instruments aren't calibrated for volcanic signatures in this region. They'd dismiss it as mining activity or natural settling."

For a long moment, the only sound was the hum of computers and Koa's increasingly anxious panting. Then Mara spoke, her voice barely above a whisper.

"Show me everything. Every data point, every correlation, every prediction. If we're going to do this—if I'm going to stake everything on your AI and animal behaviors—I need to understand it all."

Relief flooded through Elias. He pulled out the chair next to his, gesturing for her to sit. As she did, their knees touched beneath the desk, and neither pulled away.

For the next hour, they went through the data methodically. Elias explained each algorithm, each behavioral pattern, each connection Prometheus had identified. Mara challenged, questioned, demanded clarification. Sierra provided visualizations, making the abstract concrete.

Slowly, inexorably, Mara's skepticism gave way to something else. Not quite belief—not yet—but a recognition that the patterns were too consistent to ignore.

"The statistical probability of all these correlations being coincidental..." she murmured, running calculations on her tablet.

"Less than 0.0001%," Sierra supplied helpfully.

Mara set down her tablet with shaking hands. "God help us."

Elias reached out, covering her hand with his. She didn't pull away. "We need to warn people."

"They'll crucify us," she said. "The media, the scientific community, everyone. Without traditional geological evidence—"

"Then we make them see what we see." His thumb traced gentle circles on her hand, and he felt her pulse racing beneath her skin. "Together."

She looked at him then, really looked at him, and something shifted in her expression. The walls she'd built after Cross's betrayal showed the first signs of cracking. "Together," she agreed.

Sierra cleared her throat dramatically. "Should I leave you two alone, or...?"

Mara jerked her hand back, color rising in her cheeks. Elias couldn't help but smile at Sierra's knowing smirk.

"We should prepare a presentation," Mara said, all business again. "Something that shows the data without sensationalizing it. We'll need to be careful about how we frame this—"

"Already started," Sierra said, spinning her laptop around. She'd begun assembling their findings into a clean, professional presentation. "I figure we lead with the animal behavior patterns, since those are documented and verifiable, then build to the volcanic prediction."

They worked in focused silence for another hour, refining their message, anticipating objections, building an ironclad case. Elias felt the weight of what they were about to do settling on his shoulders. Going public with this prediction would change everything. Their careers, their lives, their futures—all balanced on the knife's edge of being right or catastrophically wrong.

"There's something else," Sierra said quietly, breaking into his thoughts. "I've been monitoring social media, news feeds, anything that might corroborate our data. There's... chatter."

"What kind of chatter?" Mara asked.

Sierra pulled up several browser windows. "Farmers reporting livestock acting strangely. Three different hiking groups posting about 'weird vibes' in the mountains. A Reddit thread about people's pets freaking out. It's all anecdotal, but—"

"But it matches our predictions," Elias finished. "People are already sensing something's wrong, even if they don't know what."

"Or Cross is planting stories to make us look like we're jumping at shadows," Mara countered, though her heart wasn't in the skepticism anymore.

They exchanged glances, the weight of decision pressing down. Finally, Elias stood, decision crystallizing in his mind.

"We go public tomorrow. Press conference at noon. We present our findings and let people decide for themselves what to do with the information."

Mara stood as well, squaring her shoulders. "The dean will need to approve it. The university's reputation—"

"Will be better served by being ahead of a disaster than complicit in hiding it," Elias said firmly.

She nodded slowly. Then, surprising them all—perhaps herself most of all—she stepped forward and hugged him. It was brief, almost professional, but Elias felt the tremor in her body, the fear she was mastering.

"We're really doing this," she whispered against his shoulder.

"We really are."

When she pulled back, her eyes were bright with unshed tears. "I need to... I should go prepare. Make sure my data is bulletproof."

"Mara—"

But she was already gathering her things, moving with the purposeful energy of someone who needed action to avoid thinking too hard about what they'd just committed to.

After she left, Sierra stretched, joints popping. "So, scale of one to ten, how screwed are we if Prometheus is wrong?"

"Eleven," Elias admitted.

"Cool, cool. Just checking." She paused at the door. "For what it's worth, I think you're right. And I think she knows it too. She's just scared."

"Aren't we all?"

Sierra's grin was sharp as a blade. "Terrified. But hey, at least we're terrified together, right?"

After she left, Elias sat alone in his lab, Koa pressed against his leg. The monitors continued their silent vigil, data streaming endlessly across their surfaces. Somewhere in those numbers was either their vindication or their doom.

His phone buzzed. Email notification. He almost ignored it—probably another faculty member complaining about his research methods—but something made him look.

The sender was anonymized, routed through what looked like a dozen proxy servers. The subject line was blank. But the preview showed enough to make his blood run cold:

"Dr. Quinn, I've been following your work with interest. The attached file contains your email to the National Science Foundation from three years ago. Amazing how alarmist it sounds out of context, isn't it? Wouldn't want this to surface right before your big announcement. -A concerned citizen"

With trembling fingers, he opened the attachment. It was indeed his email, but edited, words rearranged to make him sound like a doomsday prophet rather than a careful researcher. Whoever had done this had skill and access to his private communications.

His phone rang—Mara.

"Did you get—" she began.

"The email? Yes."

"Mine has a photo," she said, voice tight. "From that conference in Denver. Cross and I at dinner. Taken from an angle that makes it look... intimate."

The implications hung heavy. Someone was already moving against them, trying to discredit them before they even spoke.

"We can't let this stop us," Elias said.

"I know. I just... God, Elias, what if we're wrong?"

He closed his eyes, seeing again the data, the patterns, the undeniable convergence of evidence. "What if we're right and say nothing?"

The silence stretched between them, filled with the weight of that possibility.

Finally, she spoke. "Noon tomorrow?"

"Noon tomorrow."

After they hung up, Elias sat in the darkening lab, Koa whimpering softly beside him. On the monitors, Prometheus continued its analysis, processing new data, refining predictions. And in the corner of the screen, barely noticeable unless you were looking for it, a small alert blinked.

He clicked on it, and his heart nearly stopped.

FALSE POSITIVE DETECTED IN DATASET 7A-3. RECALIBRATING.

The timestamp showed it had appeared just minutes ago, right after he'd opened the anonymous email. As he watched, frozen, the alert vanished, deleted from the system logs as if it had never existed.

His phone buzzed again. Another anonymous message, this one just text:

"Your data is flawed. Stop now before you cause real harm. This is your only warning."

Elias stared at the message, fear and determination warring in his chest. Someone had access to Prometheus. Someone was trying to stop them. Which meant someone believed they were right.

The thought should have been comforting. Instead, it terrified him more than all the data combined.

Koa pressed closer, a low growl rumbling in his chest as if he could sense the danger gathering around them like storm clouds. Elias's hand found the dog's fur, drawing comfort from the warm, solid presence.

Tomorrow would change everything. The question was whether they'd live long enough to see if they were right.

In the distance, so faint it might have been imagination, the ground trembled.

Chapter 12: The Rift

Mara's hands trembled as she stared at the computer screen, the numbers blurring through tears she refused to acknowledge. Three in the morning, alone in her apartment, and Prometheus's data had just shattered like glass.

The discrepancy was subtle—a single variable in the correlation matrix that threw off the entire prediction model. How had they missed it? How had she missed it? The woman who'd built her career on precision, on never letting emotion cloud judgment, had allowed herself to believe in Elias Quinn's beautiful delusion.

She pulled up the raw data again, following the error back to its source. Line by line, algorithm by algorithm, until she found it: a recursive loop in the behavioral analysis that essentially had Prometheus confirming its own assumptions. Garbage in, garbage out, as her first statistics professor used to say.

Her phone buzzed. Sierra: "Can't sleep either? I'm running diagnostics on the visualization protocols."

Mara almost responded, then stopped. If Sierra was checking the visualizations, she might find the same flaw. Or worse—what if Sierra had known all along? The eager graduate student who'd appeared just when they needed help, who'd integrated herself so seamlessly into their work...

Paranoia, Mara told herself. But wasn't that what Cross had called it, too, right before he'd published her research under his name?

She dressed mechanically, gathering every piece of equipment Elias had lent her. Each item felt like evidence of her foolishness. The portable seismometer she'd used to verify his readings. The encrypted hard drive containing their shared research. The university parking pass he'd gotten her for easier access to his lab.

The drive to campus was a blur of streetlights and self-recrimination. She'd let herself believe—in the data, in the mission, in him. Had let herself feel the warmth of his hand on hers, the steadiness of his presence, the way he looked at her like she was something precious rather than broken.

Naive. She'd been so desperately naive.

The anthropology building was dark except for the basement windows. Of course, Elias would be there, probably refining his prophecy of doom, unaware that the foundation was rotten. She used her keycard—another thing to return—and descended to the lab.

She found him hunched over his computer, Koa asleep at his feet. He looked up as she entered, and his face transformed with a smile that made her chest ache.

"Mara! Perfect timing. I've been running new projections based on the cave data, and—" He stopped, registering her expression. "What's wrong?"

"This." She dropped the equipment on his desk with perhaps more force than necessary. "All of this is wrong."

His confusion was either genuine or perfectly performed. "I don't understand."

"The recursive loop in your behavioral algorithm. The one that makes Prometheus confirm its own biases." She pulled up the code on his screen, her fingers harsh on the keyboard. "Here. See it?"

He leaned forward, studying the screen. She could smell his shampoo—pine and something indefinably him—and hated herself for noticing.

"That's... that's not right," he said slowly. "This code was modified. Look at the timestamp—last night at 11:47. I was home by then, and you—"

"Don't." The word came out sharp enough to cut. "Don't try to deflect. Your entire system is built on wishful thinking and confirmation bias."

"Mara, someone tampered with this. Someone who had access—"

"Someone like your devoted graduate student? Or maybe the mysterious spy you keep hinting about?" She laughed, brittle as winter ice. "God, I can't believe I fell for this again."

He stood, reaching for her. "Fell for what? Mara, we're partners—"

"No." She stepped back, wrapping her arms around herself. "We're not partners. You're a grieving widower seeing patterns that don't exist, and I'm the fool who let another charming academic convince her to ignore the data."

His face went white. "Another... you're comparing me to Cross?"

"At least Cross was honest about his ambition. You've wrapped yours in pseudo-science and animal mysticism."

"That's not fair—"

"Fair?" Her voice rose, echoing off the concrete walls. "Was it fair when you dragged me into your conspiracy theories? When you made me believe we were saving lives? When you let me think—" She bit off the words, but they hung in the air anyway.

"Think what?" His voice was quiet now, dangerous.

"Nothing. It doesn't matter."

"It does matter. Say it."

"Fine." She met his eyes, pouring all her fear and fury into the words. "When you let me think you cared about me as more than just validation for your delusions."

The silence that followed was deafening. Koa whined, sensing the tension.

"Is that really what you believe?" Elias asked finally. "That everything between us was about Prometheus?"

"I don't know what to believe anymore." The fight drained out of her, leaving only exhaustion. "I just know I can't do this. I won't be the woman who ignored evidence because she wanted to believe in someone."

"The evidence is real, Mara. The cave samples, the historical data, the patterns—"

"Patterns you're forcing into a narrative because you can't accept that sometimes terrible things just happen. That your wife died, and there was no grand purpose, no warning you missed, no system that could have saved her."

The words hung between them like a blade. She saw them land, saw him flinch as if physically struck, and hated herself. But she couldn't take them back. Couldn't unsay the truth they both had been dancing around.

"Get out." His voice was barely above a whisper.

"Elias—"

"Get. Out."

She fled, her vision blurring. Behind her, she heard something crash—equipment thrown in anger or grief. She didn't look back, couldn't look back, even as every step away felt like tearing something vital from her chest.

***

In her office, Mara methodically erased their shared files. Each deletion felt like a small death—weeks of collaboration, late-night breakthroughs, moments when their minds had worked in perfect synchrony. Her cursor hovered over a folder labeled "Personal Notes." She knew she should delete it too, maintain the clean break.

Instead, she opened it.

Screenshots of articles about animal behavior and prediction. Links to papers she'd thought might interest him. A photo Sierra had taken of them during a late-night session, both leaning over the same screen, shoulders touching, completely absorbed in the work. In the image, Elias was looking at the data, but she was looking at him, and the expression on her face...

She slammed the laptop shut.

***

Elias sat in the wreckage of his lab, staring at the unsent email on his screen.

Mara,

I don't know if you'll read this. I don't even know if I'll send it. But I need to write it, need to put these words somewhere before they consume me.

You're right that I see patterns everywhere. It's how I've survived since Sarah died—looking for meaning, for connections, for some proof that the universe isn't just random cruelty. But the pattern I see with you isn't about grief or validation or Prometheus.

I see the way you bite your lip when you're concentrating. I see how you pretend not to care about Koa, but always save him the last bite of your sandwich. I see your brilliance, your strength, your stubborn refusal to trust even when every cell in your body wants to.

I see you, Mara Lang. And I'm falling in love with what I see.

Maybe that makes me naive. Maybe Cross broke something in you that I'm not equipped to heal. But I need you to know that nothing—not Prometheus, not the prediction, not even being right about all of this—matters as much as the fact that you walked into my life and made me remember what it feels like to hope.

I'm sorry, I'm not what you need me to be. I'm sorry the data failed. I'm sorry for so many things.

But I'm not sorry for believing in us.

—E

He highlighted the text, finger hovering over the delete key. Then, with a bitter laugh, he saved it to drafts instead. Another unsent letter in a lifetime of unspoken words.

His phone rang. Unknown number.

"Dr. Quinn? This is Dr. Harrison Cross. I believe we have a mutual acquaintance."

Elias's blood turned to ice. "What do you want?"

"To help, actually. I'm concerned about Mara. She called me earlier, quite distressed. Something about falsified data and professional misconduct?"

"She didn't call you." But even as he said it, doubt crept in. She'd been so angry, so hurt...

"Didn't she?" Cross's voice was silk over steel. "Well, perhaps I misunderstood. These things happen when emotions run high. I'm sure the security footage from the hotel in Denver would clear up any misunderstandings about professional conduct."

"What hotel? What are you talking about?"

"The conference last year. Mara and I had dinner to discuss her research. Perfectly innocent, of course, but you know how things can look when taken out of context. Camera angles can be so misleading."

"You're lying."

"Am I? Ask her about Denver, Dr. Quinn. Ask her about the wine, the conversation that ran until 2 AM, and the way she laughed at my jokes. Or don't. I'm sure she had her reasons for not mentioning it."

The line went dead.

Elias stared at his phone, pieces clicking into place. Cross knew about their relationship. Knew exactly which buttons to push. But how? Unless...

A knock at the lab door interrupted his spiraling thoughts. Sheriff Granger stood in the hallway, hat in hand, looking deeply uncomfortable.

"Doc, we need to talk."

"If this is about the prediction—"

"It's about the complaints." Granger shifted his weight. "I've got a dozen calls about you 'fear-mongering,' causing panic. People are demanding action."

"People like Harrison Cross?"

Granger's poker face slipped for just a moment. "I can't comment on who's filing complaints. But I can tell you that if you keep pushing this volcano theory without solid evidence, I'll have to take official action."

"Tom, you know me. You know I wouldn't—"

"I know you lost your wife and threw yourself into this work. I know grief makes people see things that aren't there." Granger's voice gentled. "I also know every dog in town has been acting strange for weeks, and my own horses won't go near the north pasture anymore."

"Then you believe—"

"I believe you should be careful. There's folks with deep pockets who don't like what you're stirring up. And Mara..." He paused. "She might not be as alone as you think."

"What does that mean?"

But Granger was already leaving. "Just watch yourself, Doc. And maybe ask yourself who benefits if you're wrong. Then ask who benefits if you're right."

***

Mara sat in her dark apartment, laptop open to Prometheus's code. The recursive loop stared back at her, damning in its simplicity. But something nagged at her—the timestamp Elias had pointed out.

She pulled up the access logs, cross-referencing the modification time. 11:47 PM. She'd been home, he'd been home, Sierra had been...

Her blood ran cold.

Sierra's keycard had accessed the building at 11:31 PM. But she'd messaged Mara at 3 AM about running diagnostics, as if she'd just started working.

With shaking fingers, Mara dug deeper into the system logs. More modifications, subtle changes designed to undermine the core algorithms. All traced back to authorized users, but the patterns were wrong, the coding style inconsistent with their usual work.

Her phone rang. Cross.

She almost didn't answer, then decided she needed to know what game he was playing.

"Mara, darling. I heard about your situation with Dr. Quinn. So unfortunate when personal feelings cloud professional judgment."

"How did you—"

"Oh, I make it my business to know when brilliant minds are being led astray. That surveillance footage from his lab shows quite an intimate working relationship. Very touching, really."

Surveillance footage. Her mind raced. There were no cameras in Elias's lab—she'd checked out of habit, a remnant of Cross-induced paranoia.

"You're bluffing."

"Am I? Check your personal drive, Mara. The file labeled 'Backup Analysis.' I think you'll find it illuminating."

He hung up.

With trembling fingers, she navigated to her personal drive. The file was there, created an hour ago while her laptop had been closed. Inside was a modified version of Prometheus's code—not just the recursive loop, but dozens of subtle corruptions. And at the bottom, a digital signature that looked like hers but wasn't quite right.

Someone had remote access to her system. Someone was framing her for the sabotage.

She grabbed her phone to call Elias, then stopped. The words she'd said, the accusations she'd thrown—how could she face him now? How could she ask him to believe her when she'd just shattered his trust?

But as she stared at the corrupted code, one thing became crystal clear: they'd been played. Someone wanted them separated, wanted their work discredited, wanted the prediction to fail.

Which meant, despite everything, the prediction was real.

And she'd just helped their enemy win.

In the distance, barely audible through her apartment windows, a dog began to howl. Then another. And another. Soon the night filled with the sound of animal distress, a chorus of warning that sent chills down her spine.

Her laptop screen flickered. A new file appeared on her desktop: "FINAL_WARNING.txt"

She opened it with numb fingers.

You're out of time. Both of you. Stop now, or what happens next is on your heads.

Below the text was a series of GPS coordinates. She recognized them immediately—the exact location of Elias's lab.

Mara ran for her car, praying she wasn't too late. Behind her, every dog in Morgantown continued their mournful song, and beneath their cries, almost imperceptible, the ground began to shake.

Chapter 13: Ash Dreams

Mara woke choking on sulfur and smoke that existed only in her mind.

The dream clung to her like ash—Morgantown buried under a gray shroud, buildings collapsed into rubble, the screams of those who hadn't believed until it was too late. But it was Elias's voice that had torn her from sleep, calling her name through the devastation, calling for help she couldn't give because she'd abandoned him when he needed her most.

3:47 AM. She'd managed ninety minutes of sleep after fleeing his lab, fleeing the coordinates that promised violence, fleeing her own cowardice. The apartment felt like a tomb, every shadow hiding accusations.

She stumbled to her laptop, still open to the sabotaged code. In the dream, she'd seen Cross's face as he typed, watched him plant the seeds of doubt with surgical precision. But there'd been someone else—a figure in shadow, accepting an envelope thick with cash, their face obscured but their posture familiar...

Her hands shook as she opened a new terminal window. If someone had been paid to sabotage Prometheus, there would be traces. Digital breadcrumbs that even Cross couldn't completely erase.

She started with the access logs, diving deeper than before. Past the surface timestamps to the raw system data, the kind of forensic evidence that most people didn't know existed. Line after line of code scrolled past until—

There. An SSH connection from an IP address that didn't match any of their registered devices. She traced it through three proxy servers before hitting a wall, but the connection timing told her everything: someone had been watching their every keystroke for weeks.

More disturbing were the patterns. The saboteur hadn't just corrupted random functions—they'd targeted specific algorithms, the ones that predicted timing and magnitude. Someone wanted the eruption to happen but didn't want anyone to know when.

Her phone buzzed. Sierra: "Can't sleep. Keep thinking about that recursive loop. Something's not right about the modification pattern."

Mara stared at the message. Sierra had found it too. Which meant either she was incredibly dedicated, or...

She pulled up Sierra's academic records, the ones Elias had shared when they first brought her onto the team. Honor student, glowing recommendations, a passion for data visualization that bordered on obsessive. But there, buried in her transcript, a semester's leave of absence two years ago. Medical reasons, the record said. Nothing specific.

Cross had taken his sabbatical two years ago.

"No," Mara whispered. But the pieces fit too well. Sierra's convenient appearance just when they needed help. Her eagerness to access all their systems. The way she'd integrated herself so completely that they'd stopped questioning her presence.

But if Sierra was Cross's spy, why was she pointing out the sabotage? Unless...

Mara's fingers flew across the keyboard, pulling up the visualization protocols Sierra had been working on. There, hidden in subroutines that would only activate during a real event, was code that would downplay the severity. Make a catastrophic eruption look like a manageable emergency.

Hundreds would die because the warning system would fail.

"God damn you, Cross," she breathed.

She screenshot everything, building a digital case file. But as she worked, the dream images kept intruding. Elias reaching for her through the smoke. His voice, broken: "I trusted you. We could have stopped this together."

Her phone showed seventeen unread messages from him, sent before their fight. Planning messages. Hope messages. Partnership messages that now read like prophecy.

"Running new models with the cave data. You were right about the mineral composition."

"Koa won't leave my side. I think he knows we're close to something big."

"Thank you for believing in this. In us."

That last one broke her. She typed a response, deleted it, typed again.

"Elias, I'm sorry. You were right about the sabotage. Cross has—"

Delete.

"Please forgive me. I let fear make me cruel. You deserve—"

Delete.

"The dream showed me the truth. We have to—"

Delete. Delete. Delete.

How did you apologize for choosing fear over faith? How did you explain that Cross had broken something fundamental in your ability to trust, and that breakage had made you hurt the one person who'd helped you start to heal?

You didn't. You showed up. You brought evidence. You hoped the work could bridge what words couldn't fix.

Mara saved her evidence to multiple drives, uploaded backups to secure servers, and prepared for the most important drive of her life. Outside, Morgantown slept unaware of the danger building beneath its foundations. But the animals knew. Even through her windows, she could hear the restless sounds of creatures preparing to flee.

Just like in her dream.

***

The roads to Elias's cabin should have been familiar by now. Still, the pre-dawn darkness transformed them into something alien. Mara's headlights caught eyes reflecting from the forest—deer, raccoons, possums, all moving in the same direction. Away from the mountains. Away from what was coming.

Her phone GPS showed seventeen minutes to the cabin when the first tremor hit.

It was subtle, barely enough to register, but her coffee jumped in its holder, and the radio stuttered with static. She pulled over, hands gripping the wheel, waiting. The forest had gone silent—no insects, no night birds, nothing but the tick of her cooling engine.

Then came the sound. Low, almost below hearing, like the earth clearing its throat. The trees swayed without wind, and in the distance, she saw birds erupting from their roosts in black clouds against the lightening sky.

"Please," she whispered, though she wasn't sure if she was praying for the mountain to stay quiet or for Elias to forgive her.

She drove faster, taking the mountain curves at dangerous speeds. Each mile brought new signs of disturbance—a cracked road surface that hadn't been there yesterday, a stream running muddy when there'd been no rain, the smell of sulfur growing stronger.

The cabin appeared through the trees like salvation. Elias's Jeep was there, Prometheus's mobile unit visible through the back window. Light spilled from the windows, which meant he was awake, which meant—

The front door opened before she could knock. Elias stood there in yesterday's clothes, hair disheveled, eyes rimmed with exhaustion and something that might have been grief.

"Mara?" His voice was hoarse. "What are you—the coordinates, I got your message about—"

"I didn't send a message." The words tumbled out. "Elias, I'm sorry. I'm so sorry. You were right about everything. Cross sabotaged the code, Sierra might be working for him, there's a conspiracy to hide the eruption's severity, and—"

He pulled her inside, checking the road behind her. "Slow down. Start from the beginning."

But Koa chose that moment to emerge from the back room, took one look at Mara, and began howling. Not his usual greeting, but something primal that raised every hair on her body.

"How long has he been doing that?" she asked.

"Three hours. Right around the time you—" He stopped, jaw tightening.

"The time I accused you of being delusional and compared you to the man who destroyed my career." She met his eyes, forcing herself not to look away from the hurt there. "Elias, I—"

Another tremor, stronger than the first. Books fell from shelves, and Prometheus's equipment beeped urgent warnings.

"Later," he said, already moving to the computers. "Show me what you found."

They worked side by side, Mara explaining her discoveries while Elias correlated them with Prometheus's latest readings. Every few minutes, Koa would pace to the window, whine, then return to press against their legs.

"This hidden code in the visualization," Elias muttered, "it's designed to trigger during a catastrophic event. Make it look manageable until it's too late to evacuate."

"Cross wants people to die," Mara said flatly. "He wants the disaster to be worse than predicted so he can discredit us posthumously."

"Or someone's paying him to ensure maximum damage." Elias pulled up the shadow figure from her dream, the one she'd described taking money. "Who benefits from casualties?"

"Insurance companies would lose billions. The government would face lawsuits. Unless..." Her blood chilled. "Unless someone was positioned to profit from the reconstruction. Someone who knew exactly where to buy land, exactly which companies to invest in..."

"Disaster capitalism," Elias breathed. "They're not trying to stop the eruption. They're trying to control who survives it."

A car engine growled outside. They both froze, Koa growling low in his throat.

"Were you followed?" Elias asked.

"I don't think—I was watching, but—"

He killed the lights, pulling her away from the windows. In the darkness, her hand found his, and he squeezed back—forgiveness in the simple gesture that undid her more than any words could have.

Through the curtains, headlights swept across the cabin. The engine died, and a car door opened.

"Dr. Quinn? Dr. Lang?" Voss's voice, but strained. "I need to speak with you. It's about the old stories—the ones they made me bury."

Elias looked at Mara, a silent question. She nodded. Whatever Voss knew, they needed to hear it.

He opened the door to find the elderly geologist standing in the dawn light, looking every one of her seventy-three years. But her eyes burned with purpose.

"They're moving against you," she said without preamble. "Cross has the governor's ear. By noon, there'll be warrants. Reckless endangerment, inciting panic, whatever charges they can manufacture."

"How do you know this?" Mara asked.

"Because they tried the same thing to me thirty years ago. Only I didn't have what you have—proof. And partners who believe in each other."

She looked between them, and Mara felt exposed, as if the older woman could see every harsh word, every moment of doubt, every fragile hope for reconciliation.

"The stories my family preserved," Voss continued, "they speak of twin guardians who would know the mountain's anger. One who hears the earth's creatures, one who reads the earth's bones. Apart, they fail. Tog ether..." She smiled sadly. "Together, they might just save us all."

Another tremor, the strongest yet. In the distance, a sound like thunder, but the sky was clear.

"That's not thunder," Elias said quietly.

"No," Voss agreed. "That's the mountain clearing its throat. You have perhaps days, not weeks."

"Then we need to—" Mara started, but Voss held up a hand.

"First, you need to settle whatever's broken between you. The mountain's not the only thing ready to erupt, and you'll need each other whole for what's coming."

She turned to go, then paused. "Oh, and Dr. Lang? That car that's been following you? It's parked about a quarter-mile down the road. Might want to deal with that too."

After she left, Elias and Mara stood in the doorway, dawn painting the mountains in shades of rose and gold that seemed almost obscene given what lurked beneath.

"I'm sorry," Mara said again. "For what I said about Sarah, about your grief. It was cruel and—"

"True," he interrupted. "Partially true, anyway. I did throw myself into this work because of her. But somewhere along the way, it stopped being about the past and started being about the future. A future I started imagining with you."

The words hung between them, fragile as spun glass.

"I don't know how to trust," Mara whispered. "Cross broke something in me, and I keep waiting for everyone to betray me, keep pushing people away before they can hurt me. I pushed you away because you were starting to matter too much."

"And now?"

"Now I'm terrified. Of the mountain, of Cross, of failing. But mostly of losing you before I get the chance to be brave."

He stepped closer, one hand rising to cup her face. "Then be brave now."

She kissed him. Not the desperate kiss of disaster survivors or the careful kiss of new lovers, but something deeper—acknowledgment of pain, promise of partnership, hope for whatever time they had left.

When they broke apart, Koa had stopped howling, watching them with what looked remarkably like approval.

"The car," Elias said reluctantly.

"The warrants," Mara added.

"The eruption," they said together, and despite everything, found themselves smiling.

"Together?" he asked, echoing her word from days ago that felt like years.

"Together," she confirmed.

They geared up quickly—evidence drives, emergency supplies, Prometheus's mobile unit. As they loaded the Jeep, Mara caught a glimpse of the tailing car through the trees. Black sedan, engine off but someone still inside.

"We could confront them," Elias suggested.

"Or we could let them follow us right to the press conference," Mara countered. "Let them watch us reveal everything, including their surveillance."

He grinned, the expression transforming his exhausted face. "I knew there was a reason I fell for you."

The words were casual, thrown off in the adrenaline of the moment, but they landed like small earthquakes in Mara's chest.

Another tremor—no, not a tremor. The ground rolled like ocean waves, lasting fifteen seconds that felt like forever. In the forest, trees swayed and cracked. An ancient oak near the cabin split down the middle with a sound like a gunshot.

When it stopped, they were both on their knees in the dirt, Koa between them.

"Days," Mara breathed. "Maybe hours."

"Then we'd better hurry."

They drove toward town as the sun climbed higher, the black sedan maintaining its distance behind them. But Mara kept checking the mirrors, because she'd sworn—just for a moment—she'd seen a second car following the first.

The mountain groaned beneath them, and every animal they passed was running in the opposite direction. Time was a luxury they'd already spent, and the real nightmare was just beginning.

But she had evidence, Elias, and a chance to make things right.

It would have to be enough.

Chapter 14: The Press Conference

The university's media room felt like a war zone before the battle. Sierra hunched over her laptop, fingers flying across keys as she assembled their final presentation. Mara watched her with new eyes, looking for tells, for signs of betrayal in every gesture.

"The visualization protocols are clean," Sierra announced, spinning her screen toward them. "I've quarantined the corrupted code and rebuilt everything from scratch. No hidden surprises this time."

This time. The words hung in the air like an accusation.

"Sierra," Elias began carefully, "we need to ask you about—"

"About why I accessed the lab at 11:31 PM three nights ago?" She didn't look up from her screen. "Or about my semester leave two years ago? Or about the fact that Dr. Harrison Cross was a guest lecturer in my data visualization course?"

Mara's hand found the concealed recording device in her pocket. Beside her, Elias had gone very still.

Sierra finally looked up, and her eyes were red-rimmed with exhaustion and something else. Fear.

"I know how it looks," she continued. "Convenient timing, previous connection to Cross, mysterious absence from school. You'd be idiots not to suspect me."

"Are you working for him?" Mara asked flatly.

"No." Sierra closed her laptop with deliberate calm. "But he tried to recruit me two years ago, after his guest lecture. He was impressed with my work and offered me a research position. The interview process was... intensive."

She rolled up her left sleeve, revealing a thin scar that ran from wrist to elbow.

"The stress triggered a breakdown. Hospitalization, intensive therapy, the works. When I finally got back to school, I made sure to stay far away from charismatic professors with big promises." She looked directly at Elias. "Until you."

"Why didn't you tell us?" Elias asked.

"Because I needed this. Needed to prove I could do real work, make a real difference. And because..." She hesitated. "Because I thought I could handle seeing him again. I was wrong."

Mara studied the younger woman's face, searching for deception. "He contacted you after you joined us."

It wasn't a question, but Sierra nodded anyway. "Three weeks ago. Wanted inside information. Offered to 'fix' my academic record, make the medical leave disappear." She laughed bitterly. "When I refused, he got nasty. He said he'd make sure everyone knew I was unstable and unreliable. That no one would ever trust my work."

"The sabotage code," Elias said slowly. "You found it because—"

"Because I know his style. He taught me, remember? I've been checking our systems obsessively, looking for his fingerprints." She pulled out a flash drive. "This has everything. Our clean code, plus logs of every intrusion attempt I've detected. He's not the only one watching us."

Mara took the drive, weighing it in her palm like it might bite. "Who else?"

"Government. Corporate interests. At least three foreign intelligence services." Sierra's smile was sharp. "Turns out, predicting natural disasters is a matter of national security. Who knew?"

A knock interrupted them. Voss entered, looking every inch the distinguished professor despite the early hour. She'd changed into a severe black suit that made her seem carved from stone.

"They're gathering," she announced. "Local media, science journalists, and quite a few faces I don't recognize. Security says there are protesters too—some calling you fearmongers, others begging for evacuation information."

"Cross?" Mara asked.

"Haven't seen him, but his influence is evident. Several reporters have been asking very specific questions about your," she paused delicately, "working relationship."

Heat crept up Mara's neck, but Elias just squared his shoulders. "Let them ask. We have nothing to hide."

"Don't we?" Voss moved closer, lowering her voice. "In my experience, Dr. Quinn, the truth rarely matters once the media decides on a narrative. They'll paint you as lovers who let emotion cloud scientific judgment. They'll dig into your wife's death, Dr. Lang's history with Cross, anything to discredit the message."

"Then what do you suggest?" Mara asked.

"Control the narrative. Address the relationship directly, but frame it as two scientists whose collaboration led to breakthrough discoveries. Don't hide from their attacks—redirect them."

She produced a leather journal, its pages yellow with age. "This was my grandmother's. She documented the 1847 event, the one the mining companies buried. Animal migrations, water table changes, the works. Everything you've discovered, she witnessed firsthand."

Elias accepted the journal reverently. "This is incredible. Why didn't you—"

"Because I learned the hard way that evidence means nothing if they destroy your credibility first." Voss's expression hardened. "I won't watch them do to you what they did to me. Not when lives hang in the balance."

Sierra cleared her throat. "Speaking of evidence, I've been monitoring social media. The video's about to drop."

"What video?" Mara asked, though her stomach already knew.

"Security footage from the cave yesterday. Edited to make it look like you were planting evidence rather than discovering it."

Mara's phone buzzed. Unknown number. She almost ignored it, then saw the preview: Play along or the real video surfaces.

Her blood turned to ice. What real video?

***

The auditorium was packed beyond capacity. Camera crews jostled for position while reporters sharp-elbowed their way to better seats. Mara spotted familiar faces from the science beat, but also unknown observers who watched with the flat affect of professionals paid to be present.

"Steady," Elias murmured, his hand briefly touching the small of her back. The contact was meant to be supportive, but she saw how the nearest photographer's eyes tracked the gesture.

They took their positions at the table—Elias center, Mara to his right, Sierra managing the presentation screen. Voss had positioned herself in the front row, a bastion of credibility in the coming storm.

"Thank you all for coming," Elias began, his professor's voice carrying easily through the space. "What we're about to share may be difficult to accept, but we believe the evidence is overwhelming. The Appalachian region is experiencing precursor events to a significant volcanic eruption."

The reaction was immediate. Reporters shouted questions, cameras flashed, and someone in the back actually laughed.

Elias raised a hand for silence. "Dr. Lang will present our geological findings."

Mara stood, forcing her voice steady. "Three days ago, we documented the presence of volcanic basalt in cave systems that supposedly contain only sedimentary rock. Temperature readings show a fifteen-degree anomaly at depth. Seismic activity has increased 400% in the last week alone."

She clicked through slides—data, graphs, photographs. With each piece of evidence, she felt the room's skepticism wavering. These were scientists, after all. Data spoke to them.

"Furthermore," she continued, "historical analysis reveals a pattern of suppression regarding volcanic activity in this region. Dr. Lenora Voss's 1983 study, which was buried by state authorities, correctly predicted—"

"Dr. Lang," a reporter interrupted. "Isn't it true that you were recently seen entering Dr. Quinn's residence at 4 AM?"

The room erupted. Mara felt the blood drain from her face, but before she could respond, Elias stood.

"Dr. Lang and I have been working around the clock to verify our findings. Given the urgency of the situation, conventional working hours seemed inappropriate."

"But you are romantically involved?" The reporter pressed, smirking.

"Our personal relationship is irrelevant to the data," Elias said calmly. "Would you ask this question if we were both men?"

"I might ask why someone who lost his wife to an unpredicted natural disaster might be motivated to see patterns where none exist," another reporter called out.

The cruelty of it hit Mara like a physical blow. She saw Elias flinch, saw his knuckles white as he gripped the podium.

"My wife's death taught me that ignoring warning signs has consequences," he said quietly. "If that makes me more alert to danger, I consider it a responsibility, not a bias."

"What about your responsibility to avoid causing panic?" This from a man in an expensive suit who hadn't been there when they started. "Economic damage from false evacuation could run into billions."

"And lives lost from failure to evacuate?" Mara found her voice, stepping beside Elias. "What's the economic value of those?"

Sierra clicked to the next slide—Prometheus's prediction model, showing the eruption timeline. Gasps rippled through the crowd.

"This is our AI's analysis," Elias explained. "Based on behavioral patterns, geological data, and historical precedents, we believe an eruption will occur within—"

The main screen flickered. Sierra's presentation vanished, replaced by grainy security footage. The cave, but edited—jump cuts making it appear they were planting the basalt samples rather than discovering them.

"What the hell?" Sierra frantically typed, trying to regain control.

More footage—Elias and Mara at the cabin, embracing. The angle and lighting made it look far more intimate than the comforting hug it had been. Then photos—Mara at dinner with Cross, laughing at something he'd said, his hand touching hers across the table.

"Lies!" Mara stepped forward, but the damage was done. Reporters were on their feet, shouting questions about falsified evidence and compromised objectivity.

"Dr. Lang," a woman in the third row called out, her voice cutting through the chaos. "Is it true you've expressed internal doubts about the validity of this prediction?"

Mara froze. Those were her exact words from the fight with Elias. Only three people had been in that lab—her, Elias, and Koa.

Which meant the lab was bugged.

"Any scientific theory involves internal debate," she managed. "That's how we refine our understanding—"

"But you specifically said the system was built on wishful thinking and confirmation bias," the reporter pressed, reading from her phone. "You compared Dr. Quinn to your former colleague Harrison Cross, who falsified data."

The room exploded. Through the chaos, Mara saw Cross himself enter through a side door, his expression one of manufactured concern.

"Enough!" Voss's voice cracked like a whip. The elderly professor stood, commanding attention through sheer presence. "Thirty years ago, I stood where they stand. I had evidence of volcanic activity, and I was destroyed for presenting it. Not because I was wrong, but because powerful interests needed me silenced."

She moved to the podium, shouldering past the stunned speakers.

"Dr. Cross," she said, locking eyes with him. "Since you're here, perhaps you'd like to explain why you've been systematically attempting to sabotage their work? Or shall I present the evidence myself?"

Cross's urbane mask slipped for just a moment. "I don't know what you're implying—"

"I'm not implying anything," Voss cut him off. She pulled out a tablet, connecting it to the projection system Sierra had just wrestled back under control. "I'm stating facts."

The screen filled with financial documents. Shell companies, property transfers, investment positions that would profit massively from reconstruction efforts in specific areas.

"Someone has been very busy preparing for a disaster they claim won't happen," Voss said mildly. "Buying land in zones that would become valuable refugee centers. Shorting insurance companies with Appalachian exposure. Setting up construction contracts for the rebuilding phase."

The reporters turned their cameras on Cross, who had gone pale.

"This proves nothing," he said, but his voice lacked its usual conviction.

"No?" Voss clicked again. "Then explain this."

Audio filled the room—Cross's voice, talking to someone about ensuring "maximum impact" and "discrediting the warning system." The recording was of poor quality, but it was clearly him.

In the chaos that followed, Mara felt Elias's hand find hers. She squeezed back, drawing strength from the contact.

"Where did that recording come from?" he murmured.

"I don't know," she whispered back. "But look at Cross's face. He knows who he was talking to."

Security moved in, reporters shouted questions, and through it all, Sierra worked furiously at her laptop. Suddenly, the screens around the room—meant for overflow viewing—lit up with raw data. Seismic readings from the last hour, showing a massive spike.

"Ladies and gentlemen," Sierra announced, her young voice cutting through the noise. "While you've been arguing about our credibility, the mountain has been making its own statement. These readings are from USGS sensors. In the last forty minutes, we've recorded seventeen micro-quakes, all centered beneath the dormant volcanic system we've identified."

The room fell silent except for the urgent beeping of phones as reporters received alerts from their news desks.

Elias stepped forward. "We're not asking you to believe us. We're asking you to look at the data, to remember the animals fleeing, to notice the patterns your own senses are telling you exist. Make your own decisions. But make them quickly."

"Because whether you believe us or not," Mara added, "the mountain is waking up. And when it fully opens its eyes, it won't care about our debates, doubts, or damaged reputations. It will simply erupt."

They left the podium together, moving through the crowd that parted like water. Cross had vanished, but Mara could feel hostile eyes tracking their movement. In the lobby, protesters pressed against security barriers—some holding signs calling them frauds, others begging for evacuation information.

"This way," Voss guided them through a service corridor. "My car's out back."

As they emerged into harsh afternoon sunlight, Mara's phone rang. She almost ignored it, then saw it was her mother's number.

"Hello?"

"You stupid little bitch." The voice was electronically distorted but somehow familiar. "You think you've won? This is just beginning. Everything you love, everyone you care about—we know where they are."

In the background, she heard something that made her blood freeze—the distinctive cough of her elderly neighbor, Mrs. Chen, who always watched her cat when she traveled.

"If you hurt her—"

"Then stop. Recant. Say you were wrong." The voice dropped lower. "You have six hours to release a statement admitting fraud, or we start with the old woman. Then your precious professor's students. Then his dog. We'll save you for last, so you can watch it all burn."

The line went dead.

Mara stood frozen in the parking lot, the phone slipping from numb fingers. Distantly, she heard Elias calling her name, felt his hands on her shoulders.

"They have Mrs. Chen," she whispered. "They're going to hurt people unless we recant."

"Who? Who has her?"

But Mara could only shake her head, the electronic distortion echoing in her memory. Familiar but wrong, like a song played in the wrong key.

Then it hit her. The cough in the background—Mrs. Chen's distinctive smoker's hack—but also another sound. The beep of medical equipment.

Mrs. Chen was in the hospital. Had been for three days with pneumonia.

Which meant whoever called had been there, in her room, close enough to record that cough.

The spy wasn't just watching them. They were targeting everyone around them, building a web of pressure points to force their silence.

And Mara had a terrible suspicion she knew exactly who was behind that electronic mask.

Chapter 15: The Underground Network

The basement of the Computer Science building had transformed into a digital war room. Pizza boxes towered in corners like cardboard monuments to exhaustion, energy drink cans created aluminum graveyards, and the air hummed with the electricity of three dozen laptops running simultaneously. Sierra stood at the center of it all, a general commanding her army of code.

"Alright, people, listen up!" She clapped her hands, drawing bleary eyes from screens. "The press conference was a disaster, but we're not done. We pivot. We go grassroots. We become the underground."

A hand shot up from the back. Jason Fitzgerald, senior computer science major, teacher's pet, and recent volunteer. Too recent, Elias thought, watching from the doorway. The young man had appeared two days ago, full of enthusiasm and surprisingly specific questions.

"What about authentication protocols?" Jason asked. "If we're creating a distributed warning system, we need to ensure data integrity. Maybe I could help with Prometheus's core access—"

"Prometheus stays compartmentalized," Sierra cut him off. "You want to help? Focus on the social media amplification algorithms."

Jason's smile never wavered, but Elias caught the flash of frustration in his eyes. Filed it away with the other odd moments—Jason always nearby during sensitive conversations, his code commits coming at strange hours, his questions that probed just a little too deep.

"Smart thinking," Mara murmured beside him. She'd noticed too. "Keep the spy busy with busywork."

"If he is a spy."

"In our current situation, paranoia is just another word for pattern recognition."

They entered the room together, and Elias felt the energy shift. These students had chosen to believe them despite the mockery, despite the risk to their own academic careers. That faith was humbling.

"Dr. Quinn! Dr. Lang!" Amy Chen bounced over, her enthusiasm undimmed by forty-eight hours without sleep. "We've got the hashtag trending. #MountainWarning is up to 50,000 uses. People are sharing their own animal behavior videos, earthquake prep tips, even old family stories about the mountains."

She showed them her phone, scrolling through an endless feed of citizen science. A farmer in Kentucky posting about his cows refusing to graze. A teacher in Virginia documenting her classroom pets' agitation. Ordinary people building extraordinary evidence.

"This is incredible," Mara said, then raised her voice to address the room. "All of you—what you're doing here matters. You're saving lives."

"Even if no one knows it yet," someone called out, generating nervous laughter.

"Especially then," Elias countered. "The hardest courage is standing alone with the truth."

He caught Sierra gesturing from her command station. They made their way over, weaving between workstations where students built everything from evacuation apps to data visualization tools.

"We need to talk," Sierra said quietly. "Private."

They followed her to a corner she'd converted into a server farm. The equipment hummed with processing power, jerry-rigged cooling systems keeping temperatures manageable. She'd built a fortress of technology, and Elias wondered if it was meant to keep danger out or secrets in.

"I've been enhancing Prometheus," she began, pulling up code on multiple screens. "Creating redundant backups, distributed processing nodes. If they try to sabotage us again, the system will survive."

"Smart," Mara said. "But that's not why you pulled us aside."

Sierra's fingers drummed against her thigh—a nervous tell they'd learned to recognize. "Dr. Voss sent over her family archives. Decades of geological data, indigenous oral histories, stuff that never made it into official records. But some of it's encrypted. Old-school cryptography that needs more than computing power to crack."

She handed Mara a leather journal, its pages brittle with age. Mathematical equations filled the margins, interspersed with geological diagrams and symbols that looked almost runic.

"This is..." Mara's eyes widened. "This is a substitution cipher based on mineralogical properties. Brilliant. Voss's grandmother was encoding data in the structure of the rocks themselves."

"Can you decode it?"

"Give me an hour and a pot of coffee." Mara was already lost in the puzzle, that beautiful focus Elias had learned to love, transforming her face.

While she worked, Elias helped Sierra with the technical improvements. They optimized algorithms, strengthened firewalls, and created kill switches that would preserve data even if their systems were compromised. It was meticulous work that required absolute concentration, which made Jason's interruptions even more noticeable.

"Dr. Quinn?" The student appeared at his elbow for the fourth time. "I've been thinking about the behavioral prediction matrices. If I could just see how Prometheus weighs different inputs—"

"The social media campaign needs you more," Elias said firmly. "Amy could use help with the Virginia Tech outreach."

"Of course." Jason's smile was plastic. "Just trying to help where I'm most useful."

As he walked away, Sierra muttered, "If he asks about core access one more time, I'm encoding his homework assignments in Klingon."

"You think he's—"

"I think he's got the worst case of teacher's pet syndrome I've ever seen, or he's fishing for something specific." She pulled up access logs. "Look at this. He's been trying to probe our security, but he's smart about it. Nothing overtly malicious, just... persistent."

Before Elias could respond, Mara made a sound of triumph from her corner.

"Got it!" She waved them over, the journal open to pages of decoded text. "You're not going to believe this. There weren't just volcanic events in 1847 and 1920. Voss's grandmother documented seventeen separate incidents over three hundred years, all suppressed or explained away."

"Seventeen?" Sierra's fingers flew across her keyboard, updating Prometheus's historical parameters. "That completely changes our predictive model."

"It gets better. Or worse." Mara pointed to a decoded passage. "Each eruption was preceded by the same pattern—animal migrations, water table changes, harmonic tremors. And each time, local authorities were warned. Each time, they chose economic interests over lives."

"History really does repeat," Elias murmured. "First as tragedy, then as—"

"More tragedy," Mara finished grimly.

The door burst open, admitting a stream of new volunteers. Word had spread through the academic underground—professors who'd been mocked for supporting them, graduate students risking their careers, even some townspeople who'd noticed the animal behaviors themselves.

Dr. Patricia Williams from Biology brought her decades of migration data. Professor Chen from Statistics offered predictive modeling expertise. Even Tom Granger appeared, out of uniform but carrying boxes of emergency supplies.

"Not here officially," the sheriff said gruffly. "But my dogs have been going crazy, and my granddad always said to trust the animals. Figure you could use some help with evacuation planning."

The basement became a hive of purposeful activity. Maps spread across tables as they plotted evacuation routes. Statisticians refined prediction models. Biologists correlated animal behavior patterns. It was peer review in real-time, the scientific method accelerated by desperation.

And through it all, Elias was aware of Mara. The way she commanded respect with quiet competence. How she bit her lip when concentrating. The unconscious grace of her movements as she navigated between workstations, solving problems, and offering encouragement.

During a brief lull, he caught her in the hallway outside the restrooms. The fluorescent lights flickered overhead, casting shadows that made her face look etched from marble.

"Hey," he said, eloquent as always.

"Hey yourself." She leaned against the wall, exhaustion evident in every line of her body. "This is really happening, isn't it? We're really doing this."

"Having second thoughts?"

"No. Maybe. I don't know." She laughed, but it was brittle. "Ask me when we're not running on caffeine and determination."

He stepped closer, drawn by the vulnerability she so rarely showed. "Mara—"

"I'm scared," she admitted. "Not of being wrong. Of being right. Of what comes after. Of..." She gestured between them. "This."

"I know." He raised a hand to her face, thumb tracing the curve of her cheekbone. "But isn't that when courage matters most?"

She leaned into his touch, eyes fluttering closed. "When did you become so wise?"

"Tuesday. I think it was Tuesday."

That startled a real laugh from her, and he used the moment to kiss her. Quick, soft, a promise more than a passion. When they broke apart, her eyes were bright.

"We should get back," she said.

"We should."

Neither moved.

"Elias?" Her voice was barely a whisper. "Whatever happens, I need you to know—I need you. Not just for this, for the work, but... I need you."

The words hit him like physical force. Before he could respond, she was gone, striding back to the war room with renewed purpose.

He followed more slowly, trying to process the gift she'd just given him. Trust from someone who'd had it shattered. Need from someone who'd sworn never to depend on anyone again.

The war room had erupted in controlled chaos during their absence. Sierra stood at the center, face pale, staring at her screens with horror.

"What is it?" Mara demanded.

"I found something in the backups. Hidden deep, triggered by specific queries." Sierra's voice shook. "Someone's been inside our system for weeks. Not just reading data—modifying it. Subtle changes to evacuation routes, timing predictions, safety zones."

"Show me." Mara's geological mind attacked the problem from one angle while Elias approached from another.

The modifications were clever, almost artistic in their deception. A few degrees of angle here, a couple of minutes there. Individually meaningless.

Collectively, they would funnel evacuees into specific zones—zones that corresponded to property owned by the shell companies from Cross's financial web.

"They're not just profiting from disaster," Elias realized. "They're choreographing it. Choosing who lives and dies based on land values."

"But who?" Sierra's fingers flew across keyboards. "The code style is familiar, but I can't quite—"

A chime from her phone made her freeze. Anonymous message, two words: "Eyes within."

As if summoned by the warning, Jason appeared at Sierra's shoulder. "Problems with the system? Maybe I can help debug—"

"No!" Sierra's reaction was too sharp, too sudden. Jason stepped back, hurt flashing across his features.

"I'm just trying to help," he said plaintively.

"I know. Sorry. It's just—sensitive data. University liability issues." The lie came smoothly, but Elias saw Jason's eyes narrow slightly.

An uncomfortable silence settled over their corner of the room. Around them, the underground network continued its work, oblivious to the cancer that might be growing in its heart.

"We need to check everyone," Mara said quietly after Jason drifted away. "Full background checks, code audits, the works."

"That'll take time we don't have," Sierra protested.

"Then we compartmentalize harder. Critical systems stay with the three of us. Everyone else gets pieces, never the whole."

It was paranoia, but as Mara had said, paranoia was just pattern recognition in dangerous times.

They worked through the night, building firewalls both digital and human. The basement became a maze of security protocols, and each volunteer was tracked and monitored without their knowledge. It felt wrong, treating allies like potential enemies, but the stakes were too high for trust.

As dawn light filtered through the narrow windows, Elias found himself standing before their master evacuation map. Hundreds of routes marked in different colors, each one now suspect, each decision potentially compromised.

"We'll have to verify everything manually," Granger said, joining him. The sheriff looked haggard but determined. "Drive every route ourselves if we have to."

"Tom, that would take—"

"I know what it would take." Granger's voice was steady. "Also know what it'll cost if we don't. My family's lived here six generations. I'll be damned if I let some corporate conspiracy decide who makes it to seven."

The quiet determination in his voice was echoed throughout the room. These people—students, professors, townspeople—had chosen to stand against forces they couldn't fully comprehend. Not for glory or profit, but because it was right.

Mara appeared at his side, close enough that their shoulders touched. Such a small contact, but it grounded him, reminded him why they fought.

"Updates?" he asked.

"I've decoded another section of Voss's journal. There's a pattern to the eruptions—they follow geological stress points that were mapped in the 1800s. If I'm right, we can predict not just when but exactly where the initial eruption will occur."

"That's incredible."

"That's not all." She lowered her voice. "The journal mentions a group called the Geological Preservation Society. They've been tracking these patterns for over a century, trying to warn people. Voss's grandmother was a member."

"You think they still exist?"

"I think we need to find out." She glanced around the room. "Because if they do, we're not as alone as we thought."

Before he could respond, every screen in the room flickered. For one heart-stopping moment, Elias thought they'd been hacked again. Then Sierra's triumphant whoop echoed off the walls.

"Got him! Caught our spy red-handed!"

They rushed to her station where she'd pulled up activity logs with Jason's digital fingerprints all over them.

"He's been copying everything," Sierra explained. "Sending it to an encrypted server every few hours. But he made one mistake—he accessed the system from his personal laptop. I've been running a trace, and guess where our data's been going?"

She pulled up a map with a blinking red dot. The location was familiar—a office complex on the edge of town that housed several financial firms.

Including one with documented ties to Cross's network.

"We need to—" Elias began, then stopped.

Jason was gone. His workstation sat empty, laptop missing, coffee still steaming in its cup.

"When did he—"

"Five minutes ago," Amy Chen said, confused. "Said he needed fresh air. Why?"

They ran for the exits, but even as they burst into the morning light, Elias knew they were too late. Jason Fitzgerald—if that was even his real name—had vanished into the dawn, taking their secrets with him.

But he'd left something behind. Sierra found it tucked under his keyboard—a sticky note with four words: "You can't stop this."

As if in response to the taunt, Elias's phone buzzed. Prometheus alert. The probability calculations had shifted dramatically based on the new historical data.

They now had days, not weeks.

And their enemy knew everything they planned.

"What do we do?" Sierra asked, looking younger than her years.

Elias felt Mara's hand slip into his, squeezing tight. Around them, their underground network continued its work, unaware that their sanctuary had been breached.

"We do what we've always done," he said. "We tell the truth. We save who we can. And we trust that's enough."

But as they stood in the morning light, watching the mountains that held such terrible secrets, he wondered if trust was a luxury they could no longer afford.

The spy had escaped, but he'd revealed a crucial truth: they weren't paranoid enough.

The real war was just beginning.

Chapter 16: The Cave

The morning mist clung to Backbone Mountain like a burial shroud, refusing to lift despite the rising sun. Elias checked his equipment for the third time, trying to ignore how Koa pressed against his legs with increasing desperation. The dog hadn't stopped whining since they'd loaded the Jeeps.

"Maybe he should stay behind," suggested Dr. Rachel Winters, the structural geologist Mara had recruited. She was competent, credentialed, and had appeared just two days after Jason's betrayal—which made Elias deeply suspicious.

"Koa comes," he said firmly. "His instincts have saved us before."

The expedition team gathered around their vehicles: Elias, Mara, Sierra with her arm still in a sling from yesterday's "accident" with fallen equipment, three graduate students, and Dr. Winters. Each carried advanced sensing equipment that the university's emergency fund had somehow approved overnight—another small miracle or major suspicion, depending on your paranoia level.

"Michael, you got the ground-penetrating radar?" Mara called out.

Michael Reeves, one of the grad students, patted his pack. "Yes, Dr. Lang. Though I still don't see why we need—" He fumbled with the straps, and his portable spectrometer tumbled out, smashing against a rock.

"Damn! I'm so sorry. I can run back to the lab—"

"No time," Mara said curtly. "We proceed without it."

Elias caught the flash of frustration in Michael's eyes before the student schooled his expression. Another mental note filed away. After Jason, everyone was a suspect.

The drive to the cave took forty minutes on roads that had developed new cracks overnight. Elias led in his Jeep with Mara beside him and Koa in the back, the dog's anxiety filling the vehicle like a third passenger.

"He's getting worse," Mara observed.

"The animals know. They always know." Elias glanced in the mirror at the following vehicles. "What's your read on Winters?"

"Qualified. Published. Convenient." Mara's fingers drummed against her tablet. "Her paper on magma chamber detection is solid, but..."

"But she appeared right when we needed her expertise."

"Paranoid much?"

"After Jason? Paranoid is baseline."

They reached the cave entrance to find it changed. The kudzu had been cut back, and fresh tire tracks marked the ground. Someone else had been here recently.

"Could be locals," Sierra suggested, climbing stiffly from the second vehicle. "Cave's not exactly secret."

But Koa's reaction said otherwise. The normally brave dog backed away from the entrance, a low growl building in his chest. When Elias tried to lead him forward, Koa planted all four feet and pulled against the leash hard enough to choke himself.

"I've never seen him like this," Elias muttered.

"I'll stay out here with him," Michael volunteered quickly. Too quickly.

"No." Mara's voice brooked no argument. "We stay together. Koa comes with us, even if we have to carry him."

In the end, Elias did carry him—seventy pounds of trembling Australian Shepherd who buried his face in Elias's jacket as they entered the darkness.

The cave breathed around them, cold air carrying scents of sulfur and something else—something organic and wrong. Their headlamps carved through darkness that seemed almost solid, picking out details that shouldn't exist.

"Look at these walls," Dr. Winters said, running her hand along the stone. "The scoring patterns are all wrong for natural erosion."

"Because it's not natural," Mara confirmed. "This was carved. Expanded. But not recently—these tool marks are centuries old."

They descended deeper, following the path Elias and Mara had taken before. But everything felt different with a larger group. The whispers started almost immediately—wind through stone that sounded almost like words.

Deeper... come deeper...

"Did you hear—" one of the grad students began.

"Acoustic phenomena," Mara said quickly. "The cave structure creates natural sound distortions."

But her hand found Elias's in the darkness, fingers interlacing with desperate strength.

The chamber where they'd found the collapsed rocks had been cleared. Not by them—someone else had been here, moving tons of stone with mechanical precision. The lower passage gaped open like a wound.

"Who would—" Sierra started.

That's when they heard it. Clear as a bell, echoing off the walls: "Betrayed."

Everyone froze. This wasn't wind or imagination. This was a voice, human and full of pain.

"There's someone down here," Dr. Winters breathed.

"Or something's playing recorded messages," Elias countered, though the explanation felt hollow.

Koa writhed in his arms, desperate to flee. But they pressed on, drawn by scientific necessity and something deeper—the human need to solve mysteries, even when every instinct screamed danger.

The lower passage opened into a cathedral of stone. Their lights couldn't find the ceiling, and the walls stretched beyond the beams' reach. But it was the floor that made Mara gasp.

"This is impossible."

The stone beneath their feet was smooth as glass, but shot through with veins of obsidian that shouldn't exist in this geological region. Worse, the obsidian was warm to the touch, pulsing with heat from below.

"Get samples," she ordered, her scientific mind overriding fear. "This confirms everything—there's an active magma intrusion beneath us."

They spread out, taking readings, collecting samples. Sierra worked her equipment one-handed, recording everything. The grad students seemed genuinely absorbed in the discovery. Even Dr. Winters appeared shaken by the implications.

Which is why no one noticed Michael disappearing into a side passage until they heard the rumble.

"MOVE!" Elias screamed, recognizing the sound from their last visit.

The ceiling came down in a choreographed collapse. Not random—targeted. Rocks fell in patterns designed to herd them toward the center of the chamber, away from the exit.

Sierra stumbled, her injured arm throwing off her balance. A boulder the size of a refrigerator plummeted toward her.

Time dilated. Elias saw the trajectory, calculated the physics, and knew with crystalline clarity that Sierra wouldn't make it. Neither would anyone who tried to help.

He moved anyway.

But Mara was faster, shoving Sierra aside with seconds to spare. The boulder crashed where the young woman had been, sending shrapnel in all directions. A fist-sized rock caught Mara in the ribs, spinning her around. She was falling, falling toward a fresh chasm opened by the collapse—

Elias caught her, pulling her against his chest as more rocks rained down. He curled around her, making his body a shield, feeling impacts across his back like hammer blows.

"I can't lose you too," he gasped against her hair. The words ripped out of him, raw and desperate. "Not you. Never you."

The collapse ended as suddenly as it began. Dust filled the air, turning their lights into useless cones of white. Someone was screaming—one of the grad students, hurt but alive.

"Sound off!" Mara's voice, muffled against Elias's chest but strong.

One by one, they confirmed survival. Cuts, bruises, Dr. Winters with a gashed forehead, but everyone is mobile. Everyone except—

"Where's Michael?" Sierra asked.

They found him emerging from the side passage, dusty but unharmed, face a mask of innocent concern. "I thought I saw something. Went to check. What happened?"

"You triggered a trap," Mara said flatly.

"That's ridiculous. I would never—"

"Save it." She turned away, dismissing him with contempt that cut deeper than accusation. "We have what we came for. Move out."

But as they gathered their equipment, Elias spotted something in the rubble. A piece of modern paper, edges charred but text still visible:

You're too late. The mountain wakes on our schedule, not yours. —HC

Harrison Cross. Still pulling strings even from wherever he was hiding.

"He knew we'd come back," Sierra said, reading over his shoulder. "This whole thing was planned."

"Then we spring the trap properly," Mara decided. "Complete the mission. Get the evidence out. Make his sabotage meaningless."

They formed a defensive line for the exit—those with injuries in the middle, the suspected spy under constant watch. The journey up seemed endless, each shadow potentially hiding another trap.

But it was when they emerged into daylight that the real shock waited.

Three black SUVs idled in the clearing, engines running. Men in suits stood beside them, the kind of interchangeable corporate security that could mean anything from private military to government contractors.

"Drs. Quinn and Lang?" The lead suit didn't wait for confirmation. "You're trespassing on private property. This cave system was purchased this morning by Aegis Development Corporation."

"That's impossible," Mara said. "This is state land."

"Was." He produced documents. "Emergency sale authorized by the governor's office. Something about budget shortfalls and immediate infrastructure needs."

Cross's web, spreading even now. Buy the evidence, bury the truth, control the narrative.

"We're leaving," Elias said carefully. Koa, finally free of the cave, had gone rigid in his arms, a growl building that sounded more wolf than dog.

"After we inspect your vehicles. Can't have anyone removing property that belongs to Aegis."

"You mean evidence that proves what's under this mountain?" Sierra said.

The suit's smile never wavered. "I don't know anything about that, miss. Just doing my job."

They were outnumbered, outgunned in every way that mattered. But as the suits moved toward their vehicles, Koa exploded into motion.

Seventy pounds of fury launched from Elias's arms, straight at the lead suit. Not to attack—to distract. The man stumbled backward, arms windmilling, as Koa danced around him barking furiously.

"Now!" Mara hissed.

They scattered to their vehicles. Engines roared to life, tires spinning on loose gravel. The suits scrambled for their SUVs, but Koa had done his job—those precious seconds of chaos made the difference.

Elias's Jeep fishtailed onto the access road, Mara navigating while he drove. In the mirrors, black SUVs gave chase, but these roads were Elias's territory. Every curve, every shortcut, every place where mountain driving experience trumped city reflexes.

"Hard left!" Mara called out. "The old logging road!"

He took the turn on two wheels, feeling the Jeep protest. Behind them, one SUV tried to follow and ended up nose-first in a drainage ditch.

"Two more," Sierra reported over the radio. "Coming up fast."

"The bridge," Elias realized. "If we can make it across first—"

"It won't hold their weight," Mara finished. "Do it."

The wooden bridge over Piedmont Creek had been condemned for five years, but locals still used it carefully. Elias didn't use it carefully. He floored it, feeling boards crack and splinter beneath them. The Jeep lurched sickeningly as supports gave way, but momentum carried them across.

Behind them, the lead SUV's driver saw the collapsing structure and slammed on the brakes. The vehicle skidded to a stop inches from the drop.

"Clear," Mara breathed. Then, louder: "We're clear!"

But Elias couldn't celebrate. In the back, Koa huddled on the floor, trembling worse than in the cave. And on Mara's tablet, seismic readings showed something that made his blood freeze.

"The collapse in the cave," Mara said quietly. "It wasn't just a trap. Look at these readings. The rockfall destabilized the lower chamber. Opened new fissures."

"Which means?"

"We didn't just spring Cross's trap. We accelerated the timeline." She looked at him with eyes full of terrible knowledge. "The mountain's not going to wait for our schedule either. We've got maybe 72 hours."

"Then we make them count."

She nodded, then winced, hand going to her ribs where the rock had struck.

"You're hurt," he said.

"I'm alive. Because of you." Her free hand found his on the gear shift. "What you said in the cave—"

"I meant it."

"I know." She squeezed his hand. "That's what terrifies me."

They drove in silence after that, each lost in thoughts of what came next. Behind them, Cross's web grew tighter. Ahead, a mountain prepared to wake. And somewhere between, a conspiracy worked to ensure maximum casualties when it did.

But they had evidence now. Rock samples that proved everything. Readings that couldn't be disputed. Truth that even Cross couldn't bury.

The question was whether anyone would listen in time.

As they reached the main road, Elias's phone buzzed with texts. The underground network reporting in—evacuation plans proceeding, warning systems partially restored, people beginning to listen despite the official denials.

"Sierra's traced the Aegis sale," Mara read from her own phone. "Shell company registered yesterday. Board of directors includes..." She trailed off.

"What?"

"Members of the state emergency management committee. The people who'd coordinate evacuation if we're right." Her voice was hollow. "They're not trying to stop the eruption. They're trying to control who survives it."

The mountain loomed in the windshield, peaceful in the afternoon sun. But beneath its green slopes, magma rose through ancient channels, following paths last used when the world was young.

72 hours.

And a conspiracy determined to make them the worst 72 hours in American history.

"We need help," Elias said. "Real help. Federal level."

"Who'd believe us? We're discredited academics with a doomsday prediction and evidence that's now locked in a cave owned by our enemies."

"Then we make them believe. Whatever it takes."

Mara studied him, something fierce and proud in her expression. "Together?"

"Together."

Behind them, Koa finally stopped shaking. The immediate danger had passed. But the dog remained vigilant, nose testing the air, because he knew what his humans were only beginning to understand:

The real danger hadn't even started yet.

Chapter 17: Sabotage

The smell hit Elias first, gasoline mixed with something acidic that made his eyes water. He stood frozen in his cabin doorway, Koa growling low and dangerous beside him, as his mind struggled to process the devastation.

His home had been methodically destroyed. Not ransacked in anger but systematically dismantled with surgical precision. Every piece of Prometheus equipment lay in sparking ruins. His computers had been opened, hard drives removed, circuits dissolved in acid. Twenty years of research reduced to toxic waste.

But it was the walls that made his blood run cold.

Photographs covered every surface—hundreds of them, showing him and Mara at moments they'd thought were private. Mara is asleep in her apartment, vulnerable and unaware. Elias grading papers in his office at 2 AM. The two of them in the cave, in the coffee shop, in moments of quiet conversation. Each image is annotated with timestamps and GPS coordinates.

In the center of it all, spray-painted in red across his grandmother's heirloom quilt: "YOU WERE WARNED."

"Don't touch anything," Mara's voice came from behind him. He hadn't heard her arrive, but suddenly she was there, her face a mask of controlled fury. "This is evidence."

"Evidence of what? That Cross has been stalking us for weeks?" His voice cracked. "That he's been in my home, touching my things, watching us sleep?"

"Evidence that he's escalating." She pulled out her phone, photographing everything with clinical detachment. Only the white knuckles of her grip betrayed her emotion. "He's making mistakes. Getting desperate."

Koa hadn't moved from Mara's side since she'd arrived, pressing against her legs with protective intensity. The dog's hackles remained raised, and he tracked every shadow as if Cross might materialize from the walls.

"Mara, that photo of you sleeping—"

"I know." Her voice was steady, but he saw the tremor in her hands. "My building has security cameras. We'll pull the footage, find out how he got in."

"What if he has people inside the security company? Inside the police?" The paranoia that had been building for days crystallized into certainty. "We can't trust anyone."

"Then we trust each other." She lowered her phone, meeting his eyes. "And we document everything. He wants us scared and isolated. We don't give him that satisfaction."

Through the shattered window, Elias saw movement. Three police cruisers pulling up his drive, lights flashing but sirens silent. His stomach dropped.

"They're here for me," he said quietly.

"What?"

"Cross's next move. Destroy my things, then have me arrested so I can't report it." He laughed bitterly. "Textbook gaslighting. Make the victim look crazy."

Sheriff Tom Granger stepped out of the lead vehicle, his weathered face unreadable. Two deputies flanked him, hands resting on their weapons.

"Dr. Quinn," Granger called out. "I need you to step outside. Slowly."

"Tom, you see what's been done here?" Elias gestured at the vandalism. "I need to report—"

"Sir, I need you to step outside with your hands visible. We have a warrant for your arrest."

"On what charges?" Mara demanded, moving to stand beside Elias.

"Cyber terrorism, theft of proprietary data, and criminal harassment." Granger's voice was steady, but something flickered in his eyes. "Dr. Lang, I'll need you to step aside."

"Like hell."

"Mara, don't." Elias touched her arm gently. "This is what Cross wants. Let them take me. Document everything. Call the lawyer."

"Elias—"

"Take care of Koa. And find our evidence before Cross destroys that too."

He walked toward Granger with measured steps, hands clearly visible. The sheriff's expression remained professional, but as he turned Elias around for the handcuffs, he whispered, "Bought witnesses. Three of them. Their stories don't add up, but the judge wouldn't listen."

The metal was cold against Elias's wrists. As they led him to the cruiser, he looked back to see Mara standing in the doorway of his ruined home, Koa pressed against her side, both of them watching with matching expressions of fierce determination.

"Find the spy," he called out, not caring who heard. "They're closer than we think."

***

The interrogation room at the sheriff's station hadn't been updated since the 1970s. Flickering fluorescent lights, a two-way mirror, and a metal table bolted to the floor. Elias had been sitting there for three hours, refusing water, a phone call, and everything else except the right to remain silent.

The door burst open. Not a detective—Harrison Cross himself, immaculate in a charcoal suit that probably cost more than Elias made in a month.

"You can't be here," Elias said flatly.

"My lawyers say otherwise." Cross settled into the opposite chair with predatory grace. "Amazing what a restraining order can accomplish when properly motivated. You've been harassing me, Dr. Quinn. Following me, hacking my systems, spreading libel about my business practices."

"You destroyed my home."

"I was in DC all week. Have the receipts to prove it." Cross's smile was sharp as winter. "Unlike you, I document my whereabouts. Speaking of which, where were you last Tuesday at 3 AM?"

"Asleep."

"Alone?"

"What does it matter?"

"Because that's when someone accessed my private servers using your university credentials." Cross produced a folder, sliding it across the table. "Your digital fingerprints are all over it. Your IP address, your login, even your typing patterns."

Elias didn't touch the folder. "Fabricated."

"Prove it." Cross leaned back. "That's the beautiful thing about digital evidence. It's only as reliable as the systems that create it. And who controls those systems, Professor?"

"Why?" The question escaped before Elias could stop it. "What's the point of all this? If we're right about the eruption, you'll die too."

"Will I?" Something flickered in Cross's eyes—amusement? Madness? "You assume I'm staying for the finale. But men like me, we always have exit strategies. Private jets, foreign holdings, new identities waiting in countries without extradition treaties."

"Leaving everyone else to burn."

"Natural selection." Cross shrugged. "The smart survive. The stubborn perish. You could have joined the winners, Elias. I offered partnership, profit, and safety for those you love. You chose martyrdom instead."

"I chose truth."

"Truth?" Cross laughed, the sound echoing off concrete walls. "Truth is what power says it is. And right now, power says you're a disturbed individual who let grief drive him to delusion. Your volcanic theories? The desperate fantasies of a man who couldn't save his wife from a mundane car accident."

Elias lunged across the table, but Cross had anticipated it. Security burst in, pinning Elias down while Cross straightened his tie.

"Assault. Add it to the charges." He paused at the door. "Oh, one more thing. That birthmark on Dr. Lang's shoulder? The one shaped like a crescent moon? Quite distinctive. She should really close her curtains at night."

The door slammed shut, leaving Elias with the taste of copper in his mouth and murder in his heart.

***

Mara found Cross in the parking garage beneath his office building. She'd waited three hours, sitting in shadows between concrete pillars, letting rage crystallize into purpose. When he emerged from the executive elevator, whistling something that sounded like a funeral dirge, she stepped into his path.

"Dr. Lang." He didn't seem surprised. "Come to negotiate your boyfriend's release?"

"Come to end this." She held up her tablet, showing financial records that had taken Sierra hours to decrypt. "Veridian Industries. Cascade Holdings. Prometheus Ventures. Shell companies, all funded by disaster capitalism. You're not just profiting from predictions—you're ensuring disasters happen on schedule."

"Proving that would require evidence you don't have."

"Would it?" She swiped to new screens. "Purchase orders for industrial-grade thermite. Contracts with demolition experts. Investment positions that only make sense if specific infrastructure fails at specific times."

For the first time, uncertainty flickered across Cross's face. "How did you—"

"Your mole isn't as loyal as you think. They left breadcrumbs, maybe intentionally, maybe not. But enough to trace back to you."

"Impossible. My asset is—"

"Compromised by their own conscience?" Mara stepped closer. "See, that's what you never understood about people, Cross. You can buy their actions, but not their souls. Push hard enough, and even the desperate develop spines."

"Who?" The word came out harsh. "Who betrayed me?"

"The same person who's been feeding you information. The one you've been blackmailing with forged academic records." She watched his face carefully, cataloging each micro-expression. "Oh, you didn't know about the forgery trail? Your asset covered their tracks well, but not well enough. Sierra found the digital signatures. The timestamp discrepancies."

Cross's composure cracked. "Sierra's records are real. Her breakdown, her hospitalization—"

"All real. But the academic fraud you've been holding over her? Fabricated. She figured it out yesterday. And once she knew your leverage was false..."

"She's been feeding me false data." The realization hit Cross like a physical blow. "For how long?"

"Long enough." Mara smiled coldly. "Your evacuation interference? Based on the routes Sierra provided. Routes that lead your people directly into projected lahars paths. Your safe zones? Sitting on top of methane deposits that'll turn into firebombs when the pyroclastic flows hit."

"You're lying."

"Am I? Check your models. Run the real data, not the sanitized version Sierra's been feeding you." She turned to leave, then paused. "Oh, and Cross? That photo of me sleeping? My neighbor's nanny cam caught your man placing surveillance equipment. Former NSA, wasn't he? They're usually better about checking for secondary cameras."

She left him standing there, his empire of lies beginning to crumble. But she'd only made it three blocks when her phone buzzed. Sierra, panic in her voice:

"Mara, it's not me! I'm not the mole. Someone's been using my access codes, but—"

The line went dead.

Mara ran, feet pounding pavement as her mind raced faster. If not Sierra, then who? Who had that level of access? Who knew their systems well enough to—

The answer hit her just as she reached the command center. She burst through the doors to find chaos. Computers sparked and smoked, volunteers evacuating as fire suppression systems activated. And in the center of it all, calmly downloading files to an external drive, stood someone she'd trusted completely.

"Hello, Dr. Lang," Michael Reeves said pleasantly. The eager graduate student who'd dropped the spectrometer. Who'd volunteered to stay outside with Koa. Who'd disappeared during the cave collapse. "I was hoping we'd have a chance to talk."

***

The standoff lasted thirty seconds that felt like hours. Michael held a modified cell phone—some kind of trigger device. Around them, critical data burned on dying servers.

"You were so focused on current students," he said conversationally. "Never thought to check the dropouts. The ones who left when the pressure got too much, when the bills piled too high."

"Cross recruited you before you left," Mara realized.

"Saved me, more like. My sister's medical bills were crushing us. He offered a solution—disappear for a while, come back as his inside man." Michael's smile was sad. "I really did admire your work. Under different circumstances..."

"You can still walk away. Testify against him. We'll protect you."

"With what resources? Against what power?" He shook his head. "You've seen what he can do. The reach he has. My family's only safe as long as I'm useful to him."

"And when you're not? When the eruption makes all his plans meaningless?"

"Then we'll be far away. New identities, new lives, courtesy of Aegis Corporation's relocation program." He backed toward the exit, drive in one hand, trigger in the other. "Shame about the servers. So much valuable data lost. But don't worry—Cross has copies of everything important."

"Michael, please—"

"Forty-three hours, Dr. Lang. That's the real timeline. Not seventy-two. Cross knows, I know, and now you know. Do what you want with that information."

He pressed the trigger. Not an explosion—something worse. Every screen in the command center displayed the same message: "ALL EVACUATION ROUTES COMPROMISED. TRUST NO ELECTRONIC GUIDANCE. THE MOUNTAIN CHOOSES WHO LIVES."

Then he was gone, vanishing into the smoke and chaos.

***

Two hours later, Granger personally released Elias from custody. No explanation, just a gruff "charges dropped" and a warning look that said, "don't ask questions." Elias found Mara waiting outside, soot-stained and exhausted.

"The command center?" he asked.

"Salvageable. Sierra's already rebuilding with hardened systems. No network connections, everything air-gapped." She leaned into him, drawing strength from contact. "Michael was the mole. Has been for months."

"Where is he now?"

"Wind. But he left us something—the real timeline. Forty-three hours, Elias. Less than two days."

They stood there in the sheriff's station parking lot, watching the sun set behind mountains that would soon cease to exist. Koa found them there, having escaped from wherever Sierra had tried to contain him. The dog pressed between them, whining softly.

"Cross won this round," Elias said quietly.

"Did he?" Mara pulled out her phone, showing a flood of messages. "The leaked voicemail went viral. An anonymous source sent recordings of Cross bribing officials to every major news outlet. The geology community is mobilizing. People are starting to evacuate on their own."

"Without proper routes—"

"We'll guide them. Old fashioned way. Paper maps, local knowledge, human networks." She looked up at him, fierce despite exhaustion. "Cross took our technology. He can't take our community."

A new message popped up. Granger, brief and urgent: "Federal investigators incoming. Cross's payments traced to emergency management officials. Big dominoes falling. Watch your six."

Elias felt something shift in his chest—not quite hope, but its cousin. "He overplayed his hand."

"Hubris. Gets them every time." Mara pocketed her phone. "Come on. We have forty-three hours to save thirty thousand people with stone age technology and sheer stubbornness."

"Together?"

"Together."

They walked toward her car, Koa between them, as the first emergency sirens began to wail across the valley. Not official evacuation orders—those were still tangled in bureaucracy and bribes. But volunteer fire departments, local police who'd chosen conscience over orders, ordinary people who'd decided that perhaps the crazy professors were right after all.

The mountain trembled, just once, as if acknowledging the change in the game. Cross had won the battle, but awakened something more dangerous than geological forces.

He'd awakened a community's will to survive.

And forty-three hours would have to be enough.

Chapter 18: Countdown Begins

Sierra's scream cut through the pre-dawn quiet of the makeshift command center.

Elias burst through the door to find her staring at Prometheus's main display, her face illuminated by pulsing red warnings that painted the room like a crime scene. The AI's predictive model had transformed from its usual elegant curves into a jagged nightmare of accelerating probability.

"It's not possible," Sierra whispered. "The timeline just compressed by seventy percent."

Mara was already at the secondary terminal, fingers flying across keys as she verified the data. "Magma ascent rate has tripled. Temperature spikes in all monitoring wells. Christ, Elias, it's not waiting for our schedule."

The main screen updated again, showing a three-dimensional model of the mountain's interior. Rivers of molten rock rose through ancient channels, following paths that hadn't existed in any geological survey until now. At the current rate...

"Ninety-six hours," Elias read from the display. "Four days."

"Less," Sierra corrected, pulling up her enhanced interface. "I've been incorporating Dr. Voss's historical data—the legends about animal behavior, astronomical alignments, even the indigenous lunar calculations. When I add those intuitive variables..." She tapped a final key. "Seventy-two hours. Maybe."

Through the window, the first gray light of dawn revealed birds fleeing the mountains in massive flocks, their shadows darkening the sky like smoke. Even from inside, they could hear the cacophony of their cries—a primal sound that raised primitive fears.

"We need to—" Elias began, then stopped. His phone was buzzing. Tom Granger.

"Doc? You might want to get down to the station. Your lawyer's here, and there's been a development."

***

The holding cell had been Elias's home for six hours before Granger had managed to process him out on bail. Now he sat in the sheriff's office, still wearing yesterday's clothes, while his lawyer—a public defender who looked about twelve—shuffled papers nervously.

"The charges are serious," she said. "Inciting panic, reckless endangerment, conspiracy to defraud. The prosecutor's talking about economic terrorism."

"Economic terrorism?" Mara's voice could have etched glass. "For warning people about a natural disaster?"

"For causing a panic that resulted in property damage and economic losses." The lawyer wouldn't meet their eyes. "They have witnesses saying Professor Quinn orchestrated everything for attention."

"Bought witnesses," Granger interjected from behind his desk. He'd been quiet until now, but something had shifted in his expression. "I've been sheriff here for twenty-three years. Know every troublemaker, every honest citizen, every soul in between. Those 'witnesses'? Half of them have records. The other half have sudden influxes of cash."

"You can prove that?" the lawyer asked.

"Don't need to." Granger leaned back in his chair. "Because I'm dropping all charges."

The lawyer's jaw dropped. "Sheriff, you can't—"

"Can and am. Prosecutor wants to refile? That's his business. But my department's not pursuing this farce." He met Elias's eyes. "My grandmother used to tell stories. About the time before, when the mountain spoke and folks didn't listen. Said the animals always knew first—they'd flee, and smart folk would follow."

"Tom—"

"Three days ago, my hunting dogs refused to go up the mountain. First time in fifteen years. Yesterday, every horse at the Riverside Stables broke out of their stalls trying to run. This morning?" He gestured to the window where the bird exodus continued. "That's not panic, Doc. That's a warning."

He stood, extending his hand to Elias. "I'm sorry it took me so long to listen. What do you need?"

"Evacuation support," Mara said immediately. "We have seventy-two hours to move thirty thousand people."

"Then we'd better get started." Granger turned to his deputy. "Call in everyone. Vacation's canceled. We're going to save this town whether it wants saving or not."

***

Elias's cabin felt different in the afternoon light. Smaller somehow, as if the weight of impending disaster had compressed the walls. He stood in the doorway, watching Mara move through his space with easy familiarity—making coffee, organizing their scattered research, creating order from chaos.

"You don't have to stay," he said quietly.

She turned, and the look she gave him could have melted stone. "Try to make me leave."

"Mara—"

"No." She crossed to him in three quick strides. "No noble self-sacrifice. No pushing me away for my own good. We're past that."

"My reputation's destroyed. Cross won. Even if we're right, I'll always be the professor who cried volcano."

"Good." Her hands framed his face, forcing him to meet her eyes. "Because I don't want your reputation. I want you. The man who risks every-thing for truth. Who saves students from rockfalls. Who carries his dog when he's scared."

"I'm scared now," he admitted.

"So am I." Her thumbs traced his cheekbones. "Terrified. But not of the mountain. Of wasting whatever time we have left on fear instead of—"

He kissed her. Not the desperate kisses of their near-death experiences, but something deeper. An acknowledgment of everything they'd been dancing around, every word they'd swallowed, every touch they'd cur-tailed.

When they broke apart, her eyes were bright with unshed tears.

"I love you," she said simply. "I've been falling since that first argument about intuition versus data. Fighting it the whole way, but falling nonethe-less."

"Mara—"

"Shut up. I'm not done." Despite her words, she was smiling. "You asked what I was afraid of that night in the basement. It's this—letting someone matter enough to destroy me. But you know what? The mountain's going to destroy us all anyway. Might as well bet everything on love."

He pulled her close, burying his face in her hair. "I love you too. Have since you demolished my theories in that faculty meeting? Even when you walked away, especially when you came back."

"Then stop talking," she murmured against his neck, "and show me."

They came together like tectonic plates—slow, inevitable, reshaping each other's landscapes. In his bedroom, afternoon sun painted golden bars across the floor, across skin revealed with careful reverence. Every touch was a promise, every kiss a confession of faith in whatever time remained.

"I want to memorize you," Elias whispered against her shoulder. "Every curve, every scar, every perfect imperfection."

"Why?" Her voice was breathless, arching beneath his touch.

"Because if the world ends tomorrow, I want to face it knowing I loved you completely. Without reservation or regret."

She pulled him down, her kiss fierce and tender at once. "Then love me. Like tomorrow isn't guaranteed. Like this moment is all we have."

They moved together in ancient rhythm, bodies finding harmony that had eluded their minds for so long. In the gathering dusk, they rewrote themselves—no longer separate entities but something new, forged in crisis and chosen in calm.

Afterward, they lay entwined, watching shadows lengthen across the ceiling. Mara traced lazy patterns on his chest while he played with her hair, both reluctant to break the spell of peace.

"What are you thinking?" she asked.

"That I want to do this every day for the next fifty years. Wake up beside you, argue about breakfast, save the world before lunch."

"Ambitious timeline, Professor."

"I've always been an optimist." He caught her hand, kissing her palm. "Marry me."

She went very still. "What?"

"After. When we've evacuated everyone, stopped Cross, saved the day. Marry me." He turned to face her fully. "I know it's insane. We've known each other weeks, we're facing disaster, and I'm proposing in bed like a cliché, but—"

"Yes."

"—I don't want to waste—what?"

"Yes." She was crying and laughing simultaneously. "Yes, you ridiculous, brilliant, impossible man. Of course yes."

He kissed her tears, tasting salt and joy. "You're sure?"

"I'm sure that I love you. That whatever comes next, I want to face it as your partner in every sense." She pulled back slightly. "But I have conditions."

"Anything."

"One: We survive this. Both of us. No heroic sacrifices."

"Agreed."

"Two: Koa gets to be ring bearer."

"Obviously."

"Three: We honeymoon somewhere tectonically stable. I've had enough geology excitement for a lifetime."

"Beach resort built on a solid continental shelf. Got it."

They sealed each promise with kisses, building a future on the edge of catastrophe.

***

Morning came too soon, bringing the smell of coffee and catastrophe. They cooked breakfast together, moving around each other with new-found ease—dodging elbows at the stove, sharing stolen kisses between scrambled eggs and toast.

"Domestic bliss suits you," Voss observed from the doorway.

They sprang apart like guilty teenagers, but the elderly professor just smiled.

"Don't stop on my account. Nice to see something blooming in all this ash." She helped herself to coffee. "I came to discuss evacuation routes."

They spread maps across the kitchen table, breakfast forgotten as Voss marked patterns only she could see.

"The 1847 eruption followed these valleys," she traced lines with a gnarled finger. "The indigenous peoples knew to avoid them—called them 'fire paths.' Modern development has built directly in these zones."

"Riverside Elementary," Mara realized with horror. "The new hospital complex. They're all—"

"Sitting on a superhighway for pyroclastic flows." Voss nodded grimly. "We need to evacuate these areas first."

Through the window, more signs of the mountain's growing restlessness: a murder of crows abandoning their roost, deer running through backyards in broad daylight, even Mrs. Patterson's ancient cat yowling to be let out of town.

"The animals know," Voss said quietly. "They always know."

***

The command center had transformed into organized chaos. Volunteers manned phone banks, calling every household with evacuation information. Sierra coordinated digital outreach while Granger's deputies went door-to-door in vulnerable neighborhoods. It should have felt like victory, but Elias couldn't shake his unease.

"Package for you, Prof," one of the students called out.

No return address. No delivery service markings. Just a plain brown box that felt wrong the moment Elias touched it.

"Don't open it," Mara said immediately.

But curiosity won. Inside, cushioned in foam, lay rock samples. Their rock samples from the cave expedition. But something was off—the volcanic basalt had been replaced with ordinary granite, and the labels had been switched to show different collection sites.

"He's replacing our evidence," Sierra breathed. "Making it look like we falsified everything."

A note lay beneath the samples: "Your proof is disappearing, piece by piece. Soon you'll have nothing but the word of a disgraced professor and his compromised partner. —HC"

"Son of a—" Mara's curse was cut off by her phone ringing. Unknown number.

She answered on speaker. "What do you want, Cross?"

"Just calling to congratulate you." His voice oozed false warmth. "I hear wedding bells. How romantic—finding love at the end of the world."

Ice formed in Elias's stomach. They'd been so careful, but Cross had surveillance everywhere.

"Enjoy your time together," Cross continued. "However short it might be. Oh, and Dr. Lang? That birthmark on your left shoulder blade, the one shaped like a crescent moon? Quite distinctive."

The line went dead.

Mara's face had gone pale. That birthmark was hidden by clothing—Cross could only know about it if he'd seen...

"He has cameras," she whispered. "In the cabin. He watched us—"

Before Elias could respond, the ground rolled beneath their feet. Not violently, just a gentle sway that sent coffee cups sliding and papers fluttering. A false alarm—the seismic readings showed no actual quake, just harmonic tremors playing tricks on perception.

But the psychological damage was done. Around the room, volunteers looked up with wide eyes, remembering why they were here. The mountain was waking, and Cross was still playing games while lives hung in the balance.

"Everybody back to work," Elias commanded, his professor's voice cutting through the fear. "We have seventy hours to save thirty thousand people. Cross can spy all he wants—it won't stop what's coming."

But as he met Mara's eyes across the room, he saw his own fear reflected. Cross knew their every move, their every weakness. And somewhere in the next seventy hours, he'd use that knowledge to maximum effect.

The countdown had begun in earnest. And their enemy was already three moves ahead.

Chapter 19: The Last Lecture

Elias stood in his empty classroom at 5 AM, watching dawn paint the mountains through windows that had framed twenty years of teaching. The amphitheater could hold three hundred. According to Sierra's overnight tracking, they were expecting over a thousand.

His hands trembled as he arranged his notes—not from fear, but from the weight of what this might be. His last chance to make them listen. His final opportunity to save lives before the mountain decided the debate was over.

"You're thinking too loud," Mara said from the doorway.

He turned to find her carrying two cups of coffee, her presence immediately settling his nerves. She'd stayed up all night preparing her own surprise—a paper that would either vindicate them or destroy her career forever.

"Submitted?" he asked, accepting the coffee gratefully.

"Thirty minutes ago. 'Imminent Volcanic Threat in the Appalachian Region: A Critical Warning.' Posted to every pre-print server, emailed to every geological journal, backed up in seventeen different locations." She tried for a wry smile. "If I'm going to commit career suicide, might as well be thorough."

"Mara—"

"Don't." She pressed a finger to his lips. "I chose this. Chose you. Chose truth over tenure. Besides," her smile turned genuine, "someone recently taught me that intuition matters as much as data. My intuition says this is right."

He caught her hand, kissing her palm. "What did I do to deserve you?"

"Saved my life, challenged my assumptions, made me believe in partnership again. The usual." She pulled away reluctantly. "Sierra's waiting in your office. She thinks she knows who our mole is."

***

Sierra had transformed Elias's office into a digital command center. Multiple laptops showed feed from security cameras she'd definitely not gotten permission to access, while her primary screen displayed code that looked like hieroglyphics to anyone not fluent in multiple programming languages.

"Tell me you found them," Elias said.

"Better. I found their mistake." She pulled up communication logs. "Our spy's been using a very sophisticated encryption protocol to communicate with Cross. Government-grade stuff. But here's the thing—they got cocky. Started using the same protocol for personal emails."

"Who?" Mara demanded.

Sierra's expression darkened. "You're not going to like this."

She pulled up a student ID photo. Derek Chen, one of Elias's most dedicated graduate students. The one who'd been with them since the beginning, who'd helped refine Prometheus's algorithms, who had access to everything.

"No." Elias sank into a chair. "Derek's been with me for three years. He's brilliant, dedicated—"

"And deeply in debt," Sierra continued relentlessly. "His father's medical bills, his sister's special needs care. Cross approached him six months ago with an offer he couldn't refuse. Clean his family's slate in exchange for information."

"Do we confront him?" Mara asked.

"No. We use him." Sierra's smile was sharp. "I've been feeding him false data for the last twelve hours. Cross thinks your presentation will focus on theoretical models. He's prepared to counter academic arguments. He has no idea you're about to present smoking-gun evidence from yesterday's expedition."

Elias felt something cold settle in his chest. Another betrayal, another student corrupted by Cross's web. But also an opportunity.

"Where is Derek now?"

"Helping set up the AV equipment in the amphitheater. Under the watchful eye of campus security, though he doesn't know it." Sierra's fingers danced across keys. "I've also identified seventeen other suspected assets in the audience. Cross isn't taking chances—he's flooding the zone with disruptors."

"Then we'd better give them something worth disrupting," Elias said grimly.

***

By noon, the amphitheater overflowed. They'd opened the balconies, set up screens in adjacent classrooms, and even had people sitting in the aisles. The fire marshal had given up and left, muttering about academics and death wishes.

Elias stood backstage, fighting nausea that had nothing to do with stage fright. Through the curtain, he could see the audience—colleagues who'd supported him, skeptics ready to pounce, media with cameras rolling, and scattered throughout, Cross's plants waiting for their moment.

"Nervous?" Mara appeared beside him, stunning in a simple black dress that somehow made her look both professional and warrior-like.

"Terrified," he admitted.

"Good. Use it. Channel it. Make them feel what we feel." She straightened his tie, the gesture intimate despite their surroundings. "I'll be in the front row. Sierra's managing the tech booth. Granger has plainclothes officers throughout the crowd."

"And Derek?"

"Stage left, exactly where we want him." Her expression hardened. "When he makes his move, I'll handle it."

"Mara—"

"Trust me." She kissed him quickly. "Now go save the world, Professor."

He walked onto the stage to thunderous applause mixed with skeptical murmurs. The lights were blinding, but he could feel the weight of a thousand gazes, each carrying hope or hostility.

"Thank you for coming," he began, his teacher's voice carrying easily. "I know many of you think I've lost my mind. That grief has driven me to see patterns where none exist. That Dr. Lang and I have let personal feelings cloud professional judgment."

Nervous laughter rippled through the crowd. Good—acknowledging their doubts gave him credibility.

"But I'm not here to defend myself. I'm here to show you what the mountain has been trying to tell us, if only we'd listen."

The lights dimmed, and Sierra's visualizations filled the screen. Not the corrupted versions Cross expected, but the real data—beautiful, terrible, and undeniable.

"Three days ago, we documented pyroclastic deposits in caves that shouldn't exist. Yesterday, ground-penetrating radar revealed magma chambers where geology says they're impossible. This morning, harmonic tremors began—the mountain clearing its throat before it screams."

He walked them through each piece of evidence, building the case like a master storyteller. The audience leaned forward, skepticism giving way to unease, then to dawning horror.

"But data alone isn't enough," he continued. "So let me tell you about the animals."

***

Twenty minutes into the presentation, Elias felt the shift. The audience was with him, following the logic, accepting the impossible. Which meant Cross had to act.

It started subtly. A projector "malfunction" that Sierra fixed in seconds. Audio feedback that mysteriously resolved. Then, less subtly, someone in the third row stood up to shout about fear-mongering and economic damage.

"An excellent point," Elias said calmly. "Let's discuss economic impact. Sierra, could you show the cost analysis?"

New slides appeared—not part of his original presentation. Cross's own financial documents, showing his shell companies positioned to profit from disaster. The heckler sat down very quickly.

But Cross wasn't done. Derek made his move, attempting to upload corrupted data that would show Elias falsifying evidence. Mara intercepted him in the wings, their confrontation brief and quiet. When Derek emerged moments later, his laptop was missing and his face was pale.

"Technical difficulties?" Elias asked mildly, never breaking stride.

The audience laughed, tension breaking for a moment. But Cross had one more card to play.

Dr. Harrison Cross himself entered through the main doors, his presence commanding immediate attention. He looked like what he was—successful, credible, everything Elias wasn't in his rumpled professor's jacket.

"I apologize for interrupting," Cross said smoothly, his voice carrying without amplification. "But I couldn't stand by while fear-mongering replaces science."

"By all means, join us," Elias offered. "Would you like to present your counter-evidence?"

Cross hesitated—this wasn't the panicked response he'd expected. But he recovered quickly, striding toward the stage with predatory confidence.

"I don't need to present anything. Your own student—" He turned to where Derek should have been, found only empty space. "Where is Mr. Chen?"

"Being questioned by campus security," Mara announced from the front row. "About industrial espionage, data theft, and conspiracy to commit fraud. He's been quite forthcoming about who hired him."

The audience erupted. Cameras swung between Cross and Mara, capturing the moment Cross's mask finally slipped.

"You can't prove—"

"Actually, we can." Sierra's voice came through the speakers as new documents filled the screen. "These are your communications with Mr. Chen. Your payment authorizations. Your instructions to sabotage our work. All digitally signed with your personal encryption key."

"Fake! All of it fake!" But Cross was backing toward the exit now, all composure gone.

"Is this fake too?" Elias clicked to the next slide—seismic readings from the last hour. "The mountain doesn't care about our debates, Dr. Cross. It's already decided."

The harmonic tremors were visible on the graph, building in intensity. Somewhere in the audience, a geologist gasped, recognizing the pattern.

"Forty-eight hours," Mara said, standing. "That's our current estimate. Maybe less."

The room exploded into chaos. Half the audience headed for exits while the other half pressed forward with questions. Reporters shouted into phones, scientists argued over data, and through it all, Cross tried to escape.

Tried, because Sheriff Tom Granger stood in his way, handcuffs ready.

"Dr. Harrison Cross, you're under arrest for reckless endangerment, conspiracy, and about seventeen other charges I'll think of on the way to booking."

"You can't! I have connections, lawyers—"

"You have the right to remain silent," Granger continued calmly. "I suggest you use it."

As they led Cross away, Elias found himself surrounded by colleagues, reporters, and students. Questions flew faster than he could answer, but one voice cut through the chaos.

"Professor Quinn!" A young reporter pushed forward. "Dr. Lang's paper is already going viral. Scientists worldwide are confirming your model. How does it feel to be vindicated?"

He looked across the crowd to where Mara stood, surrounded by her own circle of questioners. Their eyes met, and in that moment, vindication felt hollow compared to what they'd built together.

"It feels like responsibility," he said finally. "Now, if you'll excuse me, we have an evacuation to coordinate."

***

An hour later, they regrouped in Elias's office. The media storm raged outside, but inside was an island of calm. Sierra typed furiously, coordinating with emergency services. Mara fielded calls from geological surveys worldwide. And Elias sat with Derek Chen's confession, reading about another brilliant mind corrupted by desperation.

"He really believed Cross would help his family," Elias said quietly.

"They always do," Mara replied. "That's what makes him dangerous. He finds your weakness and offers to fix it, for a price you don't understand until it's too late."

"Speaking of which." Sierra looked up from her screens. "That judge Cross mentioned? Just issued an injunction against our evacuation plans. We're legally prohibited from causing 'public panic.'"

"Then we'll cause private panic," Granger said from the doorway. He looked tired but determined. "One family at a time, if necessary. Storm's coming whether the law admits it or not."

Through the window, the mountains looked peaceful in the afternoon sun. But Elias could feel it now—a vibration just below perception, the earth preparing for violence.

"How long?" he asked Mara.

She consulted her latest readings, face grave. "Thirty-six hours. Maybe less. The harmonic patterns are accelerating."

"Then we'd better get started."

As they prepared to leave, Elias found a note slipped under his door. Derek's handwriting, shaky but legible:

He's always one step ahead because he's not working alone. Check the evacuation routes. Some lead to safety. Others lead to Aegis.

Aegis. The company that had tried to buy the cave that morning. Another piece of Cross's web, or something bigger?

"Problem?" Mara asked.

He showed her the note. Her expression darkened. "Cross was middle management. Someone else is conducting this symphony."

"Then we'd better learn the whole score," Elias said grimly. "Before the final movement begins."

They left together, walking into a world transformed by truth finally spoken. The last lecture was over.

Now came the real test—turning knowledge into action, warnings into salvation.

The mountain was waking, and they were running out of time.

Chapter 20: Exodus

The evacuation center had become a war zone of good intentions. What started as an orderly process devolved into barely controlled chaos as word spread through Morgantown like wildfire—the mountain was waking, and Drs. Quinn and Lang had been right all along.

Elias stood atop an overturned bus, megaphone in hand, trying to coordinate the human tide. Below him, families loaded everything they could carry into vehicles already groaning under the weight of their lives. The parking lot of the high school looked like a bizarre parade—minivans next to horse trailers, motorcycles weaving between RVs, everyone fleeing with whatever would move.

"Blue zones follow Route 47 north!" His voice cracked from overuse. "Red zones take Highway 19 east! Do not—I repeat, do NOT attempt to use Backbone Mountain Road!"

Mara worked the ground level, her tablet showing real-time updates from Prometheus. She moved through the crowd with fierce efficiency, redirecting traffic, answering desperate questions, being everywhere at once. Elias watched her save an elderly man from being trampled by the surge, then immediately turn to help a mother with three young children find their vehicle.

"Professor Quinn!" Tom Granger's voice cut through the chaos. The sheriff had shed his uniform for practical gear, but his authority remained. "Need to talk to you. Now."

Elias climbed down, following Granger to a relatively quiet corner where three deputies stood guard around a figure in handcuffs.

Jason Fitzgerald looked smaller than Elias remembered. The confident spy had been replaced by a terrified kid, his face streaked with tears and dirt.

"Caught him trying to sabotage the fuel depot," Granger explained. "Would have stranded half the convoy."

"I had to!" Jason burst out. "They have my sister. Said they'd kill her if I didn't—"

"Who?" Elias demanded. "Cross?"

"I don't know! They contact me through encrypted channels. Leave dead drops. I never see faces." Jason's voice broke. "They recruited me in my sophomore year. Said it was just corporate intelligence, keeping tabs on research. I needed the money, and it seemed harmless..."

"Until it wasn't," Granger finished grimly.

"The press conference leak, the cave trap, the false routes—that was all me." Tears flowed freely now. "I'm sorry. I'm so fucking sorry. I just wanted to protect Emma."

Elias felt rage and pity war in his chest. Another brilliant student was destroyed by Cross's web. "Where's your sister now?"

"Safe house in D.C. They said after the eruption—" He stopped, face paling. "Oh God. They're not planning to let her go, are they? Loose ends."

"Give us the location," Mara said, appearing at Elias's shoulder. "Sierra can coordinate with contacts in D.C."

As Jason babbled addresses and access codes, Granger pulled Elias aside. "There's more. State police set up roadblocks on the main evacuation routes. 'Safety inspections,' they claim, but they're turning back vehicles. Someone high up wants to keep people here."

"How high?"

"Governor's office high. Maybe federal." Granger's weathered face showed strain. "I've got thirty years on the force, Doc. Never thought I'd have to choose between orders and conscience."

"And which did you choose?"

Granger smiled grimly. "I'm here, aren't I? Already told my deputies—anyone tries to stop this evacuation, they'll have to go through us first."

A tremor rolled through the ground, strong enough to set car alarms wailing. When it passed, the mountain loomed closer somehow, though that was impossible. Psychological distance collapsed as physical danger approached.

"Time to go," Mara announced, checking her readings. "Prometheus shows increasing instability. We have maybe six hours before conditions become unsurvivable."

***

The convoy grew like a living thing. Every mile brought more vehicles—farm trucks from the hollers, suburban SUVs from the development, even a school bus full of nursing home residents that someone had "borrowed" for the evacuation. Elias's Jeep led one section while Granger commanded another, Mara coordinating between them via radio.

"Prometheus update," Sierra's voice crackled through static. "I've hacked into the state emergency system. Sending real evacuation routes to everyone's phones now."

"Any pushback?" Mara asked.

"Cyber division's trying to stop me, but..." A pause filled with furious typing. "Let's just say I learned some new tricks from tracking Jason's handlers. They won't win this."

Through the windshield, Elias watched the exodus unfold. Three lanes of highway had become six as desperate drivers used shoulders and medians. But instead of chaos, something beautiful emerged—people helping each other. When a car broke down, three others stopped to give passengers a ride. When fuel ran low, neighbors shared their reserves.

Humanity at its best, forged by crisis.

"Stop ahead," Koa's low growl punctuated Mara's warning.

A state police roadblock stretched across Highway 19, officers in riot gear standing before concrete barriers. Behind them, military vehicles suggested federal involvement. The convoy ground to a halt, trapping hundreds of vehicles.

"This is illegal," Mara seethed. "They can't—"

"They are." Elias was already stepping out, Granger beside him. Together, they approached the roadblock where a captain waited with dead eyes and live ammunition.

"Turn around," the captain said without preamble. "By order of the Governor, all citizens are required to shelter in place pending assessment of the situation."

"The situation," Granger said slowly, "is that a volcano's about to erupt, and you're signing these people's death warrants."

"I have my orders."

"So did the guards at Nuremberg," Elias snapped. "How's that defense work out?"

The captain's hand moved to his weapon. "Sir, I'm warning you—"

The ground answered first. Not a tremor this time but a rolling wave that knocked everyone to their knees. The mountain roared—actually roared, a sound like the earth itself screaming. In the distance, a red glow painted the sky.

"First venting," Mara called out, helping Elias up. "We're out of time!"

The roadblock officers looked at their captain, then at the glowing mountain, then at the hundreds of families trapped between. Elias saw the moment humanity won—shoulders slumping, weapons lowering, one young officer actually starting to cry.

"Stand down," the captain said quietly. Then louder: "STAND DOWN! Let them through!"

The convoy surged forward, but Elias heard engines behind them—not evacuees, but pursuit. Black SUVs weaving through traffic with predatory intent.

"Cross's cleanup crew," Granger growled. "They're making their move."

"Sierra, we need those alternate routes now!" Mara shouted into the radio.

"Working on it! But someone's jamming GPS signals. I can only—"

Her voice cut to static. Then, horrifyingly, Cross's voice emerged from every radio in the convoy simultaneously.

"Did you really think you'd won? This mountain, these people, you—all pawns in a game you never understood. Enjoy your exodus, Dr. Quinn. It leads exactly where we want."

"He's herding us," Mara realized. "The roadblocks, the jamming—he's forcing us into a kill zone."

"Then we break the pattern." Elias yanked the wheel hard right, leaving the highway for a service road. "Local knowledge beats corporate planning."

Half the convoy followed, trusting the professor who'd warned them when no one else would. The other half continued on the main route, splitting Cross's resources. Behind them, SUVs skidded through the turn, engines screaming protest.

"They're gaining," Mara reported, then grabbed Elias's arm. "Wait. Pull over."

"Trust me. PULL OVER!"

He did, slamming brakes as several convoy vehicles shot past. In the mirrors, the lead SUV closed the distance, predator scenting wounded prey—

The sinkhole opened like a mouth, swallowing the SUV whole. Super-heated gases vented through the fresh chasm, turning the second vehicle into a funeral pyre. The third managed to stop, occupants fleeing as the ground beneath them glowed cherry-red.

"Prometheus predicted that," Mara said calmly. "Subsurface magma intrusion causing structural collapse. I've been tracking weak points for the last hour."

"You beautiful genius." He kissed her fiercely, tasting ash and adrenaline. "Remind me never to play chess with you."

"Later. Drive."

They wove through back roads Elias had biked as a teenager, leading their portion of the convoy through routes that existed more in memory than on maps. Behind them, the mountain's rage built toward crescendo—no longer venting but gathering strength for the main event.

During a brief straight stretch, Elias risked a glance at Mara. She was magnificent—covered in ash, tablet in one hand, radio in the other, coordinating salvation with the focus of a battlefield general.

"Whatever happens," he said, the words coming from somewhere deeper than thought, "we're in this together."

She looked at him, and in her eyes he saw everything—fear, determination, and love so fierce it could stand against mountains.

"Together," she agreed. "Now, next left. We need to reach the river before—"

The world exploded.

Not metaphorically. The mountain's peak simply ceased to exist, replaced by a column of fire and ash that climbed toward the stratosphere. The shockwave hit seconds later, flipping lighter vehicles, shattering windows for miles. Elias fought to keep the Jeep upright as pavement buckled beneath them.

"MOVE! EVERYONE MOVE!" Granger's voice on the radio, professional calm shattered by primal urgency.

They ran before the apocalypse. Behind them, pyroclastic flows raced down the mountainside at highway speeds, turning forests to ash, homes to memory. The convoy stretched out, faster vehicles pulling ahead while others fell behind to certain death.

"The bridge!" Mara pointed to the Columbia River crossing ahead. "If we can get across—"

"It won't hold everyone," Elias realized. The old structure was already swaying from seismic activity.

"Then we make sure the vulnerable cross first."

They reached the bridge approach to find chaos. Vehicles jammed together, drivers abandoning cars to run on foot. The nursing home bus sat trapped in the gridlock, elderly faces pressed to windows in terror.

Without hesitation, Elias and Mara plunged into the crowd. They carved a path through the panic, reaching the bus as its engine died.

"Everyone out!" Mara commanded. "Leave everything! Move!"

They formed a human chain—Elias, Mara, Granger, Sierra with her one good arm, citizens becoming heroes in the shadow of annihilation. Wheelchairs passed hand to hand. Elderly who hadn't walked in years found the strength to stumble forward. A young mother with twins got separated in the crush, screaming for her babies until Elias spotted them, scooping both children up and bulling through the crowd to reunite them.

"The bridge is failing!" someone screamed.

Cable supports snapped like guitar strings, each failure dropping the roadbed another foot. They had seconds, maybe less.

"RUN!"

The final sprint across disintegrating concrete, pyroclastic death clouds racing them to the river. Elias carried a child under each arm. Mara supported an elderly man who refused to leave his equally elderly wife. Granger literally threw people to safety as sections of the bridge vanished into the churning water below.

They made it to the far side as the bridge gave its final surrender to physics. Behind them, the structure collapsed in segments, taking dozens of abandoned vehicles into the depths. But no people. Somehow, impossibly, they'd saved everyone who'd made it that far.

Elias collapsed to his knees, lungs burning from exertion and ash. Around him, hundreds of others did the same—a congregation of the exhausted living, watching their world burn from what they hoped was a safe distance.

"Status?" Mara's voice was rough but unbroken.

"Present," he managed.

"Good. Because we're not done." She helped him stand, gesturing to the growing ash cloud. "That's going to circle the globe. Climate change, agricultural collapse, respiratory disasters—the eruption's just the first movement. This symphony of destruction is just getting started."

"Then we'd better start planning the recovery."

She smiled, fierce and beautiful. "Already am. But first..."

She kissed him, there in the ash fall with the world ending behind them. Not desperate this time but deliberate—a promise that some things survived even catastrophe.

When they broke apart, Cross's voice emerged from a radio someone had dropped: "You can't run forever."

Elias picked up the radio, meeting Mara's eyes. Together, they spoke:

"We're not running. We're leading. And you've already lost."

Behind them, Backbone Mountain continued its violent transformation. But ahead, through ash and uncertainty, a convoy of survivors rolled toward whatever came next.

They'd done the impossible—saved thousands despite sabotage, conspiracy, and the mountain itself. Now came the harder task: building something better from the ashes of the old world.

But they'd do that together, too.

The mountain had spoken its rage. Now it was humanity's turn to answer.

Chapter 21: The Mountain Awakens

4:47 AM - Elias

The first explosion wasn't what Elias expected. No dramatic mushroom cloud or Hollywood theatrics—just a sound like God clearing his throat, followed by a shockwave that turned windows into deadly rain.

Koa had been howling for three straight minutes before it hit, the sound primal enough to wake everyone in the evacuation convoy. Now the dog pressed against Elias's leg as they stood on the hill overlooking Morgantown, watching their predictions become a horrifying reality.

"Get down!" Mara screamed, tackling him backward as a second blast sent debris whistling overhead.

The sky lit up orange-red, and for one terrible moment, Elias saw the mountain's secret revealed—a glowing fissure splitting Backbone Mountain like a wound, lava fountaining into the pre-dawn darkness.

His phone buzzed with Prometheus alerts, the AI's calculations updating in real-time. But the electronics flickered and died as an electromagnetic pulse from the eruption washed over them.

"The backup systems," he gasped, struggling to his feet. "Sierra has the hardened units—"

"Already on it!" Sierra's voice crackled through their emergency radios, the only electronics still functioning. "Prometheus is tracking the ash plume. You've got maybe twenty minutes before the first fall hits your position."

Twenty minutes. To save a town that had half-believed them at best.

***

4:52 AM - Mara

The geological part of Mara's brain catalogued details even as her body moved on a survival instinct. Pyroclastic density current forming. Lahars are likely to occur when the lava hits mountain streams. Ash column reaching stratospheric levels—this would affect air travel across the continent.

But the human part of her could only focus on the screaming.

The evacuation center—a high school gymnasium—had become chaos. People who'd reluctantly gathered "just in case" now fought to escape, trampling each other in their panic. Emergency lighting failed as the power grid collapsed, leaving only the hellish glow from the mountain.

"The exits!" she shouted to the scattered volunteers. "Keep them clear!"

A teenager—one of Elias's students—stood frozen as the crowd surged toward him. Mara sprinted forward, pulling him aside just as the human tide would have crushed him against the doors.

"Thank you," he gasped. "I thought—is Professor Quinn—?"

"He's alive. Help me get these people organized."

Together they formed human chains, guiding panicked evacuees toward the buses that would—hopefully—outrun the ash fall. But Mara kept checking her phone's last cached data from Prometheus. The eruption was following the worst-case scenario, but something was off. The ash dispersal pattern showed anomalies, as if—

"The visualization code," she breathed. Cross's sabotage was still affecting the public warning systems. People were evacuating toward zones that looked safe on their phones but were directly in the path of destruction.

She grabbed her radio. "Sierra! The public alert system is compromised. It's sending people northwest, but the ash pattern—"

"I see it!" Sierra's voice was strained. "Trying to override, but someone's actively fighting me for system control. They're typing counter-commands in real-time!"

Cross. Even now, even with the mountain erupting, he was trying to maximize casualties.

***

5:03 AM - Sierra

Her fingers flew across three keyboards simultaneously, the mobile command unit's screens painting her face in shifting blues and reds. Outside the reinforced van, the world was ending. Inside, she fought a digital war for every life.

The sabotage code was elegant in its evil—every time she corrected the evacuation routes, it would subtly shift them back. Whoever was controlling it knew her style, anticipated her fixes.

"Come on, come on," she muttered, diving deeper into the system architecture.

There is a signature in the code style. Not Cross himself, but someone trained by him. Someone who'd sat in the same visualization course, learned the same tricks.

Her blood ran cold. She knew this coding signature. I had competed against it in hackathons and studied beside it in late-night sessions.

Marcus Chen. Her study partner from two years ago. The one who'd visited her in the hospital, brought her flowers, and said he understood her breakdown.

The one who'd introduced her to Cross in the first place.

"You bastard," she whispered, fingers flying faster. Now that she knew who she was fighting, she could predict his moves. Marcus had always favored elegant recursion over brute force, always hidden his best tricks in subroutines that looked like error handling.

She found his back door in ninety seconds and slammed it shut with prejudice.

The evacuation routes snapped back to reality just as the first ash began to fall.

***

5:09 AM - Tom Granger

The sheriff had lived in these mountains for fifty-seven years, and he'd be damned if he'd abandon them now. While others fled, he drove toward the danger, his cruiser loaded with every emergency supply he could grab.

The old mining road was supposed to be impassable, but Tom knew better. His grandfather had used it during Prohibition, and Tom had maintained it quietly over the years. Now it might be the only way to reach the three families who'd refused evacuation—the Hendersons, the Pikes, and old Emma Voss.

Wait. Voss.

He grabbed his radio, tried to raise Elias or Mara. Static howled back at him, mixed with what sounded like screaming wind. Or maybe just screaming.

The first ash hit his windshield like gray snow, immediately turning to concrete as his wipers smeared it. He could barely see ten feet ahead, but muscle memory guided him through turns that would have killed an outsider.

The Henderson farm materialized from the ash fall like a ghost. The family huddled on their porch, too terrified to move as the world turned gray around them.

"Get in!" Tom roared. "Now!"

Eight people crammed into his cruiser—parents, kids, and one very pregnant daughter-in-law who chose that moment to announce her contractions had started.

Because of course they had.

Tom executed a three-point turn that would have made a stunt driver proud, the overloaded cruiser fishtailing on the ash-slick road. In his mirrors, he saw the farmhouse disappear into the gray void. Twenty seconds later, a lahar—superheated mud and debris—swept through where they'd just been.

"The Pikes—" Mr. Henderson started.

"Already gone," Tom said grimly. He'd passed what was left of their house, now just a foundation swept clean by the mountain's fury.

The pregnant woman screamed, and Tom pushed the accelerator harder. He had one more stop, and he was running out of time.

***

5:17 AM - Elias

The convoy had fractured. What started as an organized evacuation became scattered groups fleeing however they could. Elias's Jeep carried eight people—him, Mara, and six others they'd gathered along the way. Koa had given up his spot and now ran alongside, occasionally darting ahead to guide them around obstacles only he could sense.

"Left!" Mara shouted. "The bridge ahead is compromised!"

She was navigating using Prometheus's last cached predictions, cross-referenced with her geological knowledge and what they could see through the falling ash. It was like driving through a blizzard in hell—the flakes glowed orange with reflected lava light, and the air tasted of sulfur and death.

A figure stumbled into their headlights. Elias slammed the brakes, nearly jackknifing on the slick road.

Harrison Cross stood in the middle of the ashfall, his expensive suit torn and gray. His Mercedes sat in the ditch, front end crumpled against a tree. In his arms, he clutched a briefcase like a life preserver.

For one moment, Elias considered driving around him. After everything Cross had done, the sabotage, the threats, the attempted murder...

But Mara was already opening her door.

"No," Cross gasped, backing away. "I don't need your help. My extraction team—"

"Your extraction team abandoned you," Mara said flatly. "We monitored their communications. They labeled you a liability three minutes after the eruption started."

Cross's face crumbled. "That's impossible. I have contracts, agreements—"

"With people who value profit over loyalty." Elias found himself stepping out too, though every instinct screamed to leave the man behind. "Imagine that."

Another explosion lit the sky. Closer this time. They were running out of road and time.

"Get in," Elias commanded. "Now."

"I'd rather die than—"

Koa chose that moment to lunge from the ash cloud, teeth bared. Cross scrambled backward, directly into Granger's arriving cruiser.

"Doc!" Tom called out. "We got a situation here!"

The pregnant woman's screams made the decision for everyone. They transferred her to the Jeep—more room to lie down—while Cross was literally thrown into the cruiser's trunk by the furious Henderson men who'd lost neighbors to his greed.

"Emma Voss," Tom said urgently. "She wouldn't leave. Said she had something to finish. Something about the old stories and—"

The mountain roared again, cutting him off. A new fissure had opened, and lava fountained directly toward the town center.

"Go!" Elias shouted. "We'll follow!"

But as they raced the advancing destruction, Prometheus's last projection burned in his mind. They had minutes, maybe less, before the main pyroclastic flow hit.

And somewhere behind them, Lenora Voss was facing the mountain alone with her grandmother's journal and a lifetime of being right too early.

***

5:23 AM - Cross's Final Gambit

In the trunk of Granger's cruiser, Harrison Cross activated his phone's last emergency function. The device had just enough battery for one final transmission, one last piece of spite.

He'd lost everything—his corporate backers, his carefully crafted reputation, his escape plan. But he still had the recordings. Every conversation with Elias and Mara, every moment of doubt, every harsh word between them. Edited, of course. Contextualized to tell the story he wanted.

His thumb hovered over "Send All."

If he was going to burn, he'd take their credibility with him. The investigation afterward would focus on their "reckless endangerment," not the lives they'd saved. His media contacts would spin it beautifully—two discredited academics whose false warnings caused panic, whose relationship compromised their judgment, whose pet AI had critical flaws they'd hidden.

The briefcase beside him held the only copies of the real data, the unedited truth. With it gone, his version would be the only one that survived.

He pressed send just as Granger took a corner too fast. The briefcase slammed against the trunk lid, popping open. Papers scattered, including one that made Cross's blood freeze.

A photo of him with Marcus Chen, dated two years ago. Sierra's handwriting on the back: "I know what you did. The truth is already uploaded. Your leverage is gone."

The clever little bitch had outplayed him.

His phone buzzed with a delivery failure notice. The files were too large, the connection too weak. His final revenge had failed to launch.

Cross laughed—a broken sound in the darkness of the trunk. Around him, the mountain's fury built toward its crescendo, and he realized with crystalline clarity that he'd orchestrated his own entombment.

***

5:28 AM - Together

The convoy reached the ridgeline just as the main pyroclastic flow hit Morgantown. Elias pulled over, unable to drive through the tears as he watched his adopted home disappear under a tide of superheated gas and ash moving at highway speeds.

Mara found his hand, squeezing hard enough to hurt. Good. Pain meant they were alive.

Around them, others had stopped too. Hundreds of vehicles lined the ridge, their occupants bearing witness to nature's terrible power. But they were alive. Against all odds, despite sabotage and disbelief, they were alive.

"How many?" Mara whispered.

Sierra's voice crackled over the radio. "Prometheus estimates 89% evacuation rate. We saved over fifteen thousand people."

Not everyone. The number who'd refused to leave, who'd been trapped, who'd trusted the corrupted warning system too long—that weight would live with them forever.

But fifteen thousand. Fifteen thousand souls who would see another sunrise because two broken people had found each other, had chosen trust over fear, had refused to stop warning even when the world called them mad.

Elias turned to Mara, ash painting her hair gray, tears cutting channels through the dirt on her face. She had never looked more beautiful.

He kissed her. Not desperately, not quickly, but with the slow certainty of a man who'd learned that tomorrow was a gift, not a guarantee. Around them, the mountain raged, but in that moment, they were the still point in a turning world.

When they broke apart, Koa was there, pressing between them, the three of them a unit forged in fire and trust.

Tom Granger's voice cut through the moment. "Folks, we need to keep moving. Wind's shifting, and that ash cloud's coming our way."

As they returned to their vehicles, Cross's voice erupted from the cruiser trunk: "You think you've won? This isn't over! I know people, have resources—"

Tom calmly turned up his radio, drowning out the threats with static.

The convoy rolled on, leaving the dying town behind. In the distance, helicopters appeared—National Guard, drawn by their warnings, ready to assist with the evacuation they'd made possible.

But Elias couldn't shake the image of Lenora Voss, somewhere in that gray hell, finishing whatever story she'd felt was worth her life.

Mara seemed to read his thoughts. "She made her choice. Just like we all did."

"I know. I just wish—"

"Look." She pointed ahead, where the ash fall was lighter. A figure stood by the roadside, thumb out like a hitchhiker from another era. Impossibly, impossibly, Lenora Voss stood there, covered in ash but very much alive, her grandmother's journal clutched to her chest.

They pulled over, and she climbed in with remarkable dignity for a woman who'd just outrun a volcano.

"Took you long enough," she said mildly. "I've been waiting for ten minutes."

"How?" was all Elias could manage.

"The old mine shafts," she replied. "My family's known about them for generations. They lead clear to the other side of the ridge. I just had to pay my respects first."

"To your grandmother?"

"To the mountain." She looked back at the ash cloud with something almost like affection. "It kept its promise. It gave us warning, through you. The least I could do was thank it properly."

As they drove on, Elias caught a glimpse of the journal's last entry, written in Voss's shaky hand: "The guardians came, as promised. The mountain spoke, and this time, we listened."

Behind them, Backbone Mountain continued its violent birth, reshaping the landscape with fire and fury. But ahead lay survival, and the chance to rebuild with hard-won wisdom.

Cross's threats faded into static and then silence. Whatever resources he thought he had, whatever revenge he planned, would have to wait until he could explain to investigators why he'd fled with falsified data while others stayed to save lives.

The mountain had made its judgment. And in the end, it had chosen mercy for those who'd chosen truth.

Chapter 22: Through the Fire

The ash fell like snow in hell, each flake a burning reminder of how quickly the world could end. Mara pressed her makeshift mask tighter against her face as she followed Elias back toward the devastation zone. Behind them, the evacuation center buzzed with controlled chaos, but ahead lay only silence—the terrible quiet of a town being buried alive.

"There!" Elias pointed through the swirling gray. The university's dormitory complex emerged from the ash cloud like a ship from fog, its upper floors still visible above the accumulation. "Sierra's infrared picked up heat signatures on the third floor."

Seven students who'd ignored the evacuation order, convinced it was all academic hysteria. Now they were trapped as the stairwells filled with hot ash and toxic gases.

Koa whined, pressing against Elias's leg. The dog had refused to stay at the evacuation center, and now his instincts proved invaluable—he'd already led them around two areas where the ground had collapsed into superheated sinkholes.

"The fire escape on the north side," Mara said, consulting the building plans on her ash-smeared tablet. "If it's still intact—"

A rumble cut her off. Not the mountain this time—the sound of a building dying. The dormitory's south wing folded in on itself with devastating grace, five floors pancaking into one.

"Move!" Elias shouted.

They ran through the ash fall, Koa leading them past abandoned cars that looked like gray monuments. The heat was oppressive even through their protective gear—makeshift assemblies of ski masks, swimming goggles, and whatever else the evacuation center had scrounged up.

The fire escape was intact but pulling away from the building, its moorings weakened by the constant tremors. Elias tested the lowest ladder, and rust showered down like red snow.

"It won't hold both of us," he said.

"Then I'll go." Mara was already moving, but he caught her arm.

"I'm lighter," he lied. They both knew he outweighed her by forty pounds, but his expression brooked no argument. "Besides, you're better at structural analysis. I need you here to tell me when this thing's about to collapse."

She wanted to argue—he could see it in her eyes behind the scratched goggles—but time was a luxury they'd spent. "The moment it shifts more than six inches from the wall, you get off. Promise me."

"Promise." He sealed it with a quick kiss to her forehead, tasting ash and fear.

The ladder shrieked with each rung, and Mara's voice in his earpiece provided a running commentary of impending doom. "Four inches separation... five... Elias, you need to move faster."

Third floor. The windows were painted shut, because of course they were. Elias used his wrapped elbow to shatter the glass, calling out, "Anyone here? We're here to help!"

Coughing, sobbing, seven shapes emerged from the smoke-filled darkness. Three girls, four boys, all looking younger than their years, beneath the terror.

"The stairs—" one boy gasped.

"Are gone. We're going out this way." Elias kept his voice professor-calm, the tone he used for panicked freshmen during finals. "One at a time, test each rung, don't look down."

"I can't," a girl whispered. "Heights—I can't—"

"What's your name?"

"S-Sarah."

The name hit him like a physical blow, but he pushed through. "Sarah, look at me. Just at me. What's your major?"

"Pre-med."

"Good. Then you understand that fear is just chemistry—adrenaline, cortisol, norepinephrine. Your body is preparing you to survive. Use it. Let it sharpen your focus."

It worked. One by one, they descended. The fire escape groaned and pulled further from the wall—eight inches, ten—but held. Elias went last, and he was halfway down when the aftershock hit.

The world lurched sideways. The fire escape tore free from its upper moorings, swinging out like a giant pendulum. Elias wrapped his arms around the ladder as students screamed below.

"Jump!" Mara's voice cut through everything. "Now! I've got you!"

He let go, trusting her completely. The fall was only ten feet, but he landed wrong, his ankle folding beneath him with a wet pop that he felt more than heard. Pain shot up his leg like lightning, and for a moment, the world went white.

"Get up!" Mara was there, her surprising strength hauling him to his feet. "The building—"

The dormitory's north face collapsed, taking the fire escape with it. They ran—or rather, Mara ran while basically carrying him, his arm around her shoulders, her arm iron-tight around his waist. The students scattered ahead, guided by Koa's barking.

They made it fifty yards before Elias's leg gave out completely.

"Just go," he gasped. "Get them to safety."

"Shut up." Mara lowered him behind an overturned car, hands already moving over his injury with clinical efficiency. "Possible fracture of the lateral malleolus. Definite ligament damage." She looked up, and tears had cut channels through the ash on her face. "You beautiful, stupid man. You promised you'd be careful."

"I promised to get off when it shifted six inches. It made it to ten."

"That's not funny."

"It's a little funny."

She kissed him then, fierce and desperate, tasting of ash and salt. When she pulled back, her hands were gentle as she wrapped his ankle with strips torn from her jacket.

"You're my intuition now," she whispered, echoing something he'd said days ago that felt like years. "When all the data fails, when the world stops making sense, you're what I trust. So please, please stop trying to die heroically."

"Can't promise that," he managed. "But I can promise to try living heroically instead."

"I'll take it."

***

Voss's voice crackled over their radios, unusually urgent. "I need assistance at the museum. There's something here—something that changes every-thing."

The Morgantown Heritage Museum was six blocks deeper into the dan-ger zone, but Voss wasn't given to dramatics. If she said it was important...

"I'll go," Sierra's voice cut in. "You two get those students to the check-point."

"Negative," Voss replied. "I need Dr. Lang's geological expertise. And there are four families trapped in the museum's basement shelter. We'll need everyone."

Mara looked at Elias, a whole conversation in a glance. His ankle was swelling despite the wrap, but stable enough to limp. Leaving him here while she went ahead went against every instinct, but—

"Together," he said firmly. "We do this together or not at all."

She nodded, helping him stand. "Koa, find Sierra. Bring help."

The dog understood—he always understood more than should be possible. With a sharp bark, he vanished into the ashfall.

Their progress was agonizingly slow. Elias leaned heavily on Mara, each step sending fresh spikes of pain up his leg. Around them, the town died in stages—a storefront collapsing here, a street buckling there, the mountain's fury made manifest in incremental destruction.

"Why the museum?" Mara asked, partly to distract him from the pain.

"Voss's grandmother... documented the 1847 event... said artifacts were stored..." He had to stop, breathing hard through the pain.

They rounded the corner to find the museum miraculously intact, its stone construction proving more resilient than modern buildings. Voss stood at the entrance, her elderly frame somehow radiating urgency.

"Quickly," she said. "Before the next wave hits."

Inside, emergency lighting cast eerie shadows on exhibits now dusted with ash. Voss led them past displays of mining equipment and settler memorabilia to a section marked "Indigenous Heritage."

"My grandmother was friends with the last keeper of the old stories," Voss explained, producing a key that looked handmade. "She was given this, told to use it only when the mountain woke again."

The key fit a display case that looked unremarkable—just pottery shards and arrowheads. But Voss pushed the false bottom aside to reveal a stone tablet covered in symbols.

Mara gasped. "This is volcanic rock. Obsidian, but worked with techniques I've never seen."

"Look closer," Voss urged.

The symbols resolved into pictographs as Mara's eyes adjusted. A mountain splitting open. Figures fleeing. And at the center, two shapes—one surrounded by animals, one holding what might be tools or instruments.

"The twin guardians," Elias breathed. "From your grandmother's stories."

"But look at the date markers." Mara traced weathered lines with her finger. "If I'm reading this right, this describes a cycle. Every 400 to 500 years, marked by specific stellar alignments."

"Which means—" Voss began.

The building shook. Not an aftershock this time—something worse. Through the windows, they could see a wall of superheated gas and debris racing down the main street.

"Pyroclastic flow!" Mara shouted. "The basement! Now!"

But even as they ran—Elias hobbling, supported between the two women—he couldn't stop thinking about the tablet. A cycle. Predictable. Which meant someone, somewhere, had always known this would happen.

The basement door was barricaded from the inside. Mara pounded on it. "Let us in! We're here to help!"

Voices argued on the other side—fear of letting in the danger versus fear of turning away help. Finally, locks turned and the door opened to reveal perhaps twenty people huddled in the museum's climate-controlled storage area.

"Thank God," a woman sobbed. "We thought everyone had left us."

They'd barely gotten the door sealed when the pyroclastic flow hit. The building shuddered but held, though the temperature spiked noticeably even in the basement. Emergency vents wheezed, trying to filter air that had become poisonous.

"We need to seal those vents," Mara commanded. "The filters won't stop everything."

They worked frantically, using plastic sheeting and duct tape to create airlocks. Elias directed from where he sat, his ankle now swollen to twice its size. The families—two with young children—huddled together, sharing the few masks available.

"How long can we last down here?" someone asked.

Mara checked her instruments. "The air quality is degrading, but slowly. If the building holds, maybe six hours."

"Sierra will find us," Elias said with more confidence than he felt. "Koa will bring help."

Voss had retreated to a corner, the tablet cradled in her lap. She was transcribing the symbols into a notebook with fevered intensity.

"There's more," she said suddenly. "The guardians weren't just warnings. They were instructions. Look—this symbol represents underground water. This one means safe passage. It's a map."

Mara joined her, bringing her geological expertise, meeting historical knowledge. "These tunnels... they're lava tubes. Formed in previous eruptions but stable enough to survive."

"The mining companies found some of them," Voss confirmed. "My grandmother said they were warned not to dig in certain areas, but they ignored the warnings."

"Where do they lead?"

Voss traced the symbols. "If I'm reading this correctly, there's a network throughout the region. And one of the entrances..." She looked up. "Is in this building's sub-basement."

A child started crying—the air was getting thicker despite their efforts. They were running out of time and options.

"I'll go," Elias said.

"Like hell." Mara's voice was steel. "You can barely walk."

"Then we go together."

"The entrance hasn't been opened in decades," Voss warned. "It could be collapsed, flooded, or—"

The building shook again. Cracks appeared in the ceiling, raining dust and debris.

"Or it could be our only chance," Mara finished. "Show us."

Voss led them to a maintenance door marked "Authorized Personnel Only." Behind it, stairs descended into darkness that predated the museum's construction. The walls changed from modern concrete to hand-laid stone, and finally to natural rock.

At the bottom, an iron door waited, its surface carved with the same symbols as the tablet.

"The miners sealed it in 1923," Voss said. "After they lost a whole crew to 'underground gases.'"

Mara examined the door. "No rust. This isn't iron—it's something else." She produced a small torch from her emergency kit, the flame burning blue-green against the metal. "Alloys I can't identify. This is old. Really old."

Together, she and Voss wrestled with the ancient locking mechanism while Elias kept watch. The families above were depending on them. Every second counted.

Finally, with a groan that sounded almost organic, the door swung open.

Cool air rushed out—clean, breathable air. Beyond the threshold, a tunnel stretched into darkness, but it was a living darkness, not the dead black of collapsed stone.

"Get everyone," Mara ordered. "Quickly."

They formed a human chain, passing children and elderly first, then supplies, then the tablet and Voss's notes. Twenty-three souls filing into the earth's embrace while above them, their town died.

Elias went last, leaning heavily on Mara. As they crossed the threshold, he looked back at the modern world one last time.

That's when they heard it—a rumbling, grinding sound from deeper in the tunnel system. Not the mountain's rage this time. Something else. Something mechanical.

"The mining equipment," Voss whispered. "Some of it was abandoned down here when they sealed the shafts."

But as they ventured deeper, following passages marked with ancient symbols, Elias realized the truth. The sounds weren't from old equipment.

Someone else was down here. Someone who'd known about these tunnels all along.

In the darkness ahead, a light flickered—electric, modern, impossible.

Mara's hand found his, squeezing tight. Whatever new mystery awaited them in the mountain's belly, they'd face it as they'd faced everything else.

Together.

Behind them, another section of the tunnel collapsed, sealing their retreat. The families cried out in fear, but Voss's voice rose above them, steady as bedrock.

"Forward is the only way now. The mountain keeps its own counsel, but it's shown us the path. We follow, or we die."

They pressed on into the ancient darkness, guided by symbols older than memory and the hope that somewhere ahead, salvation waited.

But Elias couldn't shake the feeling that they weren't just fleeing the eruption anymore.

They were being herded.

And somewhere in the maze of tunnels, whoever controlled those modern lights was waiting for them.

Chapter 23: Love in the Ashes

The emergency shelter had been a Walmart six hours ago. Now it was humanity stripped to its essence—fear, pain, hope, and the desperate need to survive pressed together under a roof that groaned with each aftershock.

Mara moved between the wounded like a ghost made of purpose, her makeshift medical supplies dwindling with each patient. The actual doctors were overwhelmed at the main evacuation center, leaving her geological first-aid training to fill gaps it was never meant to handle.

"Hold still," she murmured to a teenager with glass embedded in his shoulder. The boy—maybe sixteen—bit down on a rolled cloth as she extracted each shard with forceps sterilized in bootleg whiskey someone had produced from their emergency supplies.

Elias worked the other side of the shelter, his wrapped ankle dragging as he organized supplies, coordinated sleeping arrangements, and somehow kept three hundred terrified people from dissolving into chaos. Even injured, he moved with the calm authority that had made him a beloved professor—part shepherd, part general, all heart.

"Professor Quinn?" A woman approached him, cradling a bundle that might have been a baby or just precious possessions wrapped in blankets. "Is it true what they're saying? That you predicted this?"

"Dr. Lang and I identified the warning signs," he said carefully. "The mountain gave us time to prepare."

"My husband said you were fearmongers." Her voice cracked. "Said it was all liberal academic nonsense. He stayed behind to protect the store from looters." She pulled the blanket back, revealing not a baby but a photo album, edges already singed. "This is all I have left of him."

Elias felt the weight of every life they'd failed to save pressing down like the ash outside. "I'm sorry. We tried to warn everyone, but—"

"But we didn't listen." The woman clutched her album tighter. "My daddy used to tell stories about the mountain. Said his granddaddy knew it would wake up someday. But I thought they were just stories."

She wandered away, leaving Elias alone with the truth that being right brought no satisfaction when the cost was measured in ghosts.

***

"You need to rest." Mara appeared at his elbow, steering him toward a relatively quiet corner where they'd established a makeshift command post. "That ankle needs elevation."

"Later. The water distribution—"

"Is being handled by the Henderson family. Sit." She pressed him down onto a stack of camping chairs someone had salvaged. "Doctor's orders."

"You're not that kind of doctor."

"Tonight I am." She knelt, unwrapping his ankle with gentle fingers. The swelling had worsened, purple-black bruising spreading like spilled ink. "You need an X-ray. Could be fractured."

"Could be a lot of things. Add it to the list." He caught her hand as she rewrapped the injury. "Mara. That family in the tunnels—we left them. Twenty-three people, and we just—"

"Made the only choice we could." Her voice was firm, but her eyes betrayed her own guilt. "The tunnel collapsed. Going back would have killed everyone, including them."

"Someone was down there. Those lights, the mechanical sounds—"

"I know." She finished the wrap and sat back on her heels. "But right now, we focus on who we can still help. The mystery will keep."

A commotion near the entrance drew their attention. Sheriff Granger had arrived with another group of survivors, including—Mara's breath caught—someone she recognized.

Marcus Chen. Sierra's old study partner. The one she'd identified as Cross's digital saboteur.

He looked smaller than his coding had suggested, barely out of his teens, one arm in a makeshift sling and ash painting him gray as a ghost. His eyes darted around the shelter like a trapped animal's until they landed on Mara.

The recognition was mutual and electric.

"No," he breathed, trying to back away, but there was nowhere to go. The shelter doors had closed against the toxic air outside.

Mara was already moving, Elias limping behind her. They intercepted Marcus before he could disappear into the crowd.

"We need to talk," Mara said quietly.

"I don't—I didn't—" His words tumbled over each other. "You don't understand. He said if I didn't help, he'd destroy my sister's scholarship. She's pre-med at Hopkins. Worked her whole life for it."

"Cross," Elias said. It wasn't a question.

Marcus nodded miserably. "He had evidence that she'd cheated on her MCATs. She hadn't—God, Lily would never—but he'd manufactured enough doubt to ruin her. All I had to do was adjust some code. Make the evacuation routes a little less efficient. He said it would just slow things down, make you look incompetent."

"People died because of those routes," Mara's voice could have etched glass.

"I know!" The words ripped out of him. "Don't you think I know? I tried to minimize the damage, tried to—" He stopped, shoulders shaking. "There's no excuse. I killed them as surely as if I'd pulled a trigger."

Elias studied the young man—barely older than his students, brilliant enough to code circles around most programmers, broken by a choice between two versions of wrong.

"Where's Cross now?" he asked.

"I don't know. His extraction team dumped me when the eruption started. Said I was a liability." Marcus laughed bitterly. "Turns out he never planned to honor our deal anyway. Lily's scholarship was revoked this morning. Before the mountain even blew."

"Because he needed you desperately," Mara realized. "Needed you to have nothing left to lose."

"Sierra knew," Marcus continued. "She'd recognized my coding signature, tried to block me. We used to compete, you know? Hackathons, coding challenges. She always won." His good hand clenched. "I thought I was so clever, using the tricks Cross taught me. But she saw through it instantly."

"Where is she now?" Elias asked, alarmed. They hadn't heard from Sierra since she'd gone to coordinate the southern evacuation route.

"Last I heard, she was heading back to the university. Said something about hardened servers in the computer science building—backup data that could prove Cross's involvement."

Mara and Elias exchanged looks. The university was in the direct path of the pyroclastic flows.

"When?" Mara demanded.

"Maybe an hour ago? She had that look—you know, the one she gets when she's figured something out and won't let it go."

They knew the look. It had saved lives and nearly gotten her killed in equal measure.

"I'll go," Elias started to stand, but his ankle buckled immediately.

"You'll stay," Mara countered. "Granger and I will—"

"Nobody's going anywhere." The sheriff had approached during their conversation, his expression grim. "Radio reports have the university area at over 800 degrees ambient temperature. Nothing left but foundation and regrets."

The words hit like physical blows. Sierra—brilliant, brave, reckless Sierra—

"Wait." Marcus pulled out a battered laptop. "She uploaded something to the cloud right before she went dark. I still have admin access—Cross never knew I'd given it to her."

His fingers flew across the keyboard, the shelter's jerry-rigged WiFi barely holding. Then his face lit up.

"She did it. Everything's here—financial records, communication logs, the original Prometheus code before sabotage. And..." His expression shifted. "Oh God."

"What?"

"Cross wasn't the top of the food chain. Look at these payment authorizations." He turned the screen toward them. "Someone was paying him. Multiple someones. Defense contractors, insurance companies, foreign interests—they all wanted the eruption to happen on their terms."

"Disaster capitalism on steroids," Elias breathed.

"It's worse than that." Marcus scrolled through files with growing horror. "They've done this before. Mount St. Helens, Nevado del Ruiz, even Vesuvius—there are references to 'management protocols' going back decades. Suppressing warnings, controlling narratives, profiting from reconstruction."

"A conspiracy to weaponize natural disasters," Mara said slowly. "But that would require—"

The lights flickered. Not from power failure—the generators were holding—but from something else. The air itself seemed to vibrate.

Then they heard it. A sound like giant footsteps, rhythmic and wrong. The ground shook in time with the beats.

"Harmonic tremors," Mara whispered. "The magma chamber is reorganizing."

"English, Doc," Granger demanded.

"The eruption isn't over. It's entering a new phase." She grabbed the emergency radio. "All evacuation teams, pull back immediately. We're about to see—"

The world exploded.

Not the mountain this time—the Walmart's loading dock doors blew inward, bringing a wall of superheated air and ash. The temperature spiked twenty degrees in seconds.

"Secondary vents!" Mara shouted over the screaming. "The eruption is spreading!"

Elias ignored his ankle, helping Granger herd people toward the store's reinforced freezer section. It was designed to be airtight—their only chance against the poisonous atmosphere.

Marcus worked frantically at his laptop, uploading everything to multiple servers. "If we don't make it, someone needs to know—"

"We're making it," Mara said fiercely. She'd lost too much already. Not one more life on her watch.

They crammed three hundred people into a space meant for meat and vegetables. The freezers had been off for hours, but the insulation held. As Granger sealed the door, the last thing they heard was the roar of the pyroclastic flow hitting the building.

In the darkness, pressed against strangers who'd become family through shared terror, Elias found Mara's hand.

"I love you," he said simply. No preamble, no poetry. Just truth offered like a prayer in the dark.

"I know," she whispered back. "I've known since you tackled me in the cave. Maybe before." Her voice broke. "I just needed the world to end before I could say it back."

"Say it now."

"I love you, Elias Quinn. I love your ridiculous faith in intuition and your stupid bravery and the way you see patterns in chaos. I love that you trusted me when I couldn't trust myself."

Someone was sobbing nearby—fear or joy or both. The temperature was rising despite the insulation. They were running out of air and time.

"If we survive this," Elias said, "I want to rebuild with you. Not just the town—everything. Make something better from the ashes."

"When," she corrected. "When we survive this."

Emergency lighting flickered on—someone had found the backup power. In the pale green glow, three hundred faces emerged from darkness. Families clutched each other. Strangers had become protectors. Marcus Chen sat with the woman whose husband had stayed behind, sharing her grief and his guilt.

"Listen up!" Granger's voice carried over the murmurs. "The building's holding and the air's still good. Emergency services know our location. We just need to sit tight and—"

The harmonic tremors returned, stronger than before. The freezer walls sang with sympathetic vibration.

"That's not possible," Mara breathed. "The harmonic frequency would have to be precisely calibrated to—"

"To what?" Elias asked.

Her face had gone pale in the green light. "To target specific structures. This isn't random. Someone's using the eruption, manipulating the resonance patterns."

"The mechanical sounds in the tunnels," Elias realized. "They weren't old mining equipment."

"They were harmonic generators. Someone's literally conducting the eruption, choosing what survives and what doesn't."

The implications were staggering. Not just profiting from disaster, but orchestrating its precise effects. The ultimate insider trading, played out in lava and ash.

Marcus was typing again, correlating data with tremor patterns. "The evacuation centers. Look—every major shelter is experiencing targeted harmonic attacks except—"

"Except the ones owned by shell companies tied to Cross's benefactors," Mara finished.

They were cattle being herded to specific slaughterhouses, their survival dependent on which properties needed to remain standing for post-disaster acquisition.

"Can you stop it?" Granger asked Marcus.

"The harmonic generators must be computer-controlled. If I can access their network..." His fingers flew across keys. "There! They're using the old mining company's fiber optic lines. The idiots didn't even change the default passwords."

"Do it," Elias ordered.

"Already am." Code scrolled across the screen faster than the eyes could follow. "But they'll notice. We've got maybe three minutes before—"

The tremors stopped.

In the sudden silence, they could hear their own heartbeats, the drip of condensation, the whisper of hope.

"Got them," Marcus breathed. "Shut down the whole network. The eruption will follow natural patterns now."

Which meant chaos instead of orchestration, but at least it was honest chaos.

The building shuddered one last time, then held. Through the freezer walls, they could hear something beautiful—rain. The atmospheric disruption from the eruption had triggered a downpour, helping to settle the ash.

"We're going to make it," someone whispered.

As if in response, the radio crackled to life. "This is National Guard Search and Rescue. Any survivors in the Walmart shelter, please respond."

Granger grabbed the radio, his voice thick with relief. "This is Sheriff Granger. We have three hundred souls in the freezer section. Condition stable, but we need extraction."

"Copy that, Sheriff. Teams are en route. ETA fifteen minutes."

Fifteen minutes. After six hours of hell, fifteen minutes felt like nothing.

In the celebration that followed—tears, laughter, prayers in a dozen languages—Elias pulled Mara close.

"We did it," he murmured against her hair.

"Part of it," she corrected. "There's still a conspiracy to unravel, a town to rebuild, lives to account for."

"Tomorrow's problems."

"It is tomorrow. Has been for hours."

He pulled back to look at her—ash-covered, exhausted, beautiful. "Then I guess we survived to see it."

"Together," she said, the word that had become their touchstone.

"Together."

Around them, their community of survivors prepared for rescue. Marcus had found redemption in his code. The woman with the photo album had found a new family among strangers. Even Granger looked softer, his authority tempered by shared vulnerability.

But as the first sounds of rescue vehicles reached them, Elias couldn't shake one thought:

Someone, somewhere, had built machines to conduct volcanic eruptions like symphonies of destruction.

And whoever they were, they'd just lost their first performance.

The war was far from over, but in this freezer, surrounded by people who'd chosen courage over fear, they'd won their first real victory.

The mountain had spoken, but so had they.

And their voice—the voice of truth, community, and love forged in crisis—had proven louder than all the harmonics of hell.

Chapter 24: The Rescue

The Black Hawks appeared through the ash-laden dawn like mechanical angels, their rotors cutting vortexes in the volcanic haze that still clung to Morgantown's corpse. Elias watched them descend into the cleared football field that had become their makeshift landing zone, his arm tight around Mara's shoulders. Three days since the eruption. Three days of rationed water, dwindling medical supplies, and the constant fear that aftershocks would claim what the initial blast had spared.

"Finally," Mara breathed, but Elias caught the tension in her voice. They both knew that rescue meant scrutiny, investigation, and the inevitable battle over narrative.

The first soldier off the lead helicopter wasn't military—General Patricia Hayes wore her FEMA authority like armor, her expression professionally neutral as she surveyed the devastation. Behind her, Elias recognized Colonel Marcus Webb from the National Guard, and more troubling, Dr. Franklin Morrison from the USGS oversight committee—one of Cross's known associates, though never proven corrupt.

"Dr. Quinn, Dr. Lang," Hayes addressed them with crisp efficiency. "We need to debrief immediately. The evacuation routes you provided saved considerable resources."

"They saved lives," Mara corrected sharply. "Thousands of them."

Morrison stepped forward, his smile as thin as paper. "Yes, though we'll need to investigate why federal emergency protocols weren't followed. This unauthorized evacuation created considerable panic—"

"The panic," Granger's voice cut through as he approached, still in his ash-stained sheriff's uniform, "was from your people telling residents to ignore the warnings. I've got three dead deputies who stayed behind because the 'federal protocols' said the threat was exaggerated."

Hayes raised a hand for silence. "We'll conduct full interviews. For now, we need to establish command structure and triage priorities." She turned to Elias and Mara. "You two will report to the medical tent for evaluation, then remain available for questioning."

"Questioning?" Elias's voice carried an edge. "We're not suspects, General."

"Everyone's a suspect when the death toll reaches three digits," Morrison interjected, his satisfaction barely concealed. "Especially those who circumvented official channels."

But before the confrontation could escalate, a commotion erupted near the medical tents. Survivors were gathering around someone with a camera, their voices rising in excitement and anger.

"That's them! The ones who saved us!"

"My daughter's alive because of their warnings!"

"Where were you?" someone shouted at Morrison. "Where was USGS when the mountain exploded?"

The crowd surged forward, and suddenly Elias and Mara found themselves surrounded not by officials but by the people they'd saved. Hands reached out to touch them, voices overlapped in gratitude and grief. A woman pressed a photo into Mara's hands—her family, intact, standing in front of an evacuation bus.

"You gave us forty-eight hours," she said through tears. "It was enough."

Hayes watched the scene with calculating eyes. Morrison tried to intervene, but the crowd's emotion was a force beyond bureaucracy. Someone started clapping, then another, until the applause echoed across the ruins like thunder.

"Perhaps," Hayes said quietly to Morrison, "we should reconsider our approach."

From the edge of the crowd, Elias spotted a familiar figure being led away in handcuffs—not Cross, who was already in federal custody, but Dr. Patricia Reeves from the university board. She'd been one of the voices dismissing their warnings, and now her laptop bag bore evidence tags.

"Cross had more allies than we knew," Granger said, following his gaze. "We're finding them. Slowly."

But Elias noticed something else—a young soldier near the communications tent, speaking rapidly into an encrypted phone while watching them. When their eyes met, the soldier quickly looked away, but not before Elias caught him mouthing words that looked suspiciously like "targets confirmed."

"We're not safe yet," he murmured to Mara.

"We never were," she replied, her hand finding his as the crowd continued to surge around them, a human shield against whatever came next.

The CNN satellite truck had somehow navigated the destroyed roads, arriving just as the morning sun broke through the ash clouds. Within hours, every major network had established positions around the emergency camp, their cameras hungry for stories of survival and heroism.

Anderson Cooper stood in the ruins of what had been the university library, his silver hair dusted with ash. "I'm here with Sierra Patel, the graduate student whose technical expertise helped power the Prometheus system. Sierra, can you tell us what those final hours were like?"

Sierra, exhausted but fierce, looked directly into the camera. "Terrifying. But Drs. Quinn and Lang never wavered. Even when officials were calling them fearmongers, even when Dr. Cross was actively sabotaging our equipment, they kept working to save lives."

"You have proof of this sabotage?"

"I have everything." Sierra held up her tablet. "Every deleted file, every altered timestamp, every attempt to corrupt our data. I've been uploading it all to multiple servers for the past hour. The world needs to see what happens when profit matters more than people."

The interview went viral within minutes. #PrometheusProof began trending globally, with Sierra's data dumps being analyzed by scientists worldwide. The evidence was damning—not just Cross's direct sabotage, but a network of financial transactions, suppressed reports, and coordinated disinformation.

Meanwhile, Mara found herself surrounded by international journalists near the makeshift command center. A BBC correspondent pushed forward: "Dr. Lang, the Austrian Geological Survey is saying you abandoned your position in Vienna to pursue 'pseudoscience' in America. How do you respond?"

Mara's jaw tightened. "I respond with 3,847 lives saved. I respond with predictive models that worked when traditional methods failed. And I respond with a question—why is the Austrian Geological Survey more interested in discrediting me than understanding how we succeeded?"

"Are you suggesting a conspiracy?"

"I'm suggesting that Cross had international connections. We're finding payments to scientists in twelve countries who dismissed our warnings without examining our data. So yes, I'm suggesting something systematic."

From across the camp, Elias was deep in discussion with Japanese journalists, explaining Prometheus's integration of biological and geological indicators. But he kept one eye on Mara, watching for signs of the strain he knew she was hiding.

A Fox News reporter interrupted his explanation: "Dr. Quinn, Harrison Cross claims you stole his research. He's filed intellectual property claims from federal custody."

"Cross can claim whatever he wants," Elias replied evenly. "Our code is open-source as of this morning. Anyone can examine it, improve it, and implement it. We're not interested in ownership—we're interested in saving lives."

"Even if it costs you potential millions in patents?"

"Especially then."

The reporter seemed thrown by his response. In the background, Sierra's voice carried from her own interview: "They're uploading everything! Every line of code, every dataset, every prediction algorithm. For free! This isn't about money—it's about survival."

But the feel-good narrative was interrupted by Dr. Morrison, who'd arranged his own press conference near the National Guard command post. "While we appreciate the emotional response to this tragedy," he said into the assembled microphones, "we must investigate whether the evacuation itself contributed to casualties. The panic induced by premature warnings—"

He was cut off by a woman's scream: "Liar!"

Maria Rodriguez pushed through the crowd on her crutches, her granddaughters clinging to her sides. "This man"—she pointed at Morrison with shaking fingers—"told my neighborhood to stay put. Said the scientists were exaggerating. My neighbor listened to him. She's dead. Her whole family is dead."

The cameras swiveled between Morrison and Maria. His composed mask cracked slightly.

"That's an oversimplification—"

"It's murder," Maria spat. "You knew. The evidence says you knew, and you told us to stay anyway."

Morrison retreated as more survivors pressed forward with similar stories. The narrative was shifting in real-time, the truth too powerful for bureaucratic spin.

From her position at the medical tent, treating minor injuries, Mara watched Morrison's defeat with grim satisfaction. But her attention was drawn to a patient—a young man with ash-burned lungs who whispered urgently as she examined him.

"They're not done," he wheezed. "Cross has people... in the recovery teams... they're planning something..."

Before she could respond, the man's eyes rolled back, a seizure overtaking him. As Mara worked to stabilize him, she noticed a small tattoo on his wrist—the same geometric pattern she'd seen on the mysterious soldier's notebook.

"Elias," she called through their radio. "We have a problem."

The presidential podium had been airlifted in for the occasion, set against the backdrop of devastation with calculated political precision. President Katherine Walsh stood before the assembled media, her expression grave but resolute.

"The heroism displayed by Dr. Elias Quinn and Dr. Mara Lang represents the best of American scientific innovation," she declared. "Their Prometheus system provided forty-eight hours of warning that saved thousands of lives. Effective immediately, we're implementing Prometheus protocols nationwide."

The applause was immediate but not universal. Elias noticed several officials exchanging dark looks, Morrison among them. Cross might be in custody, but his ideology had roots throughout the system.

"Furthermore," the President continued, "Dr. Harrison Cross has been charged with federal crimes including reckless endangerment, sabotage of emergency systems, and conspiracy to commit fraud. The investigation extends to his network of associates who prioritized personal gain over public safety."

From their position in the VIP section—a dubious honor that felt more like protective custody—Elias and Mara watched the political theater unfold. Sierra sat between them, her tablet recording everything, creating backups of backups.

"Check this out," she whispered, showing them her screen. The #PrometheusHeroes hashtag had reached a billion impressions. Universities worldwide were establishing their own predictive programs. The code downloads had crashed GitHub twice.

But more interesting was an encrypted file that had just arrived in Sierra's inbox. The sender was anonymized through multiple proxies, but the message was clear: "Cross was middle management. The real architects are moving. Watch Vienna."

FBI Director James Carlton approached them as the President finished her speech. "We need to discuss your security situation," he said quietly. "We've intercepted communications suggesting you're both targets."

"From Cross's people?" Mara asked.

"From someone using Croatian intelligence protocols. Very professional, very expensive. Someone wants you silenced before you can testify."

"Testify?" Elias frowned. "Cross is already charged—"

"This is bigger than Cross. We're looking at an international conspiracy to suppress predictive technology. The Senate will convene hearings next month. Your testimony will be crucial."

A commotion near the media area drew their attention. Someone had released a batch of documents to the press—internal USGS communications showing Morrison and others discussing "containing the Quinn-Lang problem" days before the eruption.

Morrison was being escorted away by federal agents, his protests drowned out by shouted questions from reporters. But as he passed their position, he managed to lean close to Mara.

"You think you've won?" he hissed. "You've painted targets on your backs that will follow you forever. Every disaster you fail to predict, every life lost—it's on you now."

"We'll take that responsibility," Mara replied steadily. "It's better than your cowardice."

As Morrison was led away, Granger approached with a sealed evidence bag. Inside was a phone—Cross's personal device, finally cracked by FBI technicians.

"You need to see the last message he received," Granger said grimly. "Sent an hour before the eruption."

The message was brief: "Asset Prometheus compromised. Activate contingency. Eliminate primaries if necessary. —Architect"

The sun was setting over the ruins when Reuters photographer Jane Kim captured the image that would define the recovery—Elias and Mara standing on a rise overlooking the devastation, their hands clasped, silhouettes against an ash-painted sky. They were unaware of the photo being taken, lost in a moment of quiet communion after the chaos of the day.

"I keep thinking about that young man," Mara said quietly. "The one who warned me about Cross's people. He died before I could question him further."

"Another mystery," Elias agreed, pulling her closer. "We're collecting them like specimens."

Below them, the recovery camp sprawled with organized efficiency. Tents in neat rows, medical stations marked with red crosses, communication arrays reaching toward the sky. Order imposed on catastrophe, but fragile, temporary.

"They want us to be symbols," Mara observed. "The scientist couple who saved the day."

"We are symbols," Elias corrected. "But we're also targets. Morrison was right about that much."

A young girl approached them, maybe seven years old, clutching a notebook. Her mother followed nervously. "Are you the prediction people?" the child asked.

"We are," Mara said gently, kneeling to the girl's level.

"Can you predict happy things, too? Not just bad things?"

The question caught them off guard. Elias knelt beside Mara, considering his answer. "Science helps us understand patterns," he said carefully. "Both good and bad. But you're right—we should look for the good patterns too."

The girl smiled and handed them her notebook. Inside, she'd drawn pictures of the evacuation—buses and cars streaming away from a red mountain, stick figures holding hands, and at the bottom, two figures labeled "Scientist Heroes" with a heart between them.

"That's you two," she explained unnecessarily. "My teacher says love makes people brave."

After the family left, Jane Kim approached. "That photograph I just took? It's already on the wire services. You two have become the face of scientific integrity. How does that feel?"

"Terrifying," they said in unison, then laughed at their synchronicity.

But the moment of levity was shattered by an alarm from Sierra's equipment. She came running, tablet in hand.

"Prometheus is detecting something," she said urgently. "Not here—in California. Seismic patterns matching pre-eruption signatures."

They looked at each other, exhaustion warring with duty. The work never ended. The planet never stopped moving. And somewhere, the Architect was watching, waiting for them to fail.

Granger's radio crackled. "Sheriff, we've got a problem. Someone just breached the morgue. The body of that young man who died in the medical tent—it's missing."

The mysteries were multiplying faster than answers. But as Elias and Mara stood together, facing another crisis, their joined hands told a different story—one of partnership that could weather any storm, human or geological.

In his federal cell three states away, Harrison Cross smiled at the encrypted message on his lawyer's phone: "Phase Two initiated. The guardians are isolated."

The rescue was over. The real war for truth was about to begin.

Chapter 25: The Aftermath

The morning sun cast long shadows through Morgantown's skeletal remains. Where the university's clock tower once stood, only twisted metal beams reached toward the sky like blackened fingers. Elias and Mara walked hand in hand through the debris field that had been College Avenue, their boots crunching on volcanic glass that would take decades to fully clear.

"That's where we first met," Mara said quietly, pointing to a pile of rubble that had been the faculty mixer venue. A single champagne flute, somehow intact, glinted in the wreckage. "You were lecturing someone about animal intuition. I thought you were an arrogant ass."

"I was trying to impress you," Elias admitted, squeezing her ash-stained fingers. "The bartender—remember him? Older guy with the silver mustache? He told me you'd been asking about my research."

"Theodore," Mara whispered. "His name was Theodore. He didn't evacuate."

They stood in silence, the weight of the unnamed dead pressing down like the ash that still drifted from disturbed rubble. Koa, who'd refused to leave Elias's side since the eruption, whined softly and pressed against their legs.

Further down, the coffee shop where Elias had spent countless hours refining Prometheus was gone, replaced by a cooling lava flow that had hardened into grotesque ripples. But someone had planted a small American flag in the black rock, and beside it, a handwritten sign: "We'll rebuild. We survived. Thanks to Quinn & Lang."

"The bench," Elias said suddenly, pulling Mara toward the park—or what remained of it. Most of the trees were gone, either burned or knocked flat by the blast wave. But there, impossible and intact, sat the memorial bench dedicated to his late wife, Sarah.

The bronze plaque was tarnished but readable: "Dr. Sarah Quinn - 1978-2019 - 'Truth has a frequency only some can hear.'"

Mara traced the words with one finger. "She would have believed in Prometheus from the start."

"She would have loved you," Elias replied, his voice thick. "You're everything she respected—brilliant, skeptical, but willing to look beyond the data when it matters."

A distant rumble made them both tense, but it was just a bulldozer beginning the monumental task of clearing Main Street. The operator waved when he saw them, then held up a handmade sign: "You saved my daughter."

These moments of gratitude punctuated the devastation like wildflowers in ash. For every building destroyed, every life lost to those who hadn't believed or couldn't evacuate in time, there were dozens, hundreds, thousands who lived because two scientists had refused to be silenced.

"Dr. Quinn! Dr. Lang!"

They turned to find a young woman with a press badge and tired eyes. Not a reporter—her badge read "FEMA Damage Assessment."

"I'm supposed to get your input on the reconstruction zones," she said, pulling out a tablet covered in protective plastic. "Where do we rebuild, and where do we... don't?"

The question hung between them. Some areas would never be safe again. The volcanic system beneath Morgantown wasn't done—might not be done for years. Every decision they made now would echo through generations.

"Show us the geological surveys," Mara said, slipping into her professional voice even as her hand remained firmly in Elias's. "We'll need to cross-reference with Prometheus's ongoing predictions."

As they huddled over the tablet, mapping out zones of safety and danger, Elias caught their reflection in a broken storefront window. They looked older, marked by exhaustion and trauma. But also unified—two people forged by crisis into something unbreakable.

"The university will need to relocate its main campus," he said, pointing to a red zone on the map. "But the medical center is salvageable, and the evacuation proved the hospital's importance."

"Agreed," the assessor said, making notes. "What about residential areas?"

"Here," Mara indicated the eastern hills. "The lava followed predictable channels. These elevations are safe for the next century at least, assuming proper monitoring."

Behind them, someone cleared their throat. They turned to find Sheriff Tom Granger, his uniform replaced by work clothes and heavy boots, his face showing the same exhaustion they all carried.

"Thought you should know," he said without preamble. "We found something in Cross's hotel room. Before the eruption, before his arrest. My deputy just remembered to check the evidence locker we'd moved to the emergency station."

The emergency coordination center had been established in Westover's middle school gymnasium, ten miles from the disaster zone. Maps covered every wall, dotted with red pins for casualties, green for cleared areas, and yellow for zones still being searched. The air smelled of coffee, unwashed bodies, and the peculiar mixture of hope and despair that followed catastrophe.

Granger led them to a quiet corner where a laptop displayed financial records. "Cross wasn't just sabotaging your work. He was shorting disaster insurance stocks, betting against the evacuation. If people had stayed, if they'd died..." He trailed off, the implication clear.

"He would have made millions," Mara finished, her voice flat with disgust.

"Tens of millions," Granger corrected. "But that's not the worst part. Look at this."

He pulled up a series of emails, encrypted but now decoded. Cross had been corresponding with someone identified only as "Architect."

Subject: Prometheus Contingency From: Architect The primary goal remains preventing full deployment. If Quinn and Lang succeed in Morgantown, we'll need to discredit the system before global adoption. I've placed assets in Vienna, Tokyo, and São Paulo. The backdoor you requested is embedded in version 3.2.

"Backdoor?" Elias grabbed the laptop, scanning the technical details. "He built a kill switch into Prometheus?"

"Not built," Sierra's voice came from behind them. She looked haggard but determined, her tablet clutched like a shield. "I've been running diagnostics since we stabilized. The code was inserted after our last backup, during the evacuation chaos. Someone with admin access."

"The spy," Mara breathed. "The one feeding Cross information—they're still out there."

Granger nodded grimly. "We arrested the student Cross was blackmailing, but they were small-time. This 'Architect' is something else. Someone with resources, reach, and a vested interest in suppressing prediction technology."

"Oil companies," Elias said immediately. "Or insurance. Anyone whose profits depend on unpredictability."

"Or governments," Mara added quietly. "Imagine if enemies could predict each other's natural disasters. The geopolitical implications..."

They stood in silence, absorbing the magnitude of what they faced. Surviving the volcano had been the easy part. The human threats were just beginning.

"For what it's worth," Granger said, shifting uncomfortably, "I owe you both an apology. And my family's lives." His voice cracked slightly. "My wife, my seventeen-year-old daughter—they're alive because you ignored my threats, my skepticism. I came to your office to intimidate you into silence, and you saved us anyway."

"You saved yourself," Elias replied. "You chose to listen eventually. That's all we ever asked for people to look at the evidence."

"Speaking of evidence," Sierra interrupted, her fingers flying across her tablet, "I've isolated the backdoor code. It's sophisticated, but I can patch it. The question is whether we do it quietly or use it as bait."

"Bait?" Mara's eyes sharpened with interest.

"Leave it active but monitored. When the Architect tries to trigger it, we trace them."

"That's dangerous," Granger warned. "If they succeed—"

"They won't," Sierra said with absolute confidence. "I've already built redundancies. Prometheus 4.0 is running on parallel servers with different encryption. Even if they kill one version, the others survive."

A commotion outside drew their attention. Through the gym windows, they could see a convoy of construction vehicles arriving, led by a familiar figure. Lenora Voss, seemingly indefatigable despite her seventy-plus years, was directing traffic with the authority of a general.

"The reconstruction begins now," she announced, entering the gym with mud-caked boots and fierce determination. "I've called in every favor from forty years of fighting the geological establishment. We have funding, we have resources, and most importantly, we have credibility."

She pulled Elias and Mara aside, lowering her voice. "There's something else. My mentee, David Tran, was documenting the evacuation. He has something you need to hear."

David Tran was young, maybe twenty-five, with the kind of haunted eyes that came from witnessing catastrophe up close. His camera equipment sat beside him, memory cards labeled with dates and times from the eruption. But it wasn't the footage he wanted to share.

"My grandmother," he began, his voice soft with reverence. "She's from Vietnam originally, lived through earthquakes there. When she heard about your predictions, she said something I didn't understand at first."

He pulled out a worn notebook, pages filled with Vietnamese script and careful English translations.

"She said, 'The mountain speaks in pairs—one who feels, one who measures. Only together can they hear the whole truth.' It's an old legend from her village, about guardian spirits who protect against disasters."

Mara leaned forward, intrigued. "Paired guardians?"

"The story says one guardian feels the earth's pain—intuitive, emotional, connected to living things. The other counts the earth's heartbeats—logical, precise, understanding patterns. Apart, they're incomplete. Together, they can predict when the earth will shake."

David looked between them meaningfully. "She saw you two on the news, before the eruption. She packed our things immediately. 'The guardians have come,' she said. We were in the car heading out when you gave the official evacuation order."

"It's just a coincidence," Mara said, but her scientific skepticism sounded uncertain.

"Is it?" David pulled up footage on his camera. "Look at this."

The video showed the moments before the eruption. In the frame, Elias and Mara stood at the evacuation checkpoint, directing traffic. What struck them wasn't their actions but their synchronization—Elias scanning the horizon, watching Koa and the fleeing birds, while Mara checked her instruments. When Elias pointed east, Mara was already calculating that trajectory. When Mara's equipment beeped warnings, Elias was already moving people away from danger zones.

"You move like dancers," David said. "Like you're hearing the same music no one else can hear."

Another survivor approached—Maria Rodriguez, the sixty-eight-year-old Mara had mentioned in her list of saved lives. She walked with a cane now, her leg injured during evacuation but healing.

"Three minutes," she said simply. "That's how close I came. Three minutes between your warning and my house collapsing. My grandchildren were visiting. Seven and nine years old." Tears tracked down her weathered cheeks. "How do you thank someone for your grandchildren's future?"

"You live," Elias said gently. "You rebuild. You remember."

More survivors gathered, sharing fragments of gratitude and grief. Each story added weight to their success but also to their responsibility. They'd saved thousands, but the system that had tried to silence them remained partially intact.

Voss watched from the doorway, her expression unreadable. When the crowd finally dispersed, she approached with a manila envelope.

"From my personal archives," she said quietly. "Documents I've kept hidden for forty years. Names, dates, a paper trail of everyone who helped bury my volcanic predictions in the 1980s."

She handed Mara the envelope. "Some of those names are still active. Still in positions of power. The Architect you're looking for? They were part of the original suppression."

Later, in the relative quiet of their temporary housing—a FEMA trailer that felt like a palace after days of emergency shelters—Elias and Mara finally had a moment alone. Koa slept at their feet, occasionally whimpering through dreams of running.

"We're different people than we were six months ago," Mara said, studying their reflection in the small bathroom mirror. Her hair had gray streaks that hadn't been there before. Elias had new scars from flying debris.

"Better or worse?" he asked, wrapping his arms around her from behind.

"Both. Neither. Transformed." She turned in his embrace, looking up at him with eyes that held depths of experience. "I spent so long believing only in what I could measure. You taught me to feel. But more than that, we taught each other to be complete."

"Speaking of complete," Elias said, pulling out his phone. "Morrison from the university sent this."

The email was brief: The board wants you both to co-author the official account. Full access to all records, all data. "The Prometheus Prophecy: How Intuition and Data Saved Morgantown." Interested?

"A book?" Mara considered. "We'd have to include everything. Cross's sabotage, the spy, the Architect..."

"The love story," Elias added with a slight smile.

"The science," Mara countered, but she was smiling too. "We could create a template, show other communities how to build their own prediction systems."

"Fusion methodology," Elias said, the idea taking shape. "Not choosing between intuition and data, but wedding them."

"Like us," Mara said softly.

They kissed then, long and deep, a moment of peace in the ongoing storm. But even as they held each other, both knew this calm was temporary.

On the table, Sierra's tablet beeped. A message from her monitoring system: someone had just attempted to access the Prometheus backdoor from an IP address in Vienna.

The Architect was making their move.

But more unsettling was the second alert—a scan of Cross's hidden files had revealed a list of bank transfers. Payments to at least a dozen officials, scientists, and media figures. The conspiracy ran deeper than they'd imagined.

"Tomorrow," Mara said firmly, seeing Elias reach for the tablet. "Tonight, we're just us. Tomorrow, we save the world again."

But tomorrow was already bleeding into today. Outside their trailer, someone had spray-painted a message on a piece of standing wall: "QUINN & LANG LIED. PEOPLE DIED."

Cross's influence lingered like ash in the air—toxic, pervasive, and far from settled. The real fight for truth was just beginning, but at least now they knew the battlefield extended far beyond Morgantown's ruins.

In the distance, a faint tremor rippled through the earth—an aftershock, Prometheus confirmed, nothing dangerous. But Elias and Mara felt it simultaneously, their bodies attuned now to the planet's restless poetry. They were the paired guardians of David's grandmother's legend, whether they believed it or not.

And somewhere in Vienna, someone was very interested in making sure their guardianship ended.

Chapter 26: Rebuilding Trust

The stack of letters on Elias's desk had grown three inches since break-fast. Job offers from MIT, Stanford, Oxford—institutions that had once dismissed his work as "pseudoscience" now competed for the prestige of housing Prometheus. Mara sat cross-legged on his office floor, sorting through her own pile with the methodical precision that had survived even catastrophe.

"Cambridge wants us to head their new Catastrophic Prediction Department," she said, holding up cream-colored stationery. "They're offering dual professorships, unlimited research funding, and—" she paused, eyebrows raising, "—a dedicated supercomputer cluster."

"Berkeley's promising to name a building after us," Elias countered, though his heart wasn't in the competition. Through the window, Morgantown's skeletal remains stretched toward the mountains, construction crews working like ants to rebuild what the volcano had claimed. Leaving felt like abandonment.

Sierra burst through the door without knocking, her tablet clutched against her chest. "You need to see this. Now."

The video had already accumulated two million views in six hours. Someone had compiled footage from the evacuation—security cameras, cell phones, news crews—overlaid with Prometheus's predictions. The timestamp comparisons were damning in their precision. Every warning Elias and Mara had issued, every pattern they'd identified, was validated in real-time catastrophe.

"The comments," Sierra said, scrolling rapidly. "Look at the comments."

"They saved my grandmother. She lived on Oak Street, directly in the pyroclastic path."

"I called them fearmongers. I posted horrible things. I'm alive because they ignored people like me."

"My daughter's third-grade class evacuated because of their warnings. Twenty-eight eight-year-olds who get to grow up because two scientists refused to shut up."

Mara's hand found Elias's shoulder, squeezing gently as they read. But Sierra wasn't finished.

"That's not why I'm here," she said, swiping to a new screen. "The International Association of Geological Sciences wants to fund a global Prometheus network. Sixty stations, real-time monitoring, all feeding into a central AI hub. They want me to lead the technical development."

"Sierra, that's incredible—" Elias began, but she cut him off.

"I'm only taking it if we do this together. All three of us. We're a team, or we're nothing."

Through the window, a bulldozer pushed aside volcanic debris, revealing a partially melted street sign: Hope Avenue. The irony wasn't lost on any of them.

"There's something else," Sierra said, her voice dropping. "The FBI called. Cross's trial starts next week. They want you both to testify."

The warmth drained from the room. Elias felt Mara stiffen beside him, her academic excitement curdling into something harder. They'd known this was coming, but knowing didn't make it easier.

"He's been sending letters," Sierra added quietly. "From prison. To scientific journals, claiming he has proof that Prometheus was flawed. That you manipulated the data to match your predictions after the fact."

"Let him try," Mara said, her voice sharp as volcanic glass. "We have every timestamp, every backup, every—"

"He's claiming he has something else," Sierra interrupted. "A version of Prometheus's code that tells a different story. His lawyer is calling it 'evidence of scientific fraud.'"

Elias stood abruptly, pacing to the window. Below, workers installed a memorial plaque where the faculty parking lot used to be. Thirty-seven names of university staff who hadn't evacuated in time, who'd believed Cross's disinformation over Prometheus's warnings.

"We knew he'd try something," he said finally. "Narcissists like Cross can't accept defeat. They'd rather burn everything down than admit they were wrong."

"Speaking of burning things down," Sierra said, attempting levity, "President Morrison wants to see you. Something about a 'unique opportunity.'"

Twenty minutes later, they sat in the university president's temporary office—a converted classroom that still smelled of volcanic ash despite aggressive cleaning. Morrison looked older, the crisis having carved new lines around his eyes.

"I'll be direct," he said. "The university is being rebuilt with federal disaster funds. We have a chance to create something entirely new. I want you to design it. The Quinn-Lang Institute for Predictive Sciences."

"Quinn-Lang?" Mara asked, eyebrows rising.

Morrison smiled slightly. "The whole campus knows you're together. Might as well make it official. We're offering you the entire east wing of the new science complex. State-of-the-art facilities, autonomous hiring authority, and a direct line to USGS and FEMA for emergency predictions."

"Why?" Elias asked. "Six months ago, this university was ready to fire me for 'promoting panic.'"

"Because six months ago, I was a fool," Morrison said bluntly. "I let politics and optics override science. Thirty-seven members of my faculty died because I didn't mandate evacuation when you first warned us. That's on me forever. The least I can do is make sure it never happens again."

He pushed a folder across the desk. Inside, architectural renderings showed a building that looked like crystallized hope—all glass and steel, with an observation deck facing the mountains and a basement bunker for emergency operations.

"There's one condition," Morrison added. "Cross has allies. Not many anymore, but enough to cause problems. If you take this position, you're painting targets on your backs. The conspiracy theorists, the science deniers, the ones who'd rather believe this was all coincidence—they'll come after you."

"They already are," Mara said quietly, thinking of the anonymous death threats that still arrived weekly.

"Then we'll face them," Elias said, taking her hand publicly for the first time in Morrison's presence. "Together."

The laptop screen glowed in the pre-dawn darkness of their shared apartment. Elias had been writing for three hours, chasing memories through the keyboard while Mara slept beside him, one hand resting on his thigh even in dreams. The memoir had started as therapy—his psychiatrist's suggestion for processing trauma—but had evolved into something else: a historical record, a love letter to truth, an indictment of those who'd tried to suppress it.

The current chapter hurt to write.

Harrison Cross had been brilliant once. That's what made his fall so catastrophic—not just for him, but for everyone caught in his gravitational collapse. The first time I met him, at a conference in 2018, he'd presented a paper on statistical modeling that made my wife Sarah sit up straight, excited by the possibilities...

The flashback pulled him under:

Denver Convention Center, 2018. Cross commanded the stage with evangelical fervor, his projections showing perfect mathematical beauty. But Sarah had noticed something others missed.

"Look at his error bars," she'd whispered. "They're too perfect. Real data is messy. This has been cleaned."

After the presentation, she'd approached him privately, suggesting a collaboration that might reconcile his models with her biological observations. Cross's response had been swift and vicious.

"Mrs. Quinn," he'd said, deliberately using her married name rather than her professional title, "perhaps you should stick to watching birds. Leave the real science to those of us with proper training."

Sarah had laughed it off, but I'd seen the calculation in Cross's eyes—a brilliant woman who wouldn't genuflect to his genius was a threat to be eliminated.

Elias paused, remembering what came next. Sarah's grant applications were mysteriously rejected. Her papers were delayed in peer review until Cross could publish similar findings. The whisper campaign suggested she was "too emotional" for serious research.

Another memory surfaced, this one from Voss:

"Harrison destroyed my career in 1985," Voss had told them during the evacuation, her voice steady despite fleeing catastrophe. "I'd identified unusual thermal patterns in the Appalachian deep crust. He was the peer reviewer who buried my paper, then published his own work dismissing the possibility of volcanic activity in 'stable' mountain ranges. Two months later, he was appointed to the USGS advisory board. My warnings about Morgantown were classified as 'geological fiction.'"

"Why didn't you fight back?" Mara had asked.

"I did. He had me institutionalized for three months. 'Acute paranoid delusions,' the diagnosis read. Hard to argue geological theory from a psychiatric ward."

The cursor blinked. Elias struggled with how much to reveal. Cross's pattern was clear—decades of crushing anyone who threatened his supremacy, particularly women who dared challenge him. But proving it meant exposing victims who'd rebuilt their lives in silence.

"Can't sleep?" Mara's voice was soft, concerned. She propped herself on an elbow, reading over his shoulder.

"Cross's lawyer subpoenaed my early drafts," Elias said. "Claims I'm writing fiction to support our legal case."

"Let them subpoena," Mara said, her fingers tracing patterns on his back. "Truth has timestamps. Cross's lies don't."

She was right. Everything they'd documented had been backed up in triplicate, time-stamped on blockchain servers Sierra had insisted on using. But Cross's final manipulation ran deeper than data.

"He sent another letter," Elias admitted, pulling up the scanned copy. "To you, actually."

Mara read silently, her face hardening with each line:

Dear Dr. Lang,

You of all people should understand the importance of scientific integrity. I know about Vienna. I know what really happened with your first seismic study—the one you've never published. The one where you missed a 4.7 event that killed three people because you were too proud to admit your model's limitations.

We're more alike than you want to admit. We both buried our failures. The difference is, I got caught.

When this trial ends, win or lose, that study goes public unless you convince Elias to recant.

—H.C.

"He's lying," Elias said immediately. "Whatever happened in Vienna—"

"He's not," Mara whispered. "Not entirely. There was a study. I was twenty-three, cocky, certain my model was perfect. I dismissed anomalous readings as equipment error. Three construction workers died when the quake I said wouldn't happen did happen. I've been trying to atone ever since."

"Mara—"

"That's why I was so skeptical of Prometheus at first. I know what it feels like to be wrong when lives are at stake. But Cross has it backwards—my failure taught me humility. His taught him to double down on lies."

The National Press Club luncheon buzzed with controlled energy. Elias adjusted Mara's microphone, his fingers lingering against her collar. Six months ago, they'd have maintained professional distance. Now, their partnership was part of their brand—the couple who'd merged love and science to save lives.

"Remember," Mara murmured, "no tongue if they ask us to kiss for the cameras."

"You started it at the Reuters interview," he countered, earning an elbow to his ribs.

Sierra, seated at their table, rolled her eyes dramatically. "You two are disgusting. Disgustingly cute, but still."

The moderator introduced them as "the scientific power couple who redefined prediction," and cameras clicked as they took the stage hand-in-hand. The questions started soft—how did they balance personal and professional, what was it like working with a romantic partner—before veering into harder territory.

"Dr. Quinn, how do you respond to critics who say your relationship clouds scientific objectivity?"

"I'd say check our math," Elias responded, getting laughs. "But seriously, Mara challenges me more fiercely because she loves me, not despite it. She won't let me get away with sloppy thinking just because we share a bed."

"TMI," Sierra called out, causing more laughter.

"Dr. Lang," another reporter asked, "Harrison Cross claims you seduced Dr. Quinn to steal his research. Comments?"

The room went silent. Mara leaned into her microphone, her voice deadly calm.

"Harrison Cross is facing seventeen federal charges including attempted murder through willful endangerment. He sabotaged equipment that could have saved lives, destroyed data that proved imminent danger, and spread disinformation that nearly prevented thousands from evacuating. If he wants to add sexual harassment and defamation to his charges by continuing to spread lies about my relationship, he's welcome to try."

She paused, then added with surgical precision: "Also, for the record, Elias seduced me. He used differential equations. I'm weak for good math."

The tension broke. Even the hostile reporters laughed. Elias pulled her closer, pressing a kiss to her temple that every photographer captured.

Later, in the car, Sierra showed them the social media response. #ScienceCoupleGoals was trending, complete with fan art of them as superhero scientists fighting a volcano.

"We've become a meme," Mara said, horrified and amused in equal measure.

"A heroic meme," Elias corrected. "Look, someone made us into anime characters."

"Why do I have cat ears in this one?" Mara demanded.

"Because you're catastrophically cute," Sierra said, then shrieked as Mara threw a water bottle at her.

But beneath the levity, they all knew what came next. Tomorrow, Cross's trial would begin. Tomorrow, they'd face the man who'd nearly killed thousands to protect his ego.

The federal courthouse in Charleston stood like a gravestone against the October sky. Elias and Mara entered through a secure entrance, avoiding the protesters who'd gathered on both sides—supporters with signs reading "THEY SAVED US" and Cross's remaining allies claiming "SCIEN-TIFIC WITCH HUNT."

Cross looked smaller in his orange jumpsuit, his characteristic arrogance dimmed but not extinguished. He watched them enter with the intensity of a caged predator, his lawyer whispering urgently in his ear.

The prosecutor, Janet Williams, had warned them that Cross would try something dramatic. "Narcissists always do," she'd said. "They can't resist a final performance."

She was right.

Three hours into Mara's testimony, as she detailed Cross's sabotage with mathematical precision, he suddenly stood.

"Your Honor, I need to address the court," Cross announced, his voice carrying its old authority.

"Mr. Cross, sit down," the judge ordered.

"I have evidence that will change everything," Cross insisted. "Evidence that Prometheus was my creation, stolen and corrupted by these two frauds."

The courtroom erupted. The judge gaveled for order, but Cross continued, pulling a USB drive from somewhere his lawyer clearly hadn't expected.

"This contains the original Prometheus code," Cross declared. "Written by me, two years before Quinn claims to have developed it. Check the metadata. Check the timestamps. They stole my work, then framed me when I tried to reclaim it."

Mara felt the blood drain from her face. Beside her, Elias had gone rigid. They knew Prometheus's development history intimately—every line of code, every iteration. But metadata could be faked, and timestamps could be altered. If Cross had prepared this thoroughly...

"Your Honor," Williams said quickly, "the defense is introducing evidence without proper disclosure—"

"I'll allow it," the judge said, curiosity overcoming procedure. "But Mr. Cross, you're still under oath."

A technician inserted the USB drive into a secured laptop. Code filled the screen—definitely Prometheus's architecture, but subtly wrong. Variable names Elias had never used. Functions structured in Cross's characteristic style. And the metadata...

"Created January 15, 2022," the technician read. "Six months before Dr. Quinn's first documented version."

The courtroom held its breath. Cross smiled, the expression sharp as a scalpel.

"I wrote this to predict market fluctuations," he said smoothly. "Quinn attended my lecture on predictive modeling in December 2021. Two months later, suddenly, he has a 'breakthrough.' You do the math."

Elias started to stand, but Sierra's voice cut through the chaos from the gallery.

"Check the comments in line 3,847."

Everyone turned. Sierra had her laptop open, having somehow accessed the code remotely.

"Line 3,847," she repeated. "In the comments. Right there in Cross's supposed 'original.'"

The technician scrolled. There, buried in the code's documentation:

// TODO: Update this section after Mara fixes the volcanic correlation bug - EQ 03/15/2023

"That comment," Sierra said clearly, "references a bug I didn't discover until March 2023. A bug that only existed because of an update pushed in February 2023. Cross's 'original' code includes fixes for problems that didn't exist when he claims to have written it."

The courtroom erupted again. Cross's lawyer grabbed the USB, staring at the screen in horror. Cross himself had gone pale, his mouth working soundlessly.

"There's more," Sierra continued, her fingers flying across her keyboard. "The compiler signature in the metadata? It's from a version released in September 2022. Impressive time travel, Dr. Cross."

"This is—this is planted!" Cross sputtered. "They've altered—"

"The drive came from you," the judge said coldly. "From your possession, introduced by you, under oath." He turned to the bailiff. "Add perjury and evidence tampering to Mr. Cross's charges."

As security moved toward Cross, he lunged across the defense table, eyes wild.

"You don't understand!" he screamed at Elias and Mara. "I made you! Your entire career exists because I gave you something to fight against! Without me, you're nothing!"

"Without you," Mara said quietly, her voice carrying in the sudden silence, "thirty-seven people would still be alive."

Cross collapsed then, all fight leaving him. As they led him away, he looked back once, and for a moment Elias saw him clearly—a brilliant mind consumed by its own gravity, collapsing into a black hole that devoured everything, even itself.

Outside the courthouse, Williams shook their hands.

"Fifteen to twenty years, minimum," she said. "Possibly life, given the deaths his disinformation caused."

But Elias barely heard her. An email had just arrived on his phone, the sender anonymous:

Cross wasn't working alone. The real architect is still out there. Check the Prometheus backdoor you never found. —A friend

Attached was a fragment of code, elegant and malicious, that had been hidden in Prometheus's core all along. Not Cross's work—someone far more sophisticated.

"Elias?" Mara noticed his expression. "What is it?"

He showed her the screen. Her face went pale, then hard with determination.

"We're not done," she said.

"No," he agreed, pulling her close as cameras flashed around them. "But we're together. That's enough for now."

Sierra joined them, and together they walked toward the car, three minds already parsing the implications of this new threat. Behind them, the courthouse stood solid against the sky, but ahead, storm clouds gathered over the mountains.

Somewhere in those peaks, the fault lines were always shifting, always threatening. But now humanity had Prometheus. Now they had a warning.

The question was: who was trying to silence it?

The answer would have to wait. MIT had called. Oxford had doubled their offer. The world wanted Prometheus, and with it, the team that had stared down catastrophe and refused to blink.

As they drove away, Elias's phone buzzed with one final message, this one from President Morrison:

The institute funding is approved. Unlimited budget. Come home and build the future.

Home. Morgantown. Where it all began, and where, apparently, it would continue.

"So," Sierra said from the backseat, "who wants to bet our mysterious friend is Voss?"

"No bet," Mara and Elias said in unison, then laughed at their synchronicity.

Whatever came next, they'd face it as they'd faced everything else—together, with science and intuition dancing in perfect, dangerous harmony.

Chapter 27: The Fault in Our Certainty

The Vienna Convention Center hummed with the controlled chaos of three thousand scientists from sixty-seven countries. Elias adjusted his tie for the third time, catching Mara's amused glance in the mirror of their hotel room.

"You've faced down a volcano," she said, smoothing his collar with practiced intimacy. "This should be easy."

"The volcano was more predictable," he muttered, but his nervousness evaporated when she kissed him, quick and fierce.

The main auditorium's stage seemed impossibly vast. Behind them, Sierra's latest visualization of Prometheus's predictive modeling played on a screen three stories tall—magma flows rendered in bleeding reds and golds, animal migration patterns overlaying in electric blue, the fatal convergence point pulsing like a heartbeat.

"Before we begin," the moderator announced, "I must address the controversy surrounding our speakers. Dr. Richard Steinberg has requested time to present his counter-analysis."

Elias felt Mara tense beside him. Steinberg had been Cross's most vocal academic ally, though never directly implicated in the sabotage. The older geologist strode to the podium with theatrical gravity.

"Ladies and gentlemen," Steinberg began, his voice dripping condescension, "what we witnessed in West Virginia was not prescient science, but fortunate coincidence amplified by mass hysteria. The Quinns"—he deliberately used their still-unofficial shared name—"created the very panic they claimed to prevent."

The auditorium stirred. Someone booed; another shouted support. Elias started to rise, but Mara's hand on his arm stopped him.

"My turn," she whispered.

She approached the podium with the measured confidence that had first captivated him. "Dr. Steinberg raises an important point about causation versus correlation. Perhaps he'd like to explain how 'mass hysteria' accounts for the magma chamber measurements taken six weeks before our first public warning? Or how 'coincidence' explains the seventeen separate animal species that exhibited flight responses in perfect correlation with underground pressure changes?"

She clicked her remote. The screen showed Cross's falsified data next to their verified readings, the manipulation obvious in side-by-side comparison.

"More importantly," Mara continued, her voice gaining strength, "how does he explain why his mentor, Dr. Harrison Cross, spent considerable resources trying to suppress this data? Unless, of course, he knew it was accurate."

Steinberg's face flushed. "You can't prove—"

"Actually," a voice called from the audience, "she can."

Sheriff Tom Granger stood in the third row, his uniform incongruous among the suits and lab coats. "I flew here on my own dime because these folks deserve to have the truth told. I've brought sworn depositions from thirty-seven witnesses regarding Cross's sabotage campaign. Dr. Steinberg, your name appears in several of them."

The auditorium erupted. Steinberg retreated from the podium as security approached. Through the chaos, Elias heard scattered applause that grew into thunder. Scientists stood, one by one, then in waves. Mara found his hand, squeezing hard enough to hurt.

"Together?" she asked.

"Always," he replied.

They presented for ninety minutes, their rhythm perfected through crisis. Elias explained the intuitive framework, how Koa's distress had provided the first critical data point. Mara detailed the mathematical models, the fusion of behavioral and geological metrics that made Prometheus revolutionary. They finished each other's sentences, handed off concepts seamlessly, their partnership a demonstration as powerful as their data.

The questions came fast and sharp—challenges to their methodology, requests for specific parameters, demands for reproducible results. They answered them all, Sierra feeding them real-time data from her laptop in the front row.

"One final question," the moderator said. "If Prometheus detected the Morgantown event six weeks in advance, what is it detecting now?"

Elias and Mara exchanged glances. On the screen behind them, a world map bloomed with gentle yellow pulses—dozens of sites showing early-warning patterns.

"Everything," Elias said simply. "We're detecting everything."

The reception hall glittered with Nobel laureates and department heads, but Mara only had eyes for the journal in her hands. Nature had fast-tracked their paper, dedicating an entire special issue to their work. The cover showed an aerial photograph of Morgantown's evacuation—streams of headlights flowing away from danger, Prometheus's prediction overlaid in ghostly mathematical precision.

"Page forty-seven," Sierra said, appearing at her elbow with champagne. "That's my favorite part."

Mara flipped to the dedication page, her throat tightening at the words she'd written at three in the morning, Elias asleep beside her:

"To Dr. Elias Quinn, who taught me that the greatest discoveries happen when we trust what we feel as much as what we measure. And to his late wife, Dr. Sarah Quinn, whose pioneering work in biological intuition laid the foundation for everything that followed. This work is equally dedicated to the 3,847 lives saved in Morgantown—proof that when intuition and data dance together, miracles become reproducible."

"You didn't tell me about the last part," Elias said, reading over her shoulder. His voice was rough.

"Some things should be surprises," she replied, leaning into his warmth.

Dr. Lenora Voss approached, her weathered face bright with vindication. "Forty years," she said, raising her glass. "Forty years since I first proposed volcanic activity in the Appalachians. They called me crazy, destroyed my career. But you two..." She pulled them both into an unexpected embrace. "You listened to the land's whispers AND proved them with numbers. That's the real revolution."

The journal's editor-in-chief took the stage, calling for attention. "Ladies and gentlemen, I'm pleased to announce that 'Behavioral-Geological Predictive Modeling: The Prometheus Method' has become our most-downloaded paper in the journal's 150-year history. More importantly, the UN Disaster Prevention Council has officially adopted Prometheus as a standard early warning system."

Applause filled the room, but Mara noticed a commotion near the entrance. A young woman pushed through the crowd, her press credentials swinging.

"Dr. Lang!" she called. "Veronica Chen, Washington Post. How do you respond to allegations that you and Dr. Quinn manufactured evidence to support a predetermined conclusion?"

The room went silent. Mara felt Elias tense, ready to intervene, but she stepped forward calmly.

"I respond with 3,847 names," Mara said, pulling out her phone. "Would you like me to read them? These are the people alive today because we trusted our data—ALL our data, including the kind that can't always be quantified. Adam Abernethy, age seven. Susan Abernethy, age thirty-two. Michael Ackerman, age—"

"That's not necessary," the reporter interrupted, but Mara continued.

"Maria Rodriguez, age sixty-eight, pulled from her collapsed home three minutes before the pyroclastic flow hit. Tommy Chen—perhaps a relative of yours?—age nineteen, evacuated from his dorm despite university officials' initial resistance."

The reporter's face had gone pale. "Tommy's my cousin," she whispered.

"Then you know," Mara said gently, "that sometimes the fault in our certainty—that crack in absolute skepticism—is exactly where the light gets in."

The overlook stretched above Seneca Rocks, West Virginia's ancient quartzite fins catching the sunset like frozen flames. Elias had suggested the hike to "clear their heads" after the conference, but Mara knew him too well. He'd been fidgeting all day, checking his pocket with the same tell he'd had before presenting to hostile boards.

"You're going to propose," she said, amused, as they reached the summit.

Elias froze mid-step. "How did you—"

"Behavioral modeling," she laughed. "You've touched your pocket seventeen times since we left the car. Your heart rate is elevated beyond exercise parameters. And Sierra sent me a text that just said 'Say yes' with about fifty exclamation points."

"I had a whole speech planned," he said, deflating slightly.

"Then give it." She sat on a boulder, the valley spreading below them like a promise. "I want to hear it."

Elias knelt—awkwardly, catching himself on the rocky ground—and pulled out a small velvet box. Inside, a raw garnet caught the dying light, unpolished but profound, wrapped in silver that looked handmade.

"This stone," he began, his voice steady despite his racing pulse, "was in Sarah's collection. She found it on her last field expedition, the day she trusted her intuition to lead her team away from an unstable cliff. That decision saved seven lives, though she never got to catalog the specimen properly."

Mara's eyes filled, understanding the weight of the offering.

"For the longest time, I couldn't look at it," Elias continued. "It represented everything I'd lost. But then you came along—skeptical, brilliant, absolutely infuriating—and taught me that grief doesn't have to be the end of the story. You showed me that data and intuition, past and future, loss and love can coexist."

He took a breath, meeting her eyes. "You asked me once what Prometheus really predicts. It predicts patterns, convergence points where separate systems align. That's what we are, Mara. Two fault lines created something stronger at the intersection. I love your skepticism and your faith, your spreadsheets and your hunches, your fierce protection of truth and your willingness to believe in impossible things—like me."

"Elias—"

"Marry me," he said simply. "Not because we survived a volcano or saved lives or revolutionized predictive science. Marry me because when the ground shakes, you're who I want standing beside me. Marry me because you've already healed the cracks I thought would never close."

Mara slipped off the boulder, kneeling to face him on the rough granite. "You beautiful, intuitive fool," she whispered. "Yes. Of course, yes. Though I should mention—Prometheus predicted this outcome with 97.3% certainty."

"Only 97.3?"

"The remaining 2.7% was the possibility you'd chicken out."

He kissed her then, long and deep, while the sun painted the rocks around them the same warm gold as Sarah's garnet. When they finally pulled apart, Mara held up her hand, the stone catching the last light.

"She would have loved you," Elias said softly.

"I know," Mara replied. "Her research notes told me so. Page 73 of her last journal—'The best science happens when opposites attract, creating something neither could achieve alone.' I think she was writing about magnetic fields, but..."

"But she would have meant us too," Elias finished. "She always did see patterns before anyone else."

They sat together as darkness fell, the lights of recovered Morgantown twinkling below. Somewhere in the distance, a dog howled—not in warning, but in wild, unrestrained joy.

The blueprints spread across their hotel bed like a promise of the future. The Quinn Institute for Predictive Sciences decided to share the name professionally, too, which would occupy the rebuilt Morgantown University Science Center. Three floors, seventeen labs, and a specialized animal behavior observation facility that Koa had already claimed as his domain.

"Sierra's proposing a youth program," Mara said, tracing the educational wing with her finger. "Teaching kids to recognize environmental patterns."

"And Voss wants to establish an indigenous knowledge archive," Elias added. "Oral histories, traditional observations, all integrated with modern data collection."

Their phones buzzed simultaneously—another Prometheus alert. They'd grown accustomed to the constant stream of global data, but this one made them both pause. The South Pacific, showing the same early convergence patterns they'd seen in West Virginia.

"Fiji," Mara identified, already pulling up geological surveys. "Volcanic island chain, populated coastal areas, limited evacuation infrastructure."

"We could be there in eighteen hours," Elias calculated.

They looked at each other, momentarily forgetting their wedding plans and wedding designs. This was who they were now—the world's early warning system, partners in every sense.

"After the honeymoon?" Mara suggested.

"Or during?" Elias countered. "Volcanic islands are romantic."

"Your definition of romantic needs work," she laughed, but she was already opening her laptop, pulling up flight schedules.

Outside their window, Vienna slept peacefully, unaware of the tectonic forces constantly shifting beneath its historic streets. But around the world, Prometheus stations hummed with vigilance, their algorithms parsing the planet's whispers, ready to sound the alarm.

The faint tremor that rippled through the hotel was so subtle that most guests slept through it. But Elias and Mara felt it, their hands finding each other instinctively.

"Local adjustment," Mara diagnosed, checking her phone. "Nothing significant."

"This time," Elias added quietly.

They returned to their plans, designing a future built on the fault line between certainty and intuition, knowing that the earth would always keep its deepest secrets until the very moment it decided to reveal them. But they would be watching, together, ready to interpret the planet's volatile poetry into the mathematics of survival.

In the corner of Elias's laptop screen, a new alert blinked—Antarctica, showing unusual thermal patterns beneath ancient ice. He closed the laptop. Tomorrow's crisis could wait.

Tonight, they had a wedding to plan.

Chapter 28: Quiet Tremors

The rental car's tires crunched over volcanic gravel as Mara navigated the narrow road toward Bend, Oregon. Through the passenger window, Elias watched the Three Sisters peaks pierce the morning sky, their snow-capped summits deceptively serene. Koa sat in the back, nose pressed to the window, occasionally whining at something only he could sense.

"Sierra's mom makes the best tamales in Oregon," Elias said, attempting to lighten the mood that had settled over them since leaving the conference. "She'll be offended if we don't stay for dinner."

"We're not here for a social visit," Mara reminded him, though her tone was gentle. She'd been softer lately, the rigid walls she'd built after Cross's betrayal finally crumbling in the wake of their shared triumph. "Prometheus detected something. The patterns here are..."

"Different," he finished. "I know. But that doesn't mean we can't enjoy some homemade tamales while saving the world."

She smiled despite herself, reaching over to squeeze his hand. The engagement ring on her finger caught the sunlight—a piece of volcanic glass from Morgantown set in silver, Elias's idea of romantic geology.

"There," Sierra's voice crackled through the car's Bluetooth. "Turn left at the big pine with the eagle's nest."

The Patel family home sat on five acres of high desert beauty, with Mount Bachelor looming in the distance. Sierra stood in the driveway, waving enthusiastically, her mother beside her holding a steaming dish that probably contained those famous tamales.

"Dr. Quinn! Dr. Lang!" Sierra's younger brother, David, bounded over as they parked. "Is it true you predicted a volcano? Can you predict when I'll finally beat Sierra at chess?"

"Never," Sierra said, ruffling his hair. "Some disasters are inevitable."

But Mara noticed the tension in Sierra's shoulders, the way her eyes kept drifting toward the mountains. She'd mentioned the local stories on their last call—hikers who'd vanished without a trace, their cars found running at trailheads, their footprints simply stopping mid-trail as if they'd been lifted into the air.

"The earth spirits," Mrs. Patel said quietly, following Mara's gaze. "That's what my neighbor calls them. Native stories about places where the boundary grows thin."

"Boundary between what?" Elias asked, genuinely curious.

"Between our world and the world beneath," Sierra's grandmother answered from the porch, her voice carrying despite its softness. "My grandfather knew these stories. Said there were places where the earth could swallow you whole if you weren't respectful. If you didn't listen to the warnings."

Koa suddenly barked, sharp and urgent, staring at a spot near the tree line where nothing moved. The fur along his spine stood up, and he positioned himself between the humans and whatever he sensed.

"He's been doing that more often," Elias said, but Mara heard the concern beneath his casual tone.

After dinner—the tamales were indeed incredible—they spread their equipment across the Patels' dining room table. Prometheus's latest analysis painted a concerning picture: minor seismic activity was increasing along previously stable fault lines, but the pattern didn't match typical tectonic behavior.

"It's like something's moving underneath," Sierra said, manipulating the 3D visualization. "But not in a way that makes geological sense."

"Unless," Mara said slowly, pulling up historical surveys, "we're not looking at natural geology." She overlaid mining maps from the early 1900s. "Look at this. Extensive copper mining throughout this region, but half these mines aren't on any official registry."

"Ghost mines," Mrs. Patel said from the doorway. "My father worked for the forestry service. They said there were dozens of operations that never filed paperwork and never paid taxes. Just dug their holes and disappeared when the ore ran out."

"Or when something made them run," Sierra's grandmother added ominously.

Elias and Mara exchanged glances. They'd learned to take such stories seriously after Morgantown—folklore often preserved truths that official records buried.

"We should set up monitoring stations," Mara said. "Cover the area where the disappearances cluster."

"That's thirty square miles of wilderness," Sierra pointed out. "We'll need help."

"Already arranged," a familiar voice said from the front door. Dr. Lenora Voss entered, looking remarkably spry for someone who'd just driven six hours. "I've brought some students from the new indigenous knowledge program. They know these lands."

Behind her, three young people carried equipment boxes. Mara recognized one—James Littlecrow, whose paper on traditional earthquake prediction methods had caught Elias's attention months ago.

"The elders are worried," James said without preamble. "The usual signs are all wrong. Birds returning too early, then leaving again. Bears waking from hibernation, then going back to sleep. Like nature itself is confused."

As they discussed placement strategies, Mara found herself next to Voss on the porch, watching the sunset paint the mountains crimson.

"You're planning a wedding," Voss said. It wasn't a question.

"October," Mara confirmed. "Elias wants to have Koa as the ring bearer."

Voss smiled. "Sarah would have loved that. She always said Koa was more reliable than most humans." She pulled something from her pocket—a small amulet on a leather cord, carved from what looked like volcanic rock. "This was hers. She wore it during fieldwork. Said it helped her listen better."

"I couldn't—"

"You already are," Voss interrupted. "You're continuing her work, both of you. She believed the Earth speaks to those who love it enough to listen. You've learned that language."

Mara accepted the amulet, its weight surprising for its size. The moment she put it on, she felt... something. Not mystical, not magical, but a subtle awareness, like becoming conscious of her own heartbeat.

Inside, Elias was deep in discussion with James about incorporating traditional monitoring methods into Prometheus's algorithms. "The Cherokee have stories about 'pilot tremors,'" James was saying. "Small quakes that scout ahead of larger ones. They described patterns we're only now able to measure with modern equipment."

"Brilliant," Elias said, his excitement genuine. "We could create a hybrid protocol—ancient wisdom validated by modern sensors."

"Speaking of hybrids," Sierra interrupted with a grin, "can we please discuss this October wedding? If you're serious about Koa as a ring bearer, we need to start training him now. Also, Mom's already planning the catering."

The conversation shifted to lighter topics—venue options (overlooking the crater at Newberry, where geology met romance), decorations (Elias wanted wildflowers, Mara preferred mineral specimens), and the guest list (surprisingly long for two people who'd thought their careers were over two years ago).

"No volcanic activity during the ceremony," Mara said firmly. "I'm putting that in the contract with the universe."

"The universe doesn't honor contracts," James said quietly, and something in his tone made everyone pause. "My grandfather used to say the Earth keeps its own calendar. We can prepare, we can listen, but ultimately..." He shrugged.

As if in response, a tremor rippled through the house—so slight that only their trained senses detected it. Prometheus immediately logged it, algorithms churning through possible causes.

"That's the third one today," Sierra said, frowning at her screen. "All the same magnitude, all the same depth. It's almost like—"

"A heartbeat," Elias finished, and the room went cold.

Koa stood at the window, growling low and constant at something none of them could see. But Mara felt it through the amulet—a presence, vast and patient, stirring beneath their feet.

"We need more data," she said, slipping into professional mode. "Tomorrow, we set up the full array. James, can your contacts provide historical accounts of similar patterns?"

"Already working on it," he replied, but his eyes remained fixed on the window where Koa stood guard.

They worked until midnight, refining protocols and analyzing patterns. Mara and Elias found themselves alone on the porch again, wrapped in a shared blanket against the high desert chill.

"Are we making a mistake?" Mara asked suddenly. "Planning a wedding while chasing disasters?"

"We're planning a life while preventing disasters," he corrected. "There's a difference. Besides," he pulled her closer, "if we waited for the Earth to be completely quiet, we'd wait forever."

"Romantic and fatalistic. You really know how to charm a girl."

"It's worked so far," he said, kissing her temple.

In the distance, coyotes howled—but their song cut off abruptly, as if something had frightened them into silence. Koa whined from inside the house, and the amulet against Mara's chest grew warm.

"Elias," she whispered, "I think something's watching us."

He followed her gaze to the tree line, where shadows seemed to move independently of the wind. For a moment—just a moment—she could have sworn she saw eyes reflecting the porch light. Too large to be human, too deliberate to be animal.

Then Prometheus chimed with an alert. Not urgent, not critical, but noteworthy: magnetic anomalies detected in a pattern that matched no known geological phenomenon. The same location where the hikers had vanished.

"Tomorrow," Elias said firmly, though his arm tightened around her. "Whatever it is, we'll investigate tomorrow. With full equipment and back-up."

But as they went inside, Mara couldn't shake the feeling that tomorrow might not wait for their convenience. The tremors were increasing in frequency, the anomalies multiplying, and somewhere in the darkness, something that had slept for perhaps centuries was beginning to wake.

She touched the amulet, feeling its strange warmth, and wondered if Sarah had felt this too—this sense of standing on the edge of revelation, not knowing if what lay beyond was salvation or catastrophe.

"One disaster at a time," she murmured to herself, then louder, to Elias: "We should review the mine surveys tonight. If there's a connection—"

"There is," James said from the doorway, his face pale in the laptop's glow. "I just found something. Those miners who disappeared in 1923?

They reported hearing music coming from below. Music that sounded like the Earth itself was singing."

Elias and Mara looked at each other, remembering Prometheus's harmonic patterns, the frequencies too low for human ears but not too subtle for careful instruments.

"It's not random," Mara breathed. "The tremors, the patterns—something's been trying to communicate."

"Or warn," Elias added grimly.

Outside, Koa howled—a sound of recognition rather than alarm. As if he'd finally identified what he'd been sensing all along.

The Earth wasn't just waking up. It was trying to tell them something.

And they had less than twenty-four hours to learn its language before the next phase of the pattern began.

Chapter 29: The New Frontier

The Cascade Range rose like ancient titans against the Oregon sky, their peaks shrouded in clouds that seemed to pulse with their own internal weather. Mara stood at the window of the rented community center, watching the locals file in with expressions ranging from curiosity to open hostility. Two years after Morgantown, their reputation preceded them—saviors to some, fearmongers to others.

"They look thrilled to see us," Elias murmured, adjusting the projection screen. Koa lay beneath the table, his gray muzzle showing his age but his eyes still sharp, still watching.

"Can you blame them?" Mara touched her wedding ring absently—a habit she'd developed when nervous. "The last team of scientists who came here tried to condemn half the town for a dam project."

"We're not here to condemn anything," Sierra said, looking up from her laptop where Prometheus's data streams flowed like digital rivers. "Just to listen."

The word choice was deliberate. They'd learned in the months since Morgantown that "listening" opened doors that "investigating" slammed shut.

The crowd settled into metal folding chairs with squeaks and murmurs. At the front row sat three members of the Yakama Nation's council, including an elder named Joseph Wahpat whose eyes held the kind of knowledge that didn't come from textbooks. Behind them were local business owners, farmers, and skeptics who'd probably come just to heckle.

"Thank you for coming," Elias began, his professor voice warm but carrying easily through the room. "We're not here to tell you anything about your land. We're here to learn what you already know."

"Then why bring all that fancy equipment?" called out a man in a Timber Services cap. "Seems like you've already decided something's wrong."

"Our equipment helps us translate," Mara said, stepping forward. "Between what the Earth is saying and what science can measure. But the best translator we have is you—people who've lived here for generations."

Joseph Wahpat stood slowly, his weathered hands gripping a carved walking stick. "My grandmother told me stories," he began, his voice carrying the weight of generations. "About the time before, when the mountain spirits grew restless. The animals knew first—the elk moving to lower ground, the salmon swimming in circles, refusing to run upstream."

"When was this?" Sierra asked, fingers poised over her keyboard.

"1924," Joseph replied. "Three weeks before the mine collapsed near Mount Adams. Killed seventeen men." He paused, his gaze settling on Mara with uncomfortable intensity. "The surveyor who declared that mine safe—his name was Morrison. But the mining company that hired him? Cross Minerals."

The temperature in the room seemed to drop. Mara felt Elias's hand find hers under the table.

"That's... that must be a coincidence," someone said from the back.

Joseph shook his head slowly. "The Earth has a long memory. And some families have long habits. Morrison falsified his surveys, said the ground was stable when the old songs warned it was not. We called him the cursed surveyor—cursed to repeat his lies until the mountain itself stopped him."

"How did it stop him?" Mara asked, though she suspected she knew.

"He disappeared two days before the collapse. Some say he ran. Others say the mountain took him." Joseph's eyes never left Mara's face. "But his papers were found later. Full of real measurements, real warnings. Hidden in a safety deposit box while men died in the dark."

Mara's tablet chimed softly. Prometheus had found something—a pattern in the current seismic data that matched signatures from her graduate work, surveys she'd done before Cross had "corrected" them. Her hand trembled as she pulled up the comparison.

"You recognize it," Joseph said. It wasn't a question.

"This is impossible," she breathed. The harmonic patterns were identical to readings she'd taken in West Virginia eight years ago—readings Cross had dismissed as equipment malfunction. But here they were again, three thousand miles away, in a completely different geological system.

"What is it?" Elias asked quietly.

"These patterns—I've seen them before. In my original dissertation data. The data, Cross said was corrupted." She pulled up the old files, overlaying them with current readings. "But if these patterns are real, if they're consistent across different locations..."

"Then Cross didn't just suppress warnings about Morgantown," Sierra finished, her face pale. "He's been suppressing a larger pattern. Something systemic."

The room erupted in nervous chatter. Mara barely heard it, lost in the implications. If these harmonic signatures were real, they indicated something she'd theorized but never proven—a deep-Earth resonance that preceded major geological events, a kind of planetary nervous system that transmitted warnings across vast distances.

"Dr. Quinn," a woman in a business suit stood up. "I'm Deputy Mayor Harrison. While this is all very interesting, we need to know if there's immediate danger. Should we be evacuating?"

Before Elias could answer, his phone rang. The caller ID showed Tom Granger. He answered, putting it on speaker.

"Tom? You're on with about forty concerned citizens."

Granger's familiar drawl filled the room, though video showed him grayer, more worn than two years ago. "Figured you might need a character reference. Folks, I'm Sheriff Tom Granger from Morgantown, West Virginia. These two saved my town. Lost my own stubborn pride fighting them at first, nearly cost lives. Don't make my mistake."

"Sheriff," Deputy Mayor Harrison said, "with all due respect, we've heard mixed reports about what happened there."

"Mixed?" Granger laughed bitterly. "Let me unmix them for you. Without Elias and Mara, the death toll would've been in the thousands. They fought through sabotage, slander, and a conspiracy that went all the way to Washington. And they were right. Every damn prediction."

"But the media said—"

"The media said what Marcus Cross paid them to say. Until they couldn't ignore the volcano in their backyard." Granger leaned closer to his camera. "I got one piece of advice for you folks: listen to them. The Earth's trying to tell you something, and these two know how to translate."

The call ended with Granger's promise to send supporting documentation. The room was quieter now, fear replacing skepticism.

"We're not saying there's immediate danger," Elias said, moving to the projection screen where Prometheus displayed real-time data. "But we are seeing concerning patterns. Animal migrations shifting, micro-tremors in unexpected locations, and these harmonic signatures Dr. Lang identified."

"The reservation's had three wells go dry this month," an elderly woman said. "And my grandson says the eagles haven't returned to their usual nesting sites."

More stories emerged—small anomalies that meant nothing individually but painted a troubling picture collectively. Mara and Elias exchanged glances, their years of partnership allowing communication without words. They'd learned this dance in Morgantown: gather the stories, find the patterns, build trust before making predictions.

"We'd like to set up monitoring stations," Mara said. "With your permission. Not to take over, but to combine your observations with our data."

"Like a translation service," someone said, understanding dawning.

"Exactly," Elias smiled. "Your knowledge plus our technology. Together, we're—"

"Unbreakable," Mara finished, surprising herself by saying it aloud. But it was true. They'd learned that in Morgantown's ashes—separately they were vulnerable, but together they could face anything.

Joseph Wahpat stood again. "There's a place," he said slowly. "Sacred to our people. Where the Earth's voice is strongest. If you want to understand what's happening, you should start there."

"We'd be honored," Mara said.

As the meeting broke up, locals approaching with stories and offers of help, Mara felt her phone vibrate. A new email, sender unknown but the subject line made her blood freeze:

"You think Cross worked alone? The pattern you found has been hidden for a reason. Stop now or face consequences that make Morgantown look like a tremor. - A Friend of Order"

Attached was a single image: a photograph of her original dissertation committee. Five professors, including Cross. But now, looking at it with new eyes, she saw what she'd missed before. Each of them wore a small pin—barely visible unless you knew to look. A symbol she'd seen recently, in Joseph's stories about the cursed surveyor.

"Elias," she whispered, showing him the phone.

His face darkened. "Cross was part of something bigger."

Sierra looked over their shoulders, immediately screenshotting the email before it could disappear. "I'm running facial recognition on the other committee members. If they're still active, still suppressing data..."

"Then we're not just fighting old patterns," Mara said. "We're fighting an organization."

Prometheus chimed urgently. The main screen lit up with projections, algorithms processing thousands of data points into a single, terrifying conclusion. The system predicted a major event—not in weeks or days, but in hours. Location: directly beneath the sacred site Joseph had just offered to show them.

"It's accelerating," Elias said, studying the data. "Whatever's happening, our presence might have triggered something."

"Or someone triggered it because of our presence," Mara countered, thinking of the email.

They looked around the room at the locals still gathered, trusting them, counting on them. The weight of responsibility settled on their shoulders like it had two years ago. But this time, they were ready. This time, they were together.

"We need to get to that sacred site," Mara said. "Now."

Joseph nodded gravely. "I'll guide you. But know this—the mountain doesn't give up its secrets easily. And those who've tried to silence it..." He trailed off, but his meaning was clear.

As they prepared to leave, Koa suddenly stood, hackles raised, staring at the eastern window. In the distance, a low rumble—so deep it was more felt than heard—rolled across the landscape. Birds erupted from the trees in a black cloud, fleeing west.

"That's not thunder," a local whispered.

No, Mara thought, checking Prometheus's real-time feed as her heart rate spiked. It wasn't thunder.

The mountain was waking up.

And someone, somewhere, had wanted them to be right in its path when it did.

Chapter 30: Hand in Hand

The Oregon coast stretched before them, nothing like the Appalachian hills where their story began. Here, the Pacific crashed against volcanic basalt, creating tide pools that gleamed like scattered mirrors in the morning sun. The Cascade Range loomed to the east, its peaks snow-capped even in late spring, hiding secrets that Prometheus was only beginning to decipher.

Mara stood at the edge of their new research station's observation deck, tablet in hand, watching data streams flow across the screen like poetry written in numbers. Two years had passed since Morgantown—two years of rebuilding, fighting, loving, and finally, truly understanding what it meant to balance intuition with empirical evidence.

"The new sensors are online," she called to Elias, who was crouched beside Koa on the rocky shore below, both of them studying something in a tide pool. "We're getting readings from seven different fault systems."

"And the behavioral monitors?" He looked up, shielding his eyes against the sun. His hair had more gray now, earned through late nights and congressional hearings, but his smile still made her heart skip.

"Integrated and operational. Sierra outdid herself with the new algorithm." Mara pulled up the display, showing a three-dimensional map where geological data merged seamlessly with biological patterns. It was beautiful—Sarah's dream made manifest through their combined work.

Koa barked suddenly, not in alarm but in greeting. Dr. Lenora Voss emerged from the trail that connected their station to the coastal town, moving with surprising agility for someone who'd just celebrated her eightieth birthday.

"The elders are concerned," Voss said without preamble, joining Mara on the deck. "The gray whales changed their migration route yesterday. Third time this month."

"We saw," Mara said, showing her the data. "Prometheus is tracking it, but the correlation patterns are... different here."

"Different how?" Elias asked, joining them with Koa at his heels. The dog immediately went to his favorite spot on the deck, a patch of sun where he could watch both the ocean and the mountains.

"More complex. The Juan de Fuca Plate isn't like the relatively stable Appalachian geology. Here, we're dealing with active subduction, volcanic systems, and oceanic influences." Mara manipulated the display, showing layers of interconnected data. "It's like trying to conduct an orchestra where half the musicians are playing jazz and the other half are playing classical."

"And yet they're making music," Voss observed, pointing to a pattern in the animal behavior data. "Look—the same cascade effect we saw before Morgantown, just with different instruments."

Elias moved behind Mara, his hand settling naturally on her shoulder as they studied the screen together. The simple touch still sent warmth through her, even after everything they'd been through. Their wedding rings caught the light—his a simple band, hers set with a small piece of volcanic glass from Morgantown, a reminder that beauty could emerge from disaster.

"Remember our first debate?" he murmured, his breath warm against her ear. "You called me a romantic fool playing with correlation matrices."

"And you called me a data fundamentalist afraid of anything I couldn't quantify." She leaned back against him. "We were both right."

"And both wrong," he agreed.

The tablet chimed with an incoming video call. Sierra's face appeared, beaming from their new facility at MIT where she was heading the Prometheus expansion project.

"Monthly check-in time," Sierra announced. "How's the West Coast treating you?"

"Koa's developed a taste for salmon," Elias said. "Otherwise, we're adapting."

"The integration with the tsunami warning system?" Sierra asked, all business now.

"Ahead of schedule," Mara reported. "The Japanese delegation arrives next week to review the protocols. If this works, we'll have coverage across the entire Pacific Rim within eighteen months."

"Speaking of which," Sierra's expression grew serious, "I heard from Tom Granger yesterday. Cross was denied parole again."

A moment of silence settled over them. Marcus Cross had ultimately been convicted not just for data suppression and public endangerment, but for a century-old pattern of family corruption that had cost countless lives. His testimony had revealed a network of suppressed geological surveys dating back three generations, each Cover-up more elaborate than the last.

"He sent another letter," Voss said quietly. "Wanting to 'collaborate' from prison. Share his historical data in exchange for sentence reduction."

"Let him rot," Mara said flatly, then softened. "Though the data would be useful."

"That's my pragmatist," Elias said, kissing the top of her head. "Always looking for the value in everything."

She turned in his arms, looking up at him. "And that's my optimist, always believing people can change."

"Some people," he corrected. "Not Cross. But others..." He gestured toward the town where many Morgantown survivors had relocated, building new lives on more stable ground. "People can surprise you."

Prometheus chimed softly—not an alert, just a routine update. The AI had evolved far beyond its original parameters, now incorporating indigenous knowledge databases, historical patterns, and even artistic interpretations of natural phenomena. It wasn't just predicting disasters anymore; it was helping humanity read the Earth's subtle language.

"I should review the overnight data," Mara said, not moving from Elias's embrace.

"In a minute," he said, echoing their old refrain.

They stood together, watching the ocean breathe against the shore. In the distance, a pod of orcas surfaced, their movements tracked automatically by Prometheus's sensors. Everything was connected—water and stone, instinct and analysis, past and future.

"Do you ever regret it?" Mara asked suddenly. "Leaving the university, giving up the traditional academic path?"

"Do you?" he countered.

She considered, thinking of the global institute they were building, the lives they'd saved, the knowledge they'd preserved. Thinking of quiet mornings in their shared office, debates that turned into kisses, discoveries that felt like dancing.

"No," she said simply. "This is better. We're better."

"Even with all the uncertainty? Not knowing what tomorrow's data might show?"

She smiled, remembering her old self who needed everything quantified, verified, peer-reviewed. That woman wouldn't recognize who she'd become—someone who could trust both the numbers and the whispers, who could find truth in the space between data points.

"Especially with the uncertainty," she said. "You taught me that."

"You taught me that uncertainty needs structure," he replied. "That intuition without rigor is just guessing."

"Look at us," Voss interrupted with fond exasperation. "Still debating after all this time."

"It's how we flirt," Mara said, making Elias laugh.

The sun climbed higher, warming the deck. Koa stretched, then suddenly sat up, ears perked toward the mountains. A behavior Mara now recognized—not alarm, just attention. The earth was speaking, and he was listening.

"The new sensors are picking up something," Mara noted, checking her tablet. "Minor harmonics in the Cascadia Subduction Zone. Nothing urgent, but..."

"But worth monitoring," Elias finished. "Should we increase the sampling rate?"

"Already done. The system's learning, adapting to the new environment." She showed him the adjustments Prometheus had made automatically. "It's becoming more sophisticated every day."

"Like us," he said softly.

Sierra signed off with promises to visit soon. Voss departed to meet with the tribal council, working on integrating more traditional knowledge into their databases. For a moment, Elias and Mara were alone with the ocean and the mountains, the eternal dialogue between water and stone.

"I've been thinking," Elias said, his tone suggesting something he'd been considering for a while. "About expansion. Australia's reached out—they want a station. Japan's ready to fund three more. We could—"

"Create a global network," Mara finished. "I've been running models. If we place stations at key points along the Ring of Fire, integrate with existing systems, add the behavioral monitoring..."

"We could give the world a voice," he said. "Let the Earth tell us what it needs us to know."

She turned to face him fully, seeing in his eyes the same mix of excitement and trepidation she felt. They'd started with one traumatized man and one skeptical woman, brought together by disaster. Now they stood ready to reshape how humanity understood its relationship with the planet.

"It'll be dangerous," she warned. "More enemies like Cross. More stakes. More chances to fail."

"More chances to save lives," he countered. "More opportunities to prove that science and intuition aren't opposites—they're dance partners."

"You and your metaphors," she said, but she was smiling.

"You love my metaphors."

"I love you," she corrected, then added with mock seriousness, "The metaphors I merely tolerate."

He kissed her then, deep and sure, tasting like coffee and possibility. When they parted, Koa was watching them with what could only be described as approval.

A faint chime from Prometheus drew their attention. Not urgent, not even particularly notable—just a small anomaly in the pattern, something to investigate when they had time. The system would monitor, analyze, and alert them if needed. They'd learned to trust it, just as they'd learned to trust each other.

"Ready for another adventure?" Elias asked, holding out his hand.

Mara looked at his outstretched palm, remembering another moment two years ago when taking his hand had meant choosing between safety and truth. Now it meant choosing their continued journey together, whatever unknowns it might hold.

She took his hand, their fingers interlacing with practiced ease. "Always."

They stood at the edge of their new world, Prometheus humming quietly in the background, Koa settled at their feet, the ocean singing its ancient song. Somewhere in the mountains, tectonic plates shifted imperceptibly. Somewhere in the data streams, patterns emerged and evolved. Somewhere between the empirical and the intuitive, truth waited to be discovered.

The Earth was speaking. They were finally learning how to listen.

Together.

In the distance, a raven called—once, twice, three times. Koa's ears twitched, but he didn't move, didn't alarm. Not yet. But Mara had learned to read the signs, to trust the whispers as much as the data. She squeezed Elias's hand, and he squeezed back, both of them understanding without words:

The story was far from over.

The tablet chimed again, softer this time, Prometheus registering something new in the harmonics—not dangerous, not yet, but worth watching. Always worth watching. The numbers flowed like water, the patterns danced like flames, and somewhere between the two, their next chapter was already beginning to write itself.

Mara pulled up the new data with her free hand, still holding Elias with the other. The readings were fascinating—a subtle symphony playing out in frequencies too low for human ears but not too subtle for human hearts that had learned to pay attention.

"Look at this," she said, wonder creeping into her voice.

Elias leaned in, his presence warm and steady beside her. "That's beautiful," he breathed. "It's like the Earth is composing music."

"Terrible metaphor," she said automatically, but her smile gave her away.

"Accurate metaphor," he corrected. "Even you have to admit—"

She kissed him to shut him up, which had become her favorite way to win arguments. When they parted, both breathless, the sun was painting the ocean gold, and Koa was wagging his tail as if he knew something wonderful was about to happen.

Maybe he did. After everything, Mara had learned not to discount anything.

The future stretched before them, uncertain and thrilling, full of patterns yet to be discovered and disasters yet to be prevented. But they would face it as they'd learned to face everything—hand in hand, intuition and data united, love and science intertwined.

The Earth breathed. Prometheus listened. And two people who'd found each other in the space between certainty and chaos stood ready for whatever came next.

Together.

Always together.

Also by Donald J. Wright

Novels

Lilith's Garden

ASIN: B0DQX8ZWD9

The Terraforming Protocol ASIN: B0FHBVY1QS

ASIN: B0DNY8Z3WB

The Prometheus Protocol

ASIN: B0DLHFF79M

13th Moon Book I

ASIN: B0DGNTV533

13 Moons: Legacy of the Guardians Book II

ASIN: B0FDYNP7WP

Killer Ice

ASIN: B0F1G6HVMR

The Ghost Code

ASIN: B0F4FGQMG5

The Golden Book

ASIN: B0DXQGMFL8

The Golden Book II

ASIN: B0FKNNB4Z7

Tomorrow
ASIN: B0FFTS4C39
The God Equation
ASIN: B0FGZFNZTD
THE QUANTUM SCHISM:
ASIN: B0D1N9RHMQ
The Quantum Alchemist:
ASIN: B0FD43QCDB
The Quantum Heart:
ASIN: B0F9YZTRVG
The Codex Protocol:
ASIN: B0F1Z1XH89
THE QUANTUM ECHO
ASIN: B0F6KWPGG2

Non-Fiction
Beyond Climate Debates
ASIN: B0DZB8CB7K
Diamonds Under Fire
ASIN: B0CDYSTBLL
The Handbook of Lab-Created Diamonds
ASIN: B0D8V4X3CW
The Diamond Revolution
ASIN: B0FHBVY1QS
Eternal Shine
ASIN: B0DQX8ZWD9
Globe Treasure Hunting

ASIN: B0DF6RN4H8